HOWL DEADLY

HOWL DEADLY

LINDA O. JOHNSTON

WHEELER PUBLISHING
A part of Gale, Cengage Learning

GALE
CENGAGE Learning

Detroit • New York • San Francisco • New Haven, Conn • Waterville, Maine • London

GALE
CENGAGE Learning

Copyright © 2009 by Linda O. Johnston.
A Kendra Ballantyne, Pet-Sitter Mystery.
Wheeler Publishing, a part of Gale, Cengage Learning.

Wheeler Publishing Large Print Cozy Mystery.
The text of this Large Print edition is unabridged.
Other aspects of the book may vary from the original edition.
Set in 16 pt. Plantin.

LIBRARY OF CONGRESS CATALOGING-IN-PUBLICATION DATA

Johnston, Linda O.
  Howl deadly / by Linda O. Johnston. — Large print ed.
    p. cm. — (Wheeler Publishing large print cozy mystery)
  ISBN-13: 978-1-4104-2530-0 (pbk. : alk. paper)
  ISBN-10: 1-4104-2530-4 (pbk. : alk. paper)
    1. Ballantyne, Kendra (Fictitious character)—Fiction. 2. Pet
sitting—Fiction. 3. Women lawyers—California—Fiction.
4. Animal sanctuaries—Fiction. 5. California—Fiction. 6. Large
type books. I. Title.
PS3610.O387H69 2010
813'.6—dc22   2009051918

Published in 2010 by arrangement with The Berkley Publishing Group,
a member of Penguin Group (USA) Inc.

Printed in the United States of America
1 2 3 4 5 6 7 14 13 12 11 10

This book is dedicated to canines of all kinds — wild, tame, and in-between. To wolves in particular, those amazing animals who were both ancestors of our dogs today and are living evidence of how canines can survive — sometimes with protection — in the wild.

This dedication of course includes Cavalier King Charles spaniels — especially both Kendra's and Linda's Lexies, as well as Linda's little Mystie.

This book is also dedicated to all those who care about and protect the wildlife of the world, both roaming free and saved in sanctuaries. To the local Los Angeles area sanctuaries, including Wildlife WayStation and the Shambala Preserve. To the Los Angeles Zoo and the Greater Los Angeles Zoo Association.

And no dedication would be complete without a mention of Linda's husband, Fred. Linda already had her first Cavalier, Panda, when she met Fred. Fred had to learn to get along with Panda to win over Linda — not always an easy task. Since then, Fred has patiently helped Linda care for a whole pack of Cavaliers, usually two at a time. And we all absolutely appreciate him for it!

CHAPTER ONE

"Still incredibly adorable," I crooned.

"I'll say," said Dante DeFrancisco, right in my ear. When I glanced away from the sweet mama wolf and three nearly newborn pups in the glass-contained enclosure I'd been observing, I saw he was staring at me, not the latest arrivals at HotWildlife. Which made me shiver with a sensation I couldn't quite identify — a combo of lust and anticipation and just plain old pleasure that this gorgeous, sexy, and, yes, super rich guy was hot for me, too.

I smiled and slowly turned away. I was absolutely enjoying everything about this long weekend away from the bustle of L.A., at the fringe of the nearby San Bernardino Mountains.

Visiting this amazing wild animal sanctuary, founded and funded by — who else? Dante.

I'm Kendra Ballantyne, L.A. attorney and

proud pet-sitter, owner of Critter TLC, LLC. Not that I take care of wild creatures, but I'm an absolute animal aficionado, so I felt entirely in my element here at Hot-Wildlife.

Right now, we were in the critical care infirmary, a long, low structure with attractive architectural details outside, state-of-the-art housing and veterinary facilities inside. The mother wolf was in a compact, glassed-in habitat where she could roam at will without straying far from her offspring. It was the babies' dinnertime, and mama was lying contentedly on her side in an area covered with clean wood chips, nursing them.

"So how's our adorable little family?" asked a voice from the nearest doorway to the observation area just outside the habitat.

"Just fine," I responded to HotWildlife's director and caregiver-in-chief, Megan Zurich.

I'd looked up the place online last week and learned that Megan was in her early forties, with substantial experience at zoos and other wild animal parks that gave her an excellent background for being here and in control. Her hair was long and blond, and pulled back with a barrette at the nape of her neck — most likely because she didn't want her charges to be able to dig their claws into her tresses and tug them out. The golden lion's-mane shade probably wasn't natural but was streaked becomingly.

And, no, I wasn't trying to be catty, despite the fact that the sanctuary was home not only to these wolves but also to lots of felines: several lions, tigers, servals, mountain lions, and even ligers — crosses between lions and tigers. Other mammals, too, such as coyotes. A great cross section of wild animals needing a safe haven where they could thrive. Mostly ones brought up in other sanctuaries or even as illegal pets, who hadn't the skills or, sometimes, weren't healthy enough to be released into the wild.

A few of them were in the infirmary. I heard occasional growls from an injured and aging coyote a few enclosures down, and some skittering from nearby raccoons.

"Can I come in?" One of the place's volunteers squeezed around Megan's shoulder, a guy named Anthony Pfalzer. He appeared to be of high school age, with a football player's physique. Sweet, that someone so youthfully macho seemed to care so much about animals.

"Okay," Megan said, moving out of the way, "but let's all stay back so we don't bother the nursing mother. She can see us through the glass as easily as we can see her."

"Can we name her?" inquired another volunteer, who sidled in behind Anthony. "And the pups, too?" Her name was Krissy Kollings. To me, she looked like a Krissy: all cute and busty and wavy haired.

"Sure." Megan moved to allow Krissy and Anthony to draw closer to the vast window opening onto the wolf habitat. "We haven't had time to do that yet, not even with our little mother. She was brought here only last week, and gave birth almost immediately."

I knew. Thanks to Dante staying in close touch with the people in charge of the facilities he funded, he'd learned immediately from Megan about the secretive, dead-of-night deposit here of the very pregnant gray wolf. He'd told me about it, and the instant I expressed an interest in being there for the big event, we were in his car, heading to the sanctuary. For that day, I'd left my adorable Cavalier King Charles spaniel, Lexie, in the charge of my assistant at Critter TLC, LLC.

Dante had staff in his home — his Malibu home — who could care for his smart and sweet German shepherd, Wagner. He also had part-time staff at his additional home near here, at the base of the San Bernardino Mountains. How many other houses did he maintain? Damned if I knew.

We'd been here to witness the miracle of the wild wolves' birth. Then we headed home — and planned to come back for this long, lovely weekend, staying in Dante's local residence with our pampered pets and visiting HotWildlife a lot, keeping an eye on the sweet wolf pups.

"I'll bet Dante will come up with the greatest names, won't you, Dante?" Krissy asked. She now stood on his other side, and she looked up adoringly into his eyes, one hand resting on the sleeve of his blue work shirt.

Krissy had been here during the birth, too. I'd seen how she stayed way too near Dante. Obviously had a crush on him, even though he had to be at least fifteen years her senior. I figured her for mid-twenties, and Dante was forty-two.

Me? I'm thirty-six. Not cute like Krissy, but okay to look at.

"Oh, I think I'll leave that to others with more imagination than me," Dante said, smiling sexily in my flattered direction. Guess he agreed with my assessment of my appearance.

But I wasn't about to spout out a slew of

perfect names. Instead, I asked Megan, "Why not hold a contest for the public to provide possible names? Maybe people could make a contribution that would entitle them to suggest something." I glanced back at Dante, unsure whether he liked the idea of assistance in his charitable endeavors. He just winked at me.

A wink from those deep, dark, delicious eyes could have made me melt if we'd been alone. I caught Krissy's sad-eyed gaze at her hero, as if he had dared to ignore her. Which he kinda had.

"Great idea!" Megan said. "We've done that before when rescued animals have been brought in. A mini wolf pack like this should draw a bunch of media attention, get us lots of donations."

"I know a reporter who'd love something like this," I said, hoping it was so. My sometimes-friend, tabloid reporter Corina Carey at *National NewsShakers,* was right on the spot when there were little things like petnappings from Hollywood notables, or — better yet, from her perspective — unsolved murders happening around me. A sweet thing like a rescued wolf and her new pups might not be as exciting.

And, yes, in case you haven't watched Corina's awful TV show or seen the other stuff in the news about me, in addition to being a lawyer and pet-sitter, I am, most unfortunately, also a murder magnet. I've been involved in solving a lot more killings than I like to think about. But surely that trend has to come to an end eventually.

Preferably immediately.

"Hey, how's it going?" A skinny senior citizen with a goatee as gray as the hair on his head strolled in. He wore denim overalls with a white T-shirt beneath the bib as well as large bifocals perched on his parrot-beak nose. I'd met him before. He was a caretaker here at HotWildlife. His name was, incredibly, Jon Doe.

"Really well, Jon," Megan told him. "Once she's done nursing, though, I'd like to add some softer substrate for her to lie on with the pups. Any ideas?"

They talked it over for a while, discussing materials ranging from purified mulch to a fuzzy bathmat. The decision, though, was to mix some straw with the cedar chips. And if they happened to throw in some indestructible towels, too, that was fine. It would still be close to a natural habitat. Wolves in the wild might drag the softest stuff they could find into their lairs. With the way people disposed of their discards, that might, now and then, include toweling.

13

By the time they were done with the discussion, mama wolf was also through. She stood and strode away from her little balls of fur — two black and one gray — who squealed unhappily at the abandonment. Still too small for their eyes to open, they didn't see that mommy was only a few feet away, regarding them with both interest and exasperation in her intense wolfen eyes.

"Is her food ready to put inside the enclosure?" Megan asked Jon.

"Sure is," he replied.

"Let me do it, please," interjected Krissy. "I'd love to get closer to the mama wolf."

"Not a good idea," Megan chastised. "You know our routine. Only Jon or one of the other caretakers feeds our charges, so we don't confuse or upset them with a lot of intruding humans or scents."

Krissy appeared ready to protest, but she backed off when Dante shot her a stern look. She instead smiled and said, "Sure thing."

We all stood around enjoying the scene a little longer, including when Jon Doe slipped into the enclosure via the back door and left a bowl of what Megan described as a nutritious packaged doggy food enhanced with stuff wolves might find in the wild.

I didn't want to know more about the latter or how it was supplied. I had no doubt, though, that Dante had all the knowledge needed. And supplier sources. After all, he also owned HotPets, the biggest and best chain of pet supply stores in the country. It was how he'd made his millions.

Maybe. Despite the relationship I'd recently started with Dante, I knew there was a lot about him that I didn't know. Secretive stuff about his past.

That perhaps was better left there.

No matter, for now. It was time for us to leave the sanctuary, but we'd be back tomorrow before heading to L.A.

As we departed in Dante's sleek silver Mercedes, I called my pet-sitting assistant, Rachel Preesinger, who also happens to be the daughter of the tenant in my Hollywood Hills home.

Me? I live in the apartment over the garage. I moved in there over a year ago when I had problems with my law career that left me unable to pay the mortgage without assistance. I'd been accused of unethical conduct, and consequently fired from my high-powered L.A. firm. Of course I'd been exonerated, but I'd come to enjoy my revised lifestyle, so Lexie and I still reside in our home sweet garage.

15

"Everything okay with our clients, Rachel?" I asked, watching as Dante and I moved from the narrow drive leading to Hot-Wildlife onto the highway. Lots of cars around, even in this rural area.

"They're all just fine," she told me. "Wanda's checked in with me, too, about the couple she's taken on till you get back."

"Great." Wanda Villareal was a fellow member of the Pet-Sitters Club of SoCal who also owned a Cavalier King Charles spaniel, Basil. Plus, she was the girlfriend of my dearest friend in the world, Darryl Nestler, owner of Doggy Indulgence Day Resort. I'd been able to take the weekend away after getting the okay from my clients to substitute sitters. Even so, taking such time away was a real rarity for me. "See you tomorrow," I finished, and hung up.

I glanced at Dante and found his gaze on me for a moment; then it returned to the road. Lord, he was one handsome dude, even dressed casually in an ordinary blue work shirt and jeans, with his well-defined features, deep brown eyes, and black, wavy hair. And a smile that was especially smoldering just then.

"Everything okay?" He repeated the question I'd asked Rachel. He'd never met me during my high-powered law days, when my hair was highlighted and my garb was usually lady-lawyer dressy. Now, I kept my untouched-up brown hair shoulder length and wore suits only during my less frequent forays to legal meetings and court.

"Sure thing," I said, and sat back, crossing my blue-jeaned legs — still observing him from the corner of my eye, one of my favorite pastimes these days.

I'm not going to give any details about our excellent evening. Not many, at least. Suffice it to say that our dogs were delighted to see us. This time, we had brought them both to the area and left them in Dante's home. Before it got dark, we all four took a walk in the thick, fresh-smelling woods surrounding Dante's rustic mountain cabin.

Well, kinda rustic. It looked like hewn logs from the outside, but it was big and had all the amenities imaginable inside.

Including household help who ensured we all ate well after our walk, doggies included.

And despite its locale off the beaten track, the cabin was behind a big gate in a fence surrounding the property.

Lexie on my lap and Wagner on the floor beside the comfy leather sofa at Dante's feet, we watched business news, including the behavior of the big, bad stock market, on the large HD TV in the den. Dante was apparently a substantial investor, hopefully sprinkling his huge fortune around wisely. He didn't seem especially upset that night, and when we went to bed . . .

Well, that's the part that'll remain private.

Next morning, Sunday, we headed back to HotWildlife. I loved the look of it from the outside, a wrought-iron fence surrounding a huge sanctuary containing lots of habitats, each designed specially for each species of inhabitant. Inside, I meandered along the walkway and glanced in at sleeping tigers, standing lions, and pacing coyotes, Dante holding my hand. In the distance, I noticed Jon Doe head inside a nondescript building. "That's where supplies are stored," Dante responded to my inquiry.

Then we headed for the attractive critical-care structure. The wolf pups were nursing yet again. Surprise! At their young age, I assumed they did a lot of that. Today there were dozens of observers standing outside the glass, viewing them. Members of the public were encouraged to visit. And to contribute.

Several volunteers, including Anthony and Krissy, were leading tour groups of ten visitors each. Most seemed eager to stay and watch the wolves, but the tour guides were adept at encouraging them to move on.

"Hi," Anthony said as he led his gang to the exit. I gave my own greeting back, as did Dante.

Two more groups departed while Krissy and her gang remained. She soon sidled in our direction — especially toward Dante.

"How are you this morning, Krissy?" he asked her in a pleasant tone.

"Wonderful!" she gushed, looking as happy as if he'd asked her out on a date.

"Glad to hear it," I interjected. "I just love to watch that mother wolf and her pups, don't you?"

She tore her gaze from Dante, shot me a brief smile as if I didn't exactly exist, then said, "Well, gotta go. I have visitors to show around." She leaned conspiratorially toward Dante. Standing on her toes despite her open sandals beneath her capri slacks, she said, "I'll try to get them all to give Hot-Wildlife lots of money. They seem interested in paying to try to name the baby wolves."

"Great!" I said as Dante nodded his approval.

She soon departed, and Megan joined us near the wolf den. Most of the crowd was gone now.

"They look like they're thriving," I said, my tone a little quizzical.

19

She nodded. "They're getting along just fine."

We observed for a few more minutes.

"Ready to head home?" Dante eventually asked, sounding as reluctant as I felt.

"I sure am," I said anyway. "I need to take back my pet-sitting tonight."

"Oh, yes — Dante told me you're a pet-sitter," Megan said. "I guess you understand what it's like to want to take care of all these animals this way."

I nodded. "But I doubt I'd do as well with so many, especially wildlife, the way you do."

She smiled and accompanied us as we walked out of the building.

Jon Doe came up to us, pushing a cart laden with containers of animal food. "Hey, thanks for stopping by again," the grizzled older guy said. He was dressed once more in a T-shirt and grungy overalls. "Guess we'll be getting in some more high-quality stuff for these creatures' habitats pretty soon. Beats the wilderness, doesn't it? Shelters from bad weather and enemies — whoever they may be — and at least what feels like safety to them. Love 'em all, don't you?"

"Absolutely," I said. I noticed a strange look pass between Dante and Doe, but only for a second. Might even have imagined it, since afterward they shook hands.

"Keep up the good work," Dante told the caretaker.

"Count on it," was the enthusiastic reply.

We took one more meander around the compound, avoiding the gangs of visitors whenever possible. I particularly paid attention to where Krissy was with her crowd, so we could go the other way.

And then we left, drove to Dante's "shack," and picked up our pups. Dante's part-time housekeepers were there, and we soon said goodbye. We were back at my place about two hours later, after stopping for supper.

"Care to come in?" I asked Dante, bending down to pat Wagner's smooth-furred head.

To my delight, they stayed the night. Never mind that my digs would have fit in the foyer at Dante's Malibu mansion. We were definitely comfortable here. As we'd been in the mountains. Or wherever.

I wasn't sure what time it was when a song startled me awake. Not my cell phone.

Dante's. Ringing at not quite five in the morning.

He groped from where he lay near me in my small but comfortable bed. His phone was on the table by his side.

"Hello?" he grumbled with obvious irritation at being awakened this way. Had he recognized the number? He sure had. "This better be important, Megan. You know how early it is?"

I heard a muffled female voice from the other end, though I couldn't make out what she said.

But suddenly Dante sat straight up in bed, his large hand gripping the phone to his cheek — now covered in sexy dark shadow. His scowl would have made my heart skip had it been leveled at me, but he stared, apparently unseeing, across the room. We'd shut the dogs in the kitchen last night before heading for bed, and I heard them stirring in there.

"What do you mean, missing?" Dante demanded.

My hot body suddenly chilled. Something was obviously very wrong.

Who was missing?

I found out a minute later as he flipped his phone shut and looked at me with an expression that was clearly furious.

"It's the mother wolf," he said. "She's no longer with her pups, and the HotWildlife staff can't find her anywhere."

CHAPTER TWO

I made some calls to ensure that my pet charges — whose owners' consent had already been obtained — would be superbly cared for again by Rachel and Wanda. Then Dante and I raced back to HotWildlife. It was Dante's passion and mission, and he had to find out what had happened.

Me, too. Maybe because I was hooked on the place's admirable objectives. Maybe because I had kinda met the missing mama wolf — or at least had observed and fallen for her.

And maybe it was because I'd solved several mysteries during the past few months — including locating petnapped clients — and I hoped I could help with this situation, too.

Even so, I had a sense of guilt for not being there for my own pet-sitting responsibilities.

This time, I left Lexie home. Wagner was

with her. He got along fine with my pup and with Rachel's lovely Irish setter, Beggar, short for Begorrah. And Rachel would take tremendous care of them all.

Dante's silver Mercedes passed nearly everyone on the 210 Freeway heading east toward the San Bernardino Mountains. He seemed undaunted by the potential of getting a ticket. He glanced now and then into the rearview mirror, but that was his standard driving technique. Because he had intended to go home before heading for his office, he didn't have a change of clothes, so he once again wore his sexily casual outfit from yesterday.

Maybe, if we continued to see each other this way, it would make sense for him to keep some stuff at my place, and vice versa. But I was far from ready to suggest that.

"You promised to tell me what we know so far about the missing wolf," I reminded him after we'd gone a ways and chatted about unrelated things, like a new brand of healthy pet food soon to be sold by Hot-Pets.

He looked over at me, then back to the road. "She arrived at HotWildlife only last week," he said. "Brought in by a guy who claimed to have found her wandering in some mountainside woods near his home

— not far from HotWildlife. He tried to shoo her away, but she wouldn't go. And then he realized she was pregnant. He managed to coax her into the enclosed bed of his pickup and drove her to HotWildlife."

"Sounds possible," I said. "So does that mean he adopted mama wolf as a pet, then decided she was too much to care for when he realized she was about to present him with more needy wild puppies?"

"Could be."

"And if so, maybe now that the pups have been born, he's started missing his pet and stolen her back."

Dante's dark eyes looked into the rearview mirror, and I noticed that cars around us on the busy freeway seemed suddenly to go faster. Or maybe we were slowing down. Had he seen a cop car notice him?

After a moment, he continued our conversation. "Megan considered that. She already contacted him. He denies that he came back for the mama, claims she wasn't ever his pet, and even if she had been, he wouldn't take her away from her newborn pups. Too cruel to all of them."

"Sounds like a good man," I replied. "Maybe."

"Cynic." Dante aimed a grin toward me as we were passed by a California Highway

Patrol car that apparently had no issue with his current speed. I assumed it was around the limit, judging by the other cars that kept us company.

"Realist," I countered.

We talked more about how he'd founded HotWildlife seven years earlier, and some of the magnificent creatures the sanctuary had helped to save.

Soon, we approached that wonderful locale.

The place was crowded enough that Dante had a hard time locating a spot in the large, open parking lot. "Do you think word's out about the missing wolf?" I asked as he pulled into a space that seemed skinny yet accommodated the roomy sedan.

"More likely, word is out about her pups, and people are here to see them."

Turned out we were both right. The crowd was biggest around the entry to the indoor infirmary. Some of the same people I'd seen there yesterday, visitors and tourists and animal friends, milled around outside. A couple recognized Dante.

"Are you here because of the missing wolf, Dante?" called a tall, familiar-looking guy right near the door.

"That's right. And there'll be a reward for information leading to her safe return."

Dear Dante. He was adept at getting attention for something important to him — at a cost, of course. "Can anyone here share any suspicions?"

A lot of people did, including the guy who'd spoken. His name was Irwin, and he claimed to be a frequent visitor to Hot-Wildlife. "Ransom," he suggested. "A lot of people know your relationship to this animal park, and someone might figure you'd pay a lot for the wolf while she's nursing, so her pups don't suffer."

"Good thought," Dante said. "But no ransom note, at least not yet."

Not necessarily a good thing. My earlier petnapping situation had involved notes and nonsense, and I'd recovered all animals. But that was a whole other story.

Other people in the crowd tossed out possibilities, from an employee's carelessness that allowed the wolf mom to sneak away for a while, to a hidden hole in the infirmary floor where she'd gotten caught.

"We'll continue to check out the entire facility," Dante assured them, "but our able staff has already combed the area. We believe she's gone, and we're worried about both her and her babies."

"We'll make sure the public's aware of the missing wolf," I said, looking to Dante for confirmation that he didn't dislike the idea. He nodded. Soon as I had a chance, I'd call my usual media contact, Corina Carey.

We soon gently shouldered our way past the crowd and into the infirmary. Megan met us at the door.

"Any sign of the mama wolf?" I asked.

Her face was nearly as pale as her light hair. I noticed again that her golden brown eyes were as attractive as many felines' I'd seen. Maybe that was what had gotten her interested in tending to wild cats. She wore a beige safari outfit with a many-pocketed vest.

"None," she said dejectedly.

The back door opened at the far end of the hall, between the infirmary's glassed-in enclosures. Jon Doe hurried in, followed by a raft of sanctuary volunteers, including Anthony, Krissy, and others I'd seen before. Megan pivoted to look at them. But their bleak expressions solidified the situation. They hadn't found mama wolf.

I pondered the other inhabitants of the infirmary, but an injured coyote and cagy raccoons would have left evidence had they attempted to eat the wolf.

"Show me the habitat and tell me how you think she got out — or was taken out," Dante demanded.

The only way they could figure was through the sole back door. It was kept locked, and the only key was in the sanctuary director's office. And the door to the office was mostly kept locked at night, when there was only a skeleton staff keeping an eye on the residents.

The baby wolves were still in the enclosure, huddled together.

Surely, no one was allowing them to starve. I asked Megan, "How are you taking care of them with their mother gone?"

"By pretending as much as possible to be her. Want to give a baby a bottle?"

"Me?" I squeaked, and then considered it. "Heck, yeah. I thought only the caretakers could feed the animals."

"This is a special situation. We need additional help. And nurturing the babies — well, at this age they're not a lot different from doggy pups."

With no further fuss, and on Megan's okay, Jon Doe led me into the area behind the enclosures and showed me to a plastic chair. Then he handed me a small bottle with wolf formula, I supposed, and a nipple that was soft and long and might have resembled a mama wolf's — who knew?

"I've done this before at other animal sanctuaries," he explained at my inquiry.

29

And then he handed me a baby.

The little wolf was a small bundle of gray fur, eyes closed, mouth working the nipple voraciously. All I could do, sitting there with that pup in my lap, was smile and coo and make baby talk, as if I held a human infant.

Eventually, she stopped sucking and seemed to fall asleep. I looked up and noticed two others similarly engaged with the other pups: Jon Doe and Krissy. I didn't know where Dante was, but suspected he was outside somewhere attempting to track mama wolf — or her evil abductor.

Eventually, I handed my baby to Megan, hating to give her up.

"You can do it again soon, if you're still around," she said.

"Thanks," I responded gratefully.

We went back to the outside of the glassed-in enclosure. No visitors were permitted in just then, so it was empty.

Until a guy burst through the door, followed by an obviously angry Dante.

"What the hell are you doing?" Dante demanded.

"I want some answers," the guy said. He was short and stocky, with curly gray hair behind a receding hairline. "I brought that wolf here expecting her to be taken care of — her and her babies, whenever they were born. I'm here today because Megan Zurich called and all but accused me of stealing her back. I should have found someplace else to care for her. This sanctuary sucks."

"This," Megan said, glaring at him, "is Warren Beell. He brought the wolf here in the first place, but that doesn't give him the right to insult —"

"It gives him the right to question us," Dante interjected smoothly. "Just as we have the right to question him."

"You have no right to ask me anything," Beell yelled. "Especially since the questions I was asked before were nearly an accusation. I did nothing wrong. All I did was bring the wolf here. And look what happened to her."

The guy seemed justifiably upset. Maybe.

But he also seemed to sling so many accusations that I wondered whether his intent was to discourage us from asking *him* anything else.

Was that because he was trying to hide his guilt?

We got nothing useful from Warren Beell or anyone else.

Three days went by so fast I could only watch them dash. Not that I stayed an idle observer. I hung out at HotWildlife as much

31

as possible, trying to uncover clues to mama wolf's disappearance.

Good thing I had excellent backup in my pet-sitting enterprise. I again confirmed my human clients' okays. Fortunately, all were understanding — and professionally served by people whom they'd met before. Both Rachel and Wanda went out of their way to take care of the charges I was tending.

Plus, I was also lucky enough not to have any court appearances in cases I handled at the Yurick & Associates law firm. The depositions and client conferences on my schedule were deftly delayed by the sweet but firm receptionist and all-around assistant, Mignon, who was clearly eager to help me locate the missing mama wolf.

Right now, I stood in the facility's nearly full parking lot, talking on my cell phone. It was a day late in September, warm even in the mountains, and I smelled the scent of the nearby trees sheltering the sanctuary. Dante was inside the fence, and the last time I'd seen him, he was again — still — interviewing everyone around when mama wolf went missing. I hadn't met Dante long ago, but I knew that, as charming as he could be, patience in obtaining answers to a question he considered important wasn't exactly his strong suit.

Mine, either.

Which was why I'd decided to make this call. It may have been poor judgment on my part, but when faced with a problem, I always consider it best to engage all possible resources to resolve it.

"Hi, Althea," I said after pushing a button for a saved and utterly familiar number — one I hadn't used in more than a month. "This is —"

"I haven't forgotten you, Kendra," chided the voice at the other end. Althea Alton was an employee of Hubbard Security. Yes, that Hubbard. Jeff. My onetime significant other, who'd hurt me badly a while back. So badly that I'd decided we were obviously out of each other's lives.

Since then, he'd attempted to change that. I didn't mean to be an unforgiving louse, but I'd moved on.

For one thing, I'd met Dante.

Even so, it was useful, murder magnet that I am, to know a private investigator and security expert like Jeff.

More helpful yet was his employee Althea — grandmotherly in age and absolutely youthful when it came to knowing about all things technological.

Like computers. And how to get any information available online.

Using sources I knew better than to attempt to nail down.

Yes, Althea was, I believed, a hacker of outstanding skill.

"I hope you'll never forget me," I told her. "I've missed talking to you. And —"

"Cut through the crud, Kendra," she said in a dry tone. "What do you want me to find out for you?"

A car I didn't recognize drove into the Hot-Wildlife parking lot. Not that I knew more than a tiny fraction of the people whose cars were here. Even so, I kept looking for someone who could help find mama wolf. Was this the one?

I scrutinized the car and its occupant as I spoke. "It could be a matter of life and death," I advised Althea. I explained where I was and what little creatures I craved saving. And why they needed it.

The person in the white sedan got out. A woman, middle-aged. She didn't appear to be the canine kidnapping type.

But then again, who did?

She seemed somewhat hesitant as she approached the main gate. She stopped to buy a pass. Probably just a visitor.

"So," I concluded to Althea, still holding my cell tight to my ear, "I spent considerable time Googling Warren Beell, who dropped the pregnant wolf here in the first place. He seemed really bent out of shape that someone might wonder if he'd steal her back. I gather he's in the car-sales business. But I didn't get much background on him. If you could check him out, see whether there's anything available online about if he ever adopted a wild animal, legally or not, that would be great. Or anything else that might help us find the mother wolf. Maybe there's a site somewhere that says someone has just seen a female wolf wandering around the San Bernardino area. Whatever. I've used my usual resources to look, but haven't found a thing."

"Got it," she said. "And I'll be glad to help. Although, Kendra, you know that before I spend any time on it —"

"You have to clear it with Jeff." I heaved a hearty sigh. I knew that would be so. Still, I hated to get him involved. And especially to feel beholden to him again.

But I needed to exhaust every resource, especially the best. And there was no one better than Althea.

"I'll let you know what he says," she said. We completed our farewell pleasantries and hung up.

I felt like folding into a frustrated heap, right there on the pavement. Instead, I ap-

35

proached the entry. The young volunteer in the booth recognized me from my many entrances over the past few days, and waved me in.

I spotted Jon Doe walking along the path from the storage area, arms full of bags of creatures' food.

"Hi," I called. "Can I help?"

And have you seen any sign of mama wolf? But I didn't ask what was so obviously on my mind.

"Nope. I'm good." He aimed his shrewd gaze at me. "And, no, though I've looked everywhere, checked with anyone I know who's visited this place over the past few weeks, I'm still damned frustrated. I haven't found a clue about where that poor wolf went to. In case you wanted to know."

I smiled. "How did you guess? More important, are the babies still okay?"

"Sure are, and they'll continue that way as long as they're in my care." His goatee underscored his mouth's straight line of determination. "Not that I'm neglecting my other responsibilities. I want to make sure everyone's aware of that."

"That's great," I said. I believed him. He certainly seemed earnest. And if he thought it important that people around here understood his attitude, I'd do what I could to spread the word. "And . . . well, when's the next feeding time?"

He grinned. "I take it you want to participate?"

"You take it right." I smiled right back.

"You're my kind of people," he said.

Okay, so maybe I have some unsatisfied maternal genes somewhere inside. Once again, I took great pleasure in holding a small bottle for a hungry little wolflet.

Beside me, also sitting on not-so-comfortable seats in the enclosure off the infirmary's kitchen, were that same diligent Jon Doe and young Krissy, each also feeding a pup.

Too bad my hands were otherwise occupied. I'd have taken my cell phone from the bottom of my large purse and snapped a photo of our amazingly sweet activity.

"How often do you have to take care of newborn wild animals here?" I asked Jon, to make conversation.

"Not very," he said softly, hugging the pup in his lap. "Fortunately, even while in captivity, most wild mothers take good care of their offspring. And we've been really lucky that our animals after giving birth generally remain in good health."

"I helped with a baby bird not long ago,"

37

Krissy chimed in. "A little hawk, whose mother was shot by some miserable hunter." She, too, held her small charge close and looked at home here.

"HotWildlife is lucky to have devoted folks like you to help out," I said as Dante came in. Gloriously handsome as always, he looked windblown despite the stillness of the air. I again assumed he'd been busy scoping out the sanctuary for further clues on the apparent wolf abduction. At this point, after no sightings, we no longer imagined mama wolf had left her babies voluntarily to head out for a hunt.

Dante and I were on the same wavelength in other ways, too. He whipped his cell phone out of his pocket and took a couple of photos. "This is one great scene. Maybe we can use it to help publicize HotWildlife and get even more volunteers."

"Great idea!" exclaimed Krissy. She beamed an awestruck smile in his direction.

"I agree," I said. "Adding volunteers, I mean. Poor Jon, here, is making sure every-thing else he needs to do gets done, in addition to his care of the wolf pups. Extra assistance would be good."

Jon nodded and gave a modest smile while checking the bottle in his wolf baby's mouth.

But Dante didn't appear especially impressed. In fact, he seemed somewhat dour. I figured he was as worried about mama wolf as the rest of us, and hadn't fully taken in my approbation of the busy HotWildlife employee in our midst.

"There's other help on the way, too," Dante said. "A good friend of mine, Brody Avilla, really likes animals. He's coming to help look for our missing wolf."

"*The* Brody Avilla?" Krissy seemed extra impressed. Dante's buddy Brody had starred in his share of big-budget movies and now appeared often as a judge on our very own *Animal Auditions* television show.

"None other," Dante said, which got a shrill little squeal from Krissy. Much as I wanted to hold my ears, I nevertheless considered her reaction a good thing.

Maybe she'd stop panting over Dante when Brody arrived.

And of course I knew exactly why Dante had invited his longtime friend. They had a history together, one they'd yet to share with me. I suspected it was something deep, dark, and secret in their mutual past. Some military special ops, perhaps, or even something less savory.

One of these days I would ferret it out. I did, after all, have an excellent relationship with at least some ferrets, since, a few months ago, I had saved them from being murder suspects.

"That is really cool." Krissy was still so excited that she disturbed the nursing wolf pup on her lap. I saw the small creature move, and heard a teeny whimper.

"How's your little charge doing with his lunch?" I asked as a gentle reminder.

She shot me a glare that suggested I was the last person she wanted to hear speaking. Oh, well. She turned back to Dante. "I want to hear all about how you know Brody Avilla. Were you a backer for any of his films? Will you ask him if I could have just an itsy-bitsy part in one? It's so cool," she repeated. "I'm just really happy to know you, Dante." Her expression suggested that she wanted to know him better. In all ways. Especially in the biblical sense.

So much for assuming an introduction to Brody would get the young brat to stop flirting with Dante.

Not that he was mine, of course. And I wasn't convinced I wanted him to be . . . was I?

Hell, I *did* want him to be, at least for the moment. Why else would I even consider letting him keep a change of clothes at my house?

40

And that was the problem. He appeared to want more moments. Minutes. Hours. Years. Forever?

Anyhow, I needed to alter this conversation in a manner I could live with without retching.

"So when will Brody get here?" I asked Dante brightly.

"Any time," he said, smiling.

I smiled back, as if we shared some kind of secret. I heard a gruff noise emanate from the throat of someone in the room, and assumed Krissy was attempting again to usurp Dante's attention.

But when I quickly aimed my glance around, it wasn't Krissy who looked irritated, but Jon Doe.

Interesting. His expression immediately lightened as I looked at him.

Still . . . what was that about?

And why, when I looked at Dante, did a grim expression again shadow his sexy face?

CHAPTER THREE

Less than an hour later, we sat in Megan's office in the front building of the sanctuary's enclosed complex. Brody had just arrived, and he, Dante, and I had joined the director for a discussion.

"Sorry to hear about the missing wolf," Brody said. "I know you take your responsibilities here seriously, Megan, especially regarding members of endangered species."

Brody was, of course, movie-star handsome, since he was, in fact, a movie star. He'd acted in many action features — although none lately — including a remake of *Rin Tin Tin* and another about K-9 Marines. His most recent gig was as a judge for *Animal Auditions*.

Imagine how a gorgeous guy should look on the screen, and that was Brody, with his firm jaw, jutting cheekbones, and glimmering gold eyes. His hair was light brown, thick, and wavy. Today, he was clad in well-worn jeans and a black T-shirt, taut over movie-star muscles.

"Have you been to HotWildlife before?" I asked Brody. I assumed he had, since he seemed to know Megan. And, as Dante's friend, I assumed he trod many of the same paths as the chief funder of this facility.

"Several times," he said. "Love this place!" His smile was directed at Megan, and she cast a wan one right back.

Megan's face was drawn, her mouth pinched, and her usually bright brown eyes dull. The lost mama wolf obviously affected her psyche, and I felt sad for her.

Not to mention said mama wolf and her abandoned babies.

"I assume you've used the usual routes of investigation to try to find her." Brody's latest comment was addressed to Dante, who nodded.

He sat beside me, his chair abutting mine despite the roominess of this office. Now and then, he would touch my hand, lying on the metal armrest, as if in reassurance. To me or to him?

And why did that question in my mind make me want to get him alone and into my arms for a gigantic hug?

"We've gone all the usual routes," Dante confirmed. "Everyone who works here and

43

who's visited lately has been questioned. We've walked every inch, looking for a hole in the perimeter fence large enough for the wolf to get through. Nothing."

"And how about Wagner? Have you utilized him?"

"Hell!" Dante thundered as he rose. "I should have thought of him immediately. I've always kept him away from Hot-Wildlife. Didn't want his scent to aggravate the animals here, or for him to get edgy over the wild inhabitants. But he's a German shepherd."

"A well-trained one," Brody added. "He might be able to follow the scent."

"He's in L.A.," Dante grumbled.

"Can you get someone to bring him?" Megan asked. She, too, was standing, behind her neat wooden desk. A computer stand sat at her right, and its large, flat screen seemed state-of-the-art. Of course Dante would want the person running any of his operations, charitable or not, to have the finest office equipment.

"We'll go back for him," Dante said.

At the same time, I said, "My assistant, Rachel, has said she wants to see Hot-Wildlife. If I can get someone to take over all our pet-sitting clients for a day, I'm sure she'd be glad to bring him." Whether Wanda

Villareal could handle them all was doubtful, but our additional contacts in the Pet-Sitters Club of SoCal could probably take up the slack. As long as our clients were okay with it, of course.

"Sounds great." Megan looked relieved, as if she felt certain having a scent dog here would solve the missing wolf mystery. I hoped she was right, but it remained to be seen. Or scented.

"I'll make some calls," I said. "See if I can set it up." Cell phone in hand, I exited the office and made my way down the hall.

The building was separate from the rest of the sanctuary, and the infirmary and nearest habitats were many yards away. The landscaping was lush along the paths, as if in imitation of genuine wilderness that would attract wild animals.

Stopping by a tall green hedge near the facility's entrance, I saw Jon Doe outside the fence, on the pavement. He strode toward me with determination, as if eager to come back inside.

"Any sign of the mama wolf?" I asked as he approached. I'm sure he expected the repetitious question as much as I anticipated his negative answer.

I considered telling him about the upcoming assistance of Dante's dog in finding the missing mama but decided against it. Better that I start making my calls.

I soon had everything lined up. Rachel would bring Wagner here first thing the next morning, after dropping my Lexie at Doggy Indulgence Day Resort to enjoy a day of pampering by my buddy Darryl Nestler. Rachel would get a tour of HotWildlife, then head home by evening. Wanda would round up a few fellow pet-sitters and get keys and instructions for my current charges from Rachel. I'd even gotten my clients' verbal okays.

All would work out well. I hoped. I intended to keep in close touch with Wanda the next day, to make sure.

As I finished, I saw movement in the nearest animal enclosure, where a couple of coyotes resided. They'd been brought here from around L.A., where a lot of the scampish scavengers still resided. They were cunning, yet cute in their own way — as long as they weren't eating someone's pet kitty. A peek at them on the prowl inside their habitat drew me toward the walled, moated, and fenced enclosure.

Inside, Jon Doe bustled about, apparently shoveling the dirt to clean the area. It was his movement I'd seen, not the coyotes', who must have been confined in the smaller, secluded area behind.

Jon saw me at the same time and gave a wave, as he ducked into the back area. He quickly appeared outside and must have opened the inner gate, since the coyotes re-appeared in the enclosure. In moments, Jon stood beside me. I was impressed that someone who appeared more than middle-aged was as quick and agile as he.

"Did you learn anything useful?" he asked. "I noticed you were on the phone."

I opened my mouth to tell him of the impending presence of Wagner when I saw Dante, Brody, and Megan emerge from the nearby office building. I raised my hand in a wave.

And noticed, from the corner of my eye, that Jon seemed to startle. Then freeze. I glanced over at him, but he didn't look any different than usual. Had I imagined the odd reaction?

Probably.

The three approached, and soon also stood on the path outside the coyote enclo-sure. Volunteers Krissy and Anthony came down one of the nearby paths and joined us. Krissy's apparently awed gaze was on Brody. I introduced them, and she stam-mered something in greeting. Brody grinned, then looked at us all before turn-

47

ing his attention back to the coyotes.

"Fascinating animals," he said. "Sneaky and sly as all get-out. Predators of the highest magnitude." He looked at me and smiled, but his glance seemed to slide over my shoulder before returning to meet mine.

"Oh, but they're great survivors," said Jon Doe from behind me.

"Sure are," Dante said. "But they need a pack to watch their backs."

I looked over at Megan, who stood between the two men. Her expression mirrored the confusion I felt. Were these guys saying something unrelated to coyotes? I thought so, but I couldn't imagine what that was about. Krissy, on the other hand, seemed unable to decide whether to stare at Dante or Brody, and her eyes moved from one to the other. Was she clueless about anything other than her apparent dual crushes? Who knew?

"Anyway, not much more we can do here tonight — as long as you have enough people around to feed the pups." Dante looked inquiringly at Megan, who nodded.

"I'm staying!" Krissy announced. Jon Doe didn't say anything, but I felt sure that, with his dedication to the place, he'd be around as well.

"Great," Brody said. "I've got some computer work to do tonight. But I'll be back first thing tomorrow to see how else I can help while we wait for Wagner."

"Who's that?" Krissy inquired.

"Dante's dog," I said. I explained why he was on his way.

We said our good evenings and departed. Dante drove his car toward his cabin, and Brody followed.

By the time we arrived, I was ready to strangle Dante. He had responded to all my questions about any undercurrent in their comments with absolute innocence, along with incredulity at my suspicions.

I didn't buy it.

CHAPTER FOUR

A while later, we three were ensconced back at Dante's mountain retreat. We'd stopped for dinner at a sandwich shop along the highway, and now each of us sipped from a stein of icy amber beer we'd brought back.

At least Dante and I did, as we sat in front of his big-screen TV in the vast yet comfortable living room. Brody had excused himself and headed for the office at the far end of the posh cabin's first floor. Which made me mighty curious.

I knew full well that Dante and Brody had a secret history together, and suspected it had something to do with the military — maybe the K-9 corps, which was what showed up on Dante's incomplete official bio posted at the HotPets Web site. Or some kind of security ops. Whatever. My assumption now was that the hot actor Brody was not online scouting for upcoming entertainment industry gigs, but for something to do with the lost mama wolf. Would someone post a notice on a secure site about finding a stray, prowling wolf in this area?

Or was it something else Brody was after?

The curiosity drove me crazy. But I did my utmost to act normal with Dante as we watched a reality show where people competed by pruning plants into exotic and interesting topiary designs. Of course, I preferred the ones that resembled animals. No wolves, but an elephant, an iguana, and even a potbellied pig.

"They look like some of your clients you've described," Dante said. We were snuggled up together on his lush leather sofa. He had an arm around me, and I'd laid my head on his shoulder. A sweet and serene moment, sure, but I couldn't help being sexually aware of this really handsome and hot guy.

"I've never taken care of an elephant," I contradicted. Iguanas and pigs? Sure.

"So which of those pseudo artists do you think will win?" he asked.

"I'd vote for the one who snipped out the big, beautiful heart," I said.

"Hearts are supposed to be red," he countered. "Not fuzzy green plants."

"Maybe, but —"

I didn't finish, since Brody suddenly appeared in the doorway. He looked like he had something on his mind.

"Find something interesting?" Dante pulled away slightly as I lifted my head from his stiffening shoulder. I looked at him. Whatever he was hoping to hear was clearly important to him, considering how he stared so pointedly at Brody.

Brody aimed a glance in my direction. "Possibly," he said. "Some ideas on how else to look for the missing wolf."

"Right. Let's go talk about it." Dante rose and strode across the room.

I stood, too. I absolutely wanted to assist in locating mama wolf.

"Er — how about getting us another beer, Kendra?" Dante nodded toward his empty stein on the long, low coffee table, where we'd been resting our feet.

Obvious translation: this was a guy thing, a conversation to which I wasn't invited.

Which definitely suggested to me that mama wolf wasn't the topic. At least not the only topic.

What was going on? And why was I being excluded?

With a shrug, I picked up our mugs and headed to the kitchen.

But when I got there, I slowly and silently squeezed my back against the wall and sneaked into the hall. I heard hushed male voices from the den that doubled as an office. Big surprise. Brody obviously had shared the result of his research with Dante, and they were discussing it.

As quietly as I could, I went toward the office. I didn't hear much discernible, except something that sounded like "Jon Doe."

I'd gotten a sense, at HotWildlife, of an undercurrent among the men, but hadn't known what it was. Still didn't.

Did Dante and Brody think the sanctuary's employee had something to do with the wolf's disappearance? If so, why? To show off his nurturing skills with the pups?

Made no sense to me.

I heard some stirring, like the men were on the move, so I quietly hustled my bod back into the kitchen, where I opened more beer bottles and poured out the brew as if absolutely thrilled with the assignment.

As Dante and Brody entered the room, I handed Dante his refilled stein. "Where's your glass, Brody?" I asked. "Do you want more beer?"

"Sure," he said. "It's in the den."

"I'll get it," I said brightly, excited about the idea of an excuse to get into the room for a quick look at the computer.

"Don't bother." Brody hurried his movie-star self out of the kitchen toward the den.

"So, did he find something helpful about mama wolf?" I asked Dante.

"Not as much as I'd hoped," he replied cryptically, then lifted his glass to his lips.

Which I watched. I loved his talented lips. And not especially for the use of sipping beer. My insides steamed, if only for an instant. And then Brody was back with his mug. I refilled it with a bright, if false, smile.

Okay, so I enjoyed watching Dante. Liked Brody's company, too, as we all strolled into the living room and sat back down. Watched more of the reality show, followed by a flip of channels to financial news.

To which I paid little attention.

What I really wanted was to go into the den and check out the computer.

Damned if I didn't get my opportunity a little later. The men, clearly chomping at the bit to continue their conversation, eventually excused themselves to go outside. "Brody and I need to talk about some ideas I have for *Animal Auditions,*" Dante said.

"I'd love to brainstorm about it," I replied.

"It's about my financial backing and other stuff I think you'll find boring."

"Could be." I doubted it, although I also

doubted they really intended to discuss *Animal Auditions*. And so I let them head out to the rustic front porch, illuminated by lantern-shaped lights, without me.

The porch was in the front, and its windows into the house opened onto an entryway. That meant they couldn't see me leave the living room and sprint down the hall toward the den.

A good thing.

Just in case, I didn't turn on the light but saw what I could from the hall's glow behind me — enough to get me to the desk, where I pressed a key to waken the computer from sleep mode.

Not surprisingly, only the desktop showed. I got onto the Internet — this far from civilization, Dante had paid for a satellite connection — and checked the list of sites Brody had visited. To my delight and surprise, he hadn't had the foresight to delete his browsing history.

But the Web sites listed didn't make a lot of sense to me. One was something called bop.gov. I clicked on it — and learned that it was the Federal Bureau of Prisons. Another involved the U.S. Treasury. There were a couple that concerned wolves and their habitats, which was unsurprising.

The screen also showed that Brody had

Googled Jon Doe.

I was almost as confused after seeing this as I'd been before accessing the computer.

Hearing the front door open, I hurried out, hoping no one would duck into the den before the computer transferred back to sleep mode. I headed down the hall to the nearest bathroom, as an excuse not to be in the kitchen or in front of the TV.

Even as my mind continued to spin in curiosity and confusion.

Later, I considered pressing Dante with pillow talk to extort some answers. Sex in exchange for information? Well, no. I'm not that kind of woman. Sex, yes. Holding out for an unrelated request? No.

So, the next morning, I felt sensuously sated as we got ready to head to Hot-Wildlife. While Dante showered, I finished dressing. I went into the kitchen for a glass of fruit juice poured by one of the house-keepers who showed up each morning to ensure the place was perfect. As I thanked her and started sipping, my cell phone rang, and I recognized the number right away.

"Hi, Rachel," I said. "Where are you?"

"Just getting off the freeway. I should be at HotWildlife in twenty minutes."

56

"Sounds good. We may be there a little later."

But not by much. I saw Rachel standing by the front entrance with Dante's dear Wagner as the three of us — Dante, Brody and I — pulled into the partly filled parking lot about a half hour after our conversation. I grinned and waved. Rachel waved back and approached us.

"Does this entitle me to a tour of Hot-Wildlife?" she asked as she handed Wagner's leash to Dante. Rachel had recently turned twenty. When I first met her, she'd been trespassing in my large, rented-out house — kinda. Her dad was my tenant, and neither he nor I expected his offspring to move in while he was out of town.

But he'd welcomed her, and she and I had become good buddies — so much so that I'd hired her as my backup caregiver at my pet-sitting service, Critter TLC, LLC. She thrived at it. And as a wannabe actress, she wasn't doing too badly, either — often off on auditions and occasional roles — and she was doing a great job as on-air hostess of *Animal Auditions.* In fact, a good percentage of the people part of our cast was now here, with Brody around.

Rachel was waiflike, with huge brown eyes that glowed now with anticipation. She was dressed, as she often was off-screen, in jeans and a short T-shirt.

"Private tour coming up," I told her, glancing at Dante for confirmation. He nodded, and we all went in, waving at the volunteer who manned the entry booth. Inside, there were already quite a few visitors strolling the sanctuary's pathways to see the wild populace.

"Can I see the wolf pups first?" Rachel asked.

"Sure," I said. "We'll all go to the infirmary, where they're being cared for. That's where Wagner is most likely to pick up the scent of their missing mama. Right, Dante?"

"We'll start there," he confirmed, "to see if he senses anything. If not, we'll go to the enclosure where she stayed when she first got here, before the pups were born."

We passed the main office building, just as Megan Zurich exited, clad in casual jeans and a HotWildlife T-shirt. She smiled at Wagner but warned, "Better try to keep him calm and not too close to the habitats, or we'll have a lot of stressed-out animals here."

"Got it," Dante agreed.

At the infirmary, I accompanied Rachel inside, and we watched while Dante and Brody encouraged Wagner to sniff around

58

the comfortable enclosed area where the mama had given birth. The pups were nearby, in an even more comfy nest where a warming pad had been added below the surface, in a simulation of mother's heat. At the moment, the babies were alone, but I noticed Jon Doe in the rear area, apparently concocting their next nutrition.

I oohed and ahhed over them for a few minutes along with Rachel, while Dante and Brody followed Wagner, whose nose was to the concrete floor. His presence was duly noted by other infirmary inhabitants, judging by the nervous reaction of the aging coyote and young raccoons. He soon headed toward the rear exit, and I followed. Was he tracking mama's scent as she slipped out of HotWildlife?

Could be, since he continued down the main outdoor path between the large habitats of the other wild inhabitants. We passed some visitors who eyed us curiously, but we offered no explanation for the German shepherd or his entourage. I heard lots of rustles and growls from beastly residents as they, too, noted the presence of the calm, tracking canine.

At the far end of the sanctuary, Wagner stopped at the closed gate and growled. It was a locked barrier, but Megan, who'd also trailed us, used a key to get it open.

To no avail. Once Wagner was outside, he apparently lost the scent. Maybe someone with a car had scooped up mama wolf. Maybe there were simply too many other aromas that confused poor Wagner. He sat down and stared up at Dante in seeming dejection, as if aware of how important his assignment had been to the man he adored.

We all trooped back to the infirmary, Wagner included. "In a few minutes, I'll take him to the area where the wolf was before giving birth," Dante said. "But first I'll let him retrace this path in case he missed an area where she veered off."

When we got back inside, Jon Doe, Krissy, and Anthony all held wolf pups and their bottles. A crowd of visitors had gathered to watch outside the glass, all with emotional smiles. Jon gave what seemed like an impromptu educational lecture.

"In a few weeks," he said loudly, to be heard where we were, "if their mother isn't located, we'll have to prepare special food to wean them. Wild wolves eat meals generally composed of their own prey, then regurgitate it so their pups can start learning the tastes. I'd rather let my own food digest, so we'll try something else to feed them."

"I'll bet the suppliers of HotPets products can come up with something," said Krissy, who'd spotted Dante, and smiled at him as if he could do absolutely anything.

Which, maybe, he could — at least when it came to finding ideal animal supplies.

He smiled back at her. For an instant, I wanted to kick him so he'd remember my presence. But if he wanted to react to Krissy's obvious adoration, that was between them.

Even if it irritated the hell out of me.

Anthony had apparently been primed to participate in the lecture, too, since he inserted some comments about how the baby wolves felt in his arms. It seemed utterly adorable to me to see this large high school football player type being so sweet to such tiny animals. In fact, I'd learned he actually was a football player who was hoping for a college scholarship soon.

Anthony compared the wolflet he held with a domesticated canine pup. He was large enough that hanging onto the small animal seemed nearly a juggling act to him, a little awkward but absolutely tender. "When they're this little," he announced, "they don't know they're wild animals yet. Or at least they don't act any wilder than the babies of any pet dog. But when they

61

start getting weaned, they sometimes bite the face that feeds them. Of course their wild mothers quickly show them who's the alpha of their little pack, but she wants them to learn to fend for themselves."

I stayed with Rachel in the observing crowd as Dante and Brody left once more with Wagner. They soon returned, just as the pups finished their bottles. I watched as Dante took Wagner into the room behind the nesting area, where supplies were kept. Jon Doe was there, too, and Krissy and Anthony joined them.

Only, Anthony looked pissed. He aimed a glare toward Doe, and I saw his fists clench before he stomped away.

"What was that about?" I asked, curious, as I caught up with him.

"The guy's nuts," Anthony responded, not, at this moment, the easygoing big guy I'd thought he was. "He's told me I can't feed the pups anymore. Said I'm too big, liable to drop one. But I'm always careful."

"I'm sure you are," I soothed, but when I looked around to see if I could smooth things over with Jon Doe, I saw him exchange a look with Dante that I simply couldn't read. I wasn't exactly sure why, but I suspected he wasn't conveying the same message I'd intended.

Brody stayed in the observation area with Rachel and me and the rest of the on-lookers, who had just started to disperse. "I'm heading back to L.A. tonight," he told us.

"Me, too," Rachel said.

"So are we," I told Brody. "Or at least Dante said we'd go home if Wagner didn't come up with something for us to follow up on. From what I saw, he didn't."

"Finding something else is my assign-ment, too." Brody sounded grim.

"Do you think there's something going on around here that resulted in the disappear-ance of the wolf?" I attempted to assume an air of total innocence. "I mean, a wolfnap-ping or someone trying to make Hot-Wildlife look bad . . . or anything else?"

Brody shrugged his movie-star shoulders beneath his green knit shirt. "Who knows?"

You might know, I thought, but he clearly wasn't going to give me any guesses.

We hung around through most of the day. Dante only became more frustrated as he attempted to use Wagner's services to find a mama wolf clue. I accompanied Rachel to the paths outside the various wild animals' habitats, and we both had an enjoyable time observing. Midday, I slipped back into the infirmary and successfully begged Megan to let Rachel and me give the pups their bottles.

I didn't pay a lot of attention, but I noticed Jon Doe moving all over the sanctuary, doing his caretaking duties.

By the end of the day, a lot more visitors had come through the sanctuary's gates. Rachel left, wanting to hurry home to retrieve Lexie from doggy daycare and help with the evening's pet-sitting, and I thanked her again for all she'd done.

A while later, Brody, whom I hadn't seen much of during the day, said it was also time for him to go. "I've got a meeting early tomorrow on our next *Animal Auditions* season, so I need to get some sleep tonight."

I said goodbye to him, then looked idly around for Dante. Didn't see him, but I did note that Wagner was leashed beneath a shady tree in an area of the sanctuary distant from the wild animals. Where had Dante gone without his best friend?

A couple of questions had come to me about the mama wolf's disappearance, but when I dropped into Megan's office to ask them, she wasn't there.

The day was drawing to a close. We would probably hurry back to Dante's cabin, pick up our stuff, and return to L.A. within the next hour, before the sun set.

I just might have one more opportunity to hug, and feed, a wolf pup. I wasn't sure when we'd be back — especially without additional clues to mama wolf's whereabouts. Maybe not till after the babies were weaned — and they'd be more active then, with eyes open and looking around for regurgitated prey.

The crowd of visitors had thinned. Not many around now. I took the opportunity to slip into the infirmary to see if I could beg anyone to let me feed the babies.

And noticed Jon Doe in the area behind the nesting place once more. Good. I'd ask him.

As I glanced beyond the enclosure where the pups slept, I saw that Jon was sitting on the floor. That seemed a bit strange, but maybe he was getting his second wind after all his work that day.

I went to the entrance of the back room and opened the door. Walked inside.

And gasped.

Jon Doe wasn't simply resting on the floor. He was covered in blood. Unmoving. At an odd angle.

"Damn it," I muttered to myself as I approached and said aloud, "Jon? Jon, can you hear me?"

When I touched his neck, searching for a

pulse, there was none.

Jon Doe appeared to be dead.

CHAPTER FIVE

I've often said I'm a murder magnet, and it's true. As a result, I know what to do besides scream when I stumble upon a dead body.

Of course I screamed, as I stepped back on the hard concrete floor, stopped touching things that could possibly be evidence, and extracted my cell phone from my pocket to call 911.

Then I called Dante, in case he was too far away to hear my screams.

Megan must have been closer, since the sanctuary's director was the first to run into the infirmary. Strange, all the stuff I noticed. Her hair was still clipped into the same barrette, but she had changed clothes, and was again wearing her beige vest with multiple pockets. What was she doing that evening — giving a lecture on wildlife somewhere?

And was that the reason she had changed clothes, or had she gotten Jon Doe's blood on her earlier duds?

Okay, I had no particular reason to suspect her, except that she was here and had known Jon Doe.

"What's the matter, Kendra?" she immediately demanded, then followed my line of sight along the back room's floor, and gasped.

She hurried toward the body. "Jon? Jon, are you okay?"

I grabbed her as she started to kneel. "Don't touch anything," I said in a quivering voice. "We don't want to destroy any evidence."

"Evidence?" She stood up again and looked at me with shocked, enormous eyes. "Is he — did someone — ?"

I finished it for her. "Yes, it looks like someone stabbed him, and I think . . . he's gone."

No, my initial reaction hadn't been to believe that a wild animal, in this sanctuary for feral creatures, was the killer.

Not with a bloody knife lying on the floor beside Jon. And I had to assume that the suspect watched at least some of the same crime shows on TV that I did. I'd have bet a week's worth of pet-sitting proceeds that there were no fingerprints on the weapon.

I heard sounds from inside the infirmary,

including the shrill cries of the wolf pups. Oh, heavens, were they okay? I hadn't noticed anything wrong with them as I'd dashed in. They'd seemed to be sleeping. But had anything happened to them, too? Although I heard multiple yaps, I couldn't really tell if there were two or three yappers. As people started streaming in from outside, I hurried to the viewing area and checked our little charges.

Yes! All three stood on wobbly legs, eyes still closed, most likely shrieking from being awakened by my screams — and, oh, by the way, if we happened to want to feed them now, they'd be pleased.

No, I don't know wolf-pup-speak any more than I can speak Barklish with Lexie, Wagner, or my pet-sitting doggy charges, but I'm often intuitive in discerning what animals attempt to communicate. Or at least I think I am.

I moved back the way I'd come, to block the hordes from heading into the back area. Not everyone would try it, of course, but among the crowd were Krissy, Anthony, caretakers and other employees, and volunteers. I took a deep breath and said, "There's been an accident, folks. I need for you to step outside and hang around until the authorities arrive."

Which was when Dante plowed in. I'd bawled enough into my cell phone to convey what I'd discovered, and he gallantly started backing up my orders.

Only later did I wonder where he'd been from the time I'd called until the time he arrived.

The EMTs arrived only a few minutes before the cops. I wasn't sure what was communicated to the volunteer staffing the front gate, but presumably she knew better than to keep the authorities out. In any event, I was herded outside by the San Bernardino Sheriff's Department to join the milling crowd I had commanded to wait there.

It was hot as the sun beat down. I longed to stroll the paths of the sanctuary, peek into the carefully constructed habitats, and spy on the cheetahs and coyotes and mountain lions. Predators all, they wouldn't blink at the presence of a dead body. But they used teeth and claws, not a human-manufactured blade, to bring down their prey. They hadn't had anything to do with Jon Doe's demise.

I would rather have departed HotWildlife, but I knew the drill. No one could leave until the authorities had released them. And that wouldn't occur until we'd all been interrogated.

I looked around in the crowd for Dante, wondering why he hadn't joined me. Surprisingly, he seemed deeply engaged in a conversation — with Brody! I thought Brody had left a long while ago to head back to L.A. Why was he here?

Wagner sat at their feet. Krissy hovered nearby in the mass of people, as if she, too, was hanging on every word of Dante's. Anthony was at her side.

I stood in a group of strangers. Maybe that was a good thing, for now. I used the opportunity to make a call.

"Hi, Ned," I said when Detective Ned Noralles of the Los Angeles Police Department answered his cell. "Guess what?"

"I know that tone," my former nemesis and now buddy — since I'd helped clear his sister and him from being murder suspects recently — said to me. "Don't tell me you're involved in another murder."

"I can't not tell you," I grumbled as quietly as I could so those around me couldn't easily eavesdrop. "I need your advice."

"Where are you?" he asked in apparent resignation. Or so it sounded, as best as I could hear amid the hubbub in the parking

71

lot and the static in our connection. "Do you want me to join you?"

"Not necessarily," I said. "I'm at Hot-Wildlife."

"If it's where I think it is, that's the jurisdiction of the San Bernardino County Sheriff-Coroner's Department, right?"

Looking toward the nearest uniformed cop who was engaged in crowd control, I studied the official green and yellow patch on the sleeve of her khaki-colored cotton shirt that was tucked into deep green slacks. "Seems so," I agreed.

"That could be a good thing. I've got a couple of buddies there. Tell me what happened."

I eased my way to the perimeter of the crowd, earning a glare from the same exasperated cop. I smiled as disarmingly as I could, then told Ned what had occurred.

"So this Jon Doe was an employee there?"

I confirmed it.

"Do you know anyone who had anything against him?"

"Not unless he'd located the missing mama wolf and whoever took her was peeved about it." I'd filled Ned in on that angle of what was going on, too. And I purposely didn't mention how I'd sensed an undercurrent that seemed generated by

72

Dante and Brody. And my wondering why Brody so conveniently was here just now. Or had he ever left?

"Okay, I'll call one of my buddies there. I'll ask him to keep an eye on whoever questions you. Just be as candid as you were with me, and you should be released fairly soon."

Which I knew, in cop time, could be anywhere from an hour to a few days, but I hoped for the former.

As I hung up my cell, I started meandering through the crowd toward Dante and Brody. Brody spotted me first and lifted his hand in a wave. When I reached them, I basked for an instant under Dante's warm smile, then said to Brody, "What are you doing here?"

"Dante called when he heard what had happened. I hadn't gotten far, so I came back to see what was going on."

And help Dante with whatever investigation he intended to conduct, I suspected. One of these days, I really had to get a grip on their mutual background.

I immediately recalled what I'd seen on the computer after Brody's search last night. Stuff I didn't understand.

And stuff about Jon Doe.

Very convenient that Brody hadn't gotten too close to L.A., and was able to return here at Dante's call.

Unless he hadn't gotten far at all for some other reason. Like something to do with Jon Doe's death?

Damn! I absolutely hoped not. I liked Brody. And if he'd been involved in killing Jon Doe, that undoubtedly meant Dante was an aider and abettor . . . or worse.

With the large crowd at HotWildlife, the local authorities had to make do with the available facilities. I watched as most people were sorted into groups in the warm September air. Sanctuary visitors were herded to several areas, and those with presumably closer ties to HotWildlife were shown to others.

As a person who was present mainly because of close acquaintanceship with the place's chief money source, I didn't fit neatly into any characterization. Then again, I had a credential more exciting than most: the person who'd discovered the body. Lucky me.

I mentally kicked my behind for my silent sarcasm. I, in fact, *was* lucky — compared with poor Jon Doe.

I was soon debriefed by a professional and particularly curt woman in a suit. She said she was a detective with the Homicide

Detail. But before I'd related the entire story — excluding my concerns and suspicions about Dante and Brody, of course — we were joined by a large guy, also in a suit, whose dark complexion and features suggested Hawaiian extraction.

"I'm Sergeant Frank Hura, Kendra," he said, holding out his beefy hand to me. His smile suggested I should know him, but I didn't.

"Hi," I said tentatively as we shook.

His round face folded into a hint of a frown. Not a good sign, since this cop just might be in charge. "Didn't Ned Noralles tell you about me?"

I hid my sigh of relief. "No, but I called him to ask his advice a little while ago. He said he had some friends in San Bernardino. You're one of them?"

"Sure am. I know some of your background with Ned, too, and how irritated he used to be with you — till you helped him out of an ugly situation." He glanced at the lady detective from the Homicide Detail. "Thanks, Liz. I'll take over now."

She seemed to work at erasing an even more annoyed expression and said, "Of course, sir," before moving off.

"Let's take a walk," Frank Hura said. "It's been a long time since I've been here, and I like to look at the animals."

"Me, too." And the idea of strolling made me happy; much more relaxed than standing, or sitting, face-to-face during an interrogation.

We skirted some pockets of people and headed down the main HotWildlife path, staying on the slightly shadier side, although there were few trees in the sanctuary. We stopped outside the liger enclosure and stared over the moat at the mostly striped feline that was a cross between a lion and tiger.

"So tell me what happened," Frank said.

I did so, repeating what I'd told the Homicide Detail woman, and then some. I described the disappearance of mama wolf, our worried attempts to find her, and more — up through my entering the infirmary and finding Jon Doe's crumpled, bloody body.

"So you're here with Dante DeFrancisco and Brody Avilla?" For a Sheriff's Department sergeant, he sounded rather starstruck.

"Yes. I'm sure they're being questioned by someone from your department, but I'd be glad to introduce you to them."

"Let's go!" But then he stopped and looked down at me. "They're potential murder suspects as much as everyone else around here, at least till they're cleared. But Dante DeFrancisco and Brody Avilla — a megabillionaire and a movie star — how likely is it that either would come here and kill a guy who cleaned animal enclosures for a living?"

"Not likely," I agreed, hoping it was true.

"Do you know if they knew Jon Doe?" I could tell from his tone that he was hoping I'd say no.

"Well, they talked to him here, of course," I dissembled. "Jon was helping to nurture the baby wolves and teach everyone how to care for them."

"I mean other than here," Frank said.

"Not that I'm aware of," I said. I crossed my fingers behind my back, just in case. I wasn't exactly lying. I didn't really know why Brody had been Googling strange stuff on the Internet and also looking up Jon Doe. And the fact that Dante and Brody exchanged unreadable looks didn't mean they knew him. Did it?

I intended to assume all things positive. I had no reason to believe Dante or Brody could have harmed the senior citizen who cared for HotWildlife animals.

And even if my murder-magnet mind made me wonder *if,* there was no reason to mention that to this deputy sheriff. Not yet, at least.

I had some checking to do.

CHAPTER SIX

But the checking would have to wait till later, when I could follow up on it.

In a while, Sergeant Hura conducted his own informal follow-up interview of Dante and Brody. I don't know what the official session was like, but this one was uneventful for the two interviewees, who were absolutely polite and cooperative like the good citizens they were. All their answers supported the position that they were both appalled at Jon Doe's untimely death, and that they had nothing to do with it.

We all stood in the shade beside a coyote compound at the far end of the sanctuary as the three of them talked and commiserated. Wagner lay down on some grass-covered earth and panted as he watched each of us in turn.

Frank Hura acted utterly star-struck while questioning the two men deferentially, his tone apologetic, as if he had to do this to fulfill his duty while knowing full well they were absolutely innocent. He had spent only a few minutes alone with the detectives who'd done the formal sessions, so for all I knew, this could be a Columbo kind of intended trap. But I didn't think so.

And me? It was all I could do not to roll my eyes in exasperation at this whole absurd exchange. I certainly didn't want Dante or Brody to have had anything to do with the ending of Jon Doe's life, but my suspicions remained that they out-and-out lied about not knowing him.

Or maybe it was simply a matter of semantics. Maybe they didn't actually *know* him, but I believed they knew something *about* him. Especially since Brody had looked him up on the Internet.

But, okay, even if they were absolutely guilty, I didn't want them arrested right then and there. I needed to conduct my own inquiry. Hopefully, it would exonerate them as fully as their own proclaimed innocence. If it didn't? What then? I'd really come to like Brody a lot, especially as an *Animal Auditions* judge with a star's appearance and a droll and delightful sense of humor.

And Dante? Well, I was an attorney, an officer of the court, and I might owe it to the world to turn over any evidence I found of his guilt. But I was also a woman in deep infatuation, one who lusted after this gorgeous, rich, and powerful pet-supply magnate. And —

"Kendra?"

My name spoken by that very same magnate kicked me out of my reverie. I'd been staring at some pacing coyotes as I'd stood there thinking and listening to the guys chatter near me. But now I turned back toward Dante.

"Those coyotes," I said. "They seem so grumpy, don't you think, the way they're acting?"

"I think you're projecting 'grumpy,' lady," he said in a tone so sweet that I couldn't completely focus on his insult. "Anyway, Frank is done with us, at least for now."

I aimed a glance at the deputy, who still smiled broadly, as if basking in having had the honor of interrogating Dante and Brody as potential murder suspects.

"With me, too, I assume." I attempted to keep the aforesaid grumpiness out of my voice, although I wasn't too successful.

"Of course, Kendra," Frank effused. "I'll want your contact information, all of you, as a formality and in case any further questions come up during our investigation, but you're free to go. I assume you'll head back to L.A., but be sure to get in touch with me next time you're around here." Something quizzical and perhaps defensive must have shown on my face, since as he watched me, his expression grew apologetic. "I mean, just so I can say hi. Show you around. Answer any questions you may have — as long as they're not confidential because of our inquiries. That kind of thing."

"Of course," Dante said smoothly. "Let's definitely stay in touch, Frank. We want to do all we can to make sure that whoever did this to Jon is captured and punished." He pulled his wallet from his jeans pocket and extracted a business card, which he handed to the sergeant.

As long as whoever did it isn't you, I thought. To Frank, I said, "Thanks for your discretion and understanding." I, too, handed him a card after waffling for an instant whether it should be my card as a partner of the law firm of Yurick & Associates or as the managing member of Critter TLC, LLC. I decided on the first, not that my playing the lawyer card would necessarily remove me from the suspect list. It was easier to field calls directed to my official place of legal employment.

Dante took my hand. "Let's head back to L.A.," he said. "We'll stop at my place first, to pick up our stuff. Brody will leave straight from here."

"Okay," I said, suddenly especially eager to be as far away from HotWildlife as possible. For the moment. Murder magnet that I'd become, I knew I'd stay involved until the case was resolved.

And no matter how star-struck Sergeant Hura might be, I wouldn't be swayed by the fact that these two guys with whom I was leaving happened to be celebrities.

Which meant I had a phone call to make to stay in the good graces of one of my contacts who'd become a friend: tabloid reporter Corina Carey. We scratched each other's backs, so to speak, when expedient. I'd sometimes found that having a murder I was looking into show up in the media helped me figure out whodunit. Corina had been interested, but not overwhelmingly so, about the missing mama wolf. But she would never forgive me for failing to tell her of yet another situation in which I knew a murder victim.

I also knew a host of potential suspects, which could include myself . . . as well as Dante. Reporters would undoubtedly drool about a story that involved something more than that hot entrepreneur's power, wealth, and benevolence to beasts.

And though I had no control over Corina, I could bargain with her to make her story an exclusive, at least for an instant, if she kept it less biased, and less sensational than other media slime might make it.

I decided not to make the call in front of Dante. He'd undoubtedly be at least somewhat displeased. Sure, he had come to know Corina during the murder investigation of an *Animal Auditions* judge. But talk to her now? I didn't think so.

So, when we reached his mountain getaway, I got away from him while he readied his stuff to go. I went into the backyard, just my cell phone and me, to make my call.

"Hi, Kendra," Corina said. She'd captured my cell number long ago. "How are things?" Her tone was as inquisitive as always, saying silently, *Have you come across any more murders?*

I stood near the trunk of a stately, sharp-scented tree — perhaps a ponderosa pine — staring toward the back door of the pseudo log cabin. Didn't see Dante or any of the part-time housekeeping staff. I could talk.

I told her about my latest deceased discovery. "We'd been having such a wonderful time here, helping those poor baby wolves," I finished with a sigh, leaning dejectedly against the tree trunk.

"Do you think the murder was related to the disappearance of the wolf bitch?" Corina sounded ecstatic with excitement. She'd already expressed her delight at my call and that I'd (hopefully) given her one up on any other reporter.

"I wouldn't be surprised," I said, "although right now I haven't a clue how that could be."

"I'll head to HotWildlife right away," she said. "Can you stay there so I can interview you?"

Not! I said to her softly, "No, but I can call the director, Megan Zurich, and ask her to cooperate with you. No guarantees, of course, but as long as you promise to cover this story like an unbiased reporter, and not an intrusive paparazzo, that'll help."

"Absolutely," she gushed, making me certain the opposite was most likely. "Thanks, Kendra. Say hi to Dante for me. And I owe you."

"You sure do," I said sweetly, and hung up. Okay, maybe calling her wasn't the most comfortable thing I could do, but I'd learned that keeping her not mad at me could come in quite handy. Dante would surely understand that . . . I hoped.

I called Megan Zurich, explained the situation, and warned her to be as forthright with Corina as she could be. "She comes on awfully strong at times," I said, "and she is, at heart, a tabloid type, but I've learned I can mostly trust her. Don't guess any answers to questions she asks, and feel free to refuse to discuss anything."

"How about if I refuse to discuss anything at all?" Megan clearly disliked everything about this.

"I'd suggest you stay courteous — and cooperative — without making any accusations against anyone in Jon Doe's death. She'll love you. Might even give Hot-Wildlife lots of good publicity that can only help bring in even more donations and visitors when all this is over." I explained how Corina had helped me in the past when I'd needed a little publicity to help bring a killer out from undercover — and how cooperating with her had helped to keep the rest of the media hordes at bay.

"Okay, Kendra," Megan finally said with a sigh. "I assume Dante's okay with it, too?"

"I'll make sure he is," I told her — with a bit more optimism than I actually felt.

I told Dante about my call to Corina a little after he'd turned onto the freeway. That way he couldn't easily stop and stare daggers at me.

To my surprise and delight, he didn't seem too angry. "Your friend Corina's a straight shooter as a reporter," he said, sounding somewhat pensive. He looked pensive, too, with his high forehead creased and his marvelous lips pursed. Too bad I couldn't kiss that pursing away. Well, maybe later. "Or at least pretty much so. Obviously this'll get a lot of publicity — the kind I don't really want. But having her on our side again might be useful. Good call, Kendra."

I basked in his praise for a little while, at least, as I watched the buildings at the sides of the freeway whiz by — shopping centers, residential areas, and all. I also pondered how to plunge into the topic that had been driving me nearly nuts for what seemed like forever, but had actually only been hours.

"So do you get involved with who Megan hires to help out at HotWildlife?" I commenced somewhat nonchalantly.

"If you mean, was I involved with her decision to employ Jon Doe in the first place, the answer is no."

So much for my employing even a little subtlety. He already knew what I was after.

"Then you didn't know him well," I

surmised. Or at least he wouldn't admit otherwise.

"No, but from what I could see, he was an asset. Worked hard. Cared about the animals. He always seemed to dig in to do what was needed at the facility."

"Then you have no ideas who might have killed him?"

Dante's gaze darted from the road ahead for an instant, and his gorgeous, dark eyes bored into me. Then he returned his attention to the road. "No," he said. "I don't."

I really had come to think a lot of this guy. Loved our intimate interludes. Even thought, now and then, that I might even, someday, come to love *him*.

Had gotten to know him fairly well over the past few exciting, enjoyable weeks. Or thought I had.

Right now, he sounded absolutely sincere. Utterly honest. Trustworthily truthful.

So why, then, didn't I believe him?

Did it have anything to do with my suspicions that he hadn't been entirely within the law in his enigmatic past?

Okay, so I stayed suspicious. That didn't serve to alleviate my hurt feelings when Dante simply dropped me off at my house late that evening. Even when he offered a kind of apology.

"I've got a lot of meetings lined up tomorrow, things I've missed after spending so much time at HotWildlife over the last couple of weeks. I need a good night's sleep first, Kendra, so I'd better not come in." Still sitting in the driver's seat of his Mercedes sedan, he regarded me beneath the lights on my curved and steep street. Was that regret I saw in his shining, dark eyes — or relief?

And why was I feeling so paranoid?

Maybe because I wasn't sure whether to trust the guy?

Behind us, in the backseat, Wagner woofed.

"See ya soon, guy," I called to him as I opened the car door. Dante was gentleman enough to come around to help me out and walk me to the wrought-iron gate. He gave me one heck of a sexy and suggestive kiss, considering it wasn't intended to be a harbinger of anything exciting for the rest of the night.

"Good night, Kendra," he said breathily against my mouth. "Think about me tonight."

"In your dreams," I countered airily, turning toward the nearest concrete pillar to enter the security code that turned off the alarm and opened the gate.

"Exactly. Yours, too." Dante smiled.

With a final look at him intended to be both enticing and irritated, I went inside and locked up again. In the chilly night air, I walked down the driveway past my nearly new SUV, a blue hybrid Escape, and up the stairs at the side of the garage to my apartment. I stopped at the top of the steps and waved at him, then went inside.

Where Lexie awaited me with such enthusiasm that you'd have thought I'd been gone for ages, not just a few days. The dynamic little ball of black and white fur trimmed in red was all over, leaping and snuggling and licking as I stooped beside her.

"I missed you, too, girl," I said, then stood. Nothing like a great greeting from a loving Cavalier to help defuse a sense of sorrow at being dumped at the doorstep by Dante. Cheered a bit, I headed into the kitchen with my cell phone at my ear, and called next door.

"Hi, Kendra," said my assistant and tenant's daughter, Rachel. "I just saw you come home and thought about letting Beggar out to greet you, but I didn't get there in time."

"How is your sweet Irish setter tonight?"

"Fine," she said. "I walked Lexie and him together an hour ago, just before it got dark.

Are you calling about our pet-sitting schedule tomorrow? I hope so."

Fortunately, I was already sitting at my cramped, round kitchen table in my cramped, square kitchen. Otherwise, I might have sunk down in anticipation. Rachel's words sounded like a harbinger of her unavailability tomorrow, which would mean I'd need to double up on my own pet-sitting obligations.

Well, I owed her for doubling up on hers for me.

"That's one reason I called," I acknowledged, "besides making sure you knew I was home. And to thank you again for stepping in and also making sure I had enough additional pet-sitting backup while I was gone."

"No problem. Only —"

"Only?"

"I heard on the news about the guy who was killed at HotWildlife. It's not enough that you're hunting a missing wolf. Are you investigating another murder?"

I sighed and stared at the phone. Word was already out. "Looks that way," I finally said with a sigh.

"Awesome!" she exclaimed. "You're so good at it, too. The way you solved the murder of Sebastian Czykovski for us at

Animal Auditions — that was my favorite case of yours so far."

Rachel had been a tenant, an assistant, and a friend during several murders I'd found myself involved in resolving. I wasn't surprised that she was especially interested in the one at *Animal Auditions,* since she's one of the hosts of the show. She had helped Brody come up with scenarios for our next mini-season, and he'd said planning was already moving along.

"Thanks," I said drolly.

"Do you have any clues yet? Any favorite suspects so far?"

"It just happened earlier today," I said. "It'll take time to unravel, I assume, like the others I've unfortunately been involved in."

She must have caught my less-than-ecstatic tone at last. "Oh. That makes sense. I hope this was another guy like Sebastian, who you weren't especially fond of in the first place."

I answered her partially unasked question. "I didn't know him well at all, but I'd no reason to dislike him."

"Was his name really Jon Doe?"

"That's right," I said, although her query kicked a little button inside my brain. I'd lots of questions about Jon Doe, especially regarding anything he might have done to bring himself onto Brody's computer screen for a search.

As part of attempting to ascertain who killed him, I might have a lot of digging to do.

"Anyway," Rachel said, "I have a really big audition tomorrow, Kendra. I guess my being on *Animal Auditions* may have helped my acting career. It's for a small part in a really big film. Do you . . . I mean, is it okay if I . . . ?"

"If you're asking if I can fill in for you and do all tomorrow's pet-sitting, the answer is yes," I said. "That's our deal. You help me when you can, without being chained to what I do. And you've gone above and beyond that over the past few days. Go for it, Rachel. Break a leg!"

I didn't know if she'd get the role, or how much time it might involve, but I hoped she'd still be able to help me out.

"You're the greatest, Kendra," she said, and I felt her warm hug leap from the mansion on my property, through the phone, and into my apartment.

"Of course I am," I said, then hung up.

A little while later, I'd walked Lexie for the last time that night, showered, and gotten ready for bed.

And willed the phone to ring, as it always

used to do a while back, when I was dating Jeff Hubbard, the P.I. and security guy.

Dante was a whole lot less predictable.

I wasn't about to call him, since he'd said his reason for dropping me off alone was that he needed sleep.

But the fact he didn't call kept me awake long into the night.

Or maybe it was because my mind churned over how I would approach solving this latest murder, especially from so many miles away.

CHAPTER SEVEN

We woke early the next morning, Lexie and I. I had lots of pets to sit, or rather, to walk, feed, play with, and — possibly — clean up after. For the first visits, in and around the San Fernando Valley, I took Lexie with me. She got along great with Meph, a little terrier who was a longtime client. It was too early, though, to stop in next door to Meph and visit with my friend Maribelle Openheim and her shepherd mix, Stromboli. Then there was Beauty, a golden retriever.

By the time we'd hung out with these pups for a while and lavished a lot of attention, it was nearly nine o'clock. Since the day promised to be a busy one — with more pets to visit — I decided not to impose my feelings of stress on Lexie, so I headed for Doggy Indulgence Day Resort.

My good friend Darryl Nestler was with his human staff at the tall desk near the door of the canine care center, greeting doggy guests for the day. Long, lanky, and lovable, Darryl was the reason I'd taken up pet-sitting in the first place. Doggy Indulgence didn't board pets, and he had given me a lot of referrals over time, none more critical than the first. Back then, I'd been unjustly accused of ethics violations that resulted in the temporary suspension of my license to practice law. For Lexie and me to eat, I had to do something — and that something consisted of my first pet-sitting assignments.

"Hi, Kendra," Darryl said enthusiastically as I walked in the door. "Hi, Lexie." He stooped and scooped my eager pup into his arms, hugging her gently as she stood on her hind legs and licked his pointed chin. Then he rose once more. As he nearly always did, he wore a green henley-style shirt with a Doggy Indulgence logo on the pocket. "Is Lexie staying here today?"

I nodded, then let her loose to join the already significant contingent of canines in the place that smelled of doggies and cleaning stuff. One of her favorite areas in Doggy Indulgence was the part with people furniture for pets to veg out on. Today, though, she obviously had some pent-up energy. She headed for a section where a few other doggies already played keep away with canine toys.

"I'm going to be on the go all day." I explained Rachel's unavailability to pet-sit due to her potentially exciting audition — and why I especially owed her the time off, which I'd have given her anyway.

"A missing wolf and a dead body? Boy, Kendra, you've been busy. Again. Don't you ever get tired of being a murder magnet?"

I saw the twinkle in his kind brown eyes beneath his wire-rims, and decided to tease him back. "I sure do. I'm ready to turn that pleasure over to you anytime. How about" — I pulled my cell phone from my purse and regarded the time on its screen — "immediately?"

"Sorry, I've got a full day planned. Full week, too. Full year . . ."

"I get it," I said with a laugh. "But I wish I could pass along this responsibility to someone. Anyone. Preferably someone I don't like — so that excludes you."

He gave me a big hug, even as I caught the eye of Kiki, my least favorite of his employees. The blond bombshell was a wannabe actress, as were so many people in L.A. And she was good with pets, which was why she was able to stay at Doggy Indulgence. But she had a nasty, somewhat slimy personality with people. And now she glared at me, as if I was muscling in on someone else's territory.

But I was just accepting a platonic embrace from my closest bud, not intruding on his relationship with his girlfriend. As I backed away slightly, I said, loud enough for her to hear, "How's Wanda?" That would be Wanda Villareal, a fellow pet-sitter and now Darryl's significant other. "She's been great about filling in for me when I've been out of town." We chatted briefly about Wanda and her Cavalier, Basil. And then I let him know I had to leave. "Lots of pet-sitting clients to visit," I told him. "See you and Lexie later."

First thing, when I returned to my Ford Escape to escape to my next pup to care for, I used my hands-free phone system to make one of a couple of pending calls. "Mignon, it's me," I said to the receptionist at my law firm. "I'll be in later, I promise, but I have some things to take care of first."

"Animals always come first, don't they, Kendra?" she said in a giggly, nonjudgmental voice. Like Borden Yurick, the senior partner of our firm that specialized in practicing law for senior citizens, she understood my priorities. "Want me to check your calendar and call you back if there's anything pressing later today?"

98

"Yes, and please ask Borden, too."

When I hung up, I took a deep breath and called Althea Alton for the second time in only a few days. I kind of regretted having had her check her unusual online sources for the missing wolf mama — since I was about to ask her for an even huger favor.

"Hi, Kendra!" she greeted me effusively. "Sorry, I haven't found anything on the sudden appearance of a loose wolf in the area. I wanted to touch base with you, though, to let you know."

"Thanks," I said as I stopped for a traffic light and saw a cop in the car in the next lane staring at me. Better that it appear I was talking to myself than violating the California law against use of hand-held cell phones in automobiles. "But I have another favor to ask."

"Oh?" I heard her backing-away tone. I was pressing my luck in pushing for more help, especially under the current circumstances.

"Check with Jeff, of course, but . . . well, I'm looking into who could have committed another murder."

"Another one? Oh, Kendra, that's so weird. Unless — did you go looking for this one?"

"Hardly." The light changed, and I accelerated slowly, not wanting to give the cop a reason to harass me. He went on ahead, and I sighed in relief. "Anyway, I would love it if you could find out all you can about a man named Jon — that's J-O-N — Doe, who worked at HotWildlife. I checked with the director, and she said he applied with excellent credentials. He'd worked at zoos and other animal sanctuaries. But I'd really, really appreciate a whole history of the guy." Like anything that gave me insight into why Dante and Brody were so interested in him.

"You know what Jeff's going to say, don't you?" Althea's young but grandmotherly voice was filled with warning.

"Yes, and you can tell him I'll schedule a lunch with him soon. I'll even come to your office." Which was located in Westwood, not exactly convenient to my mostly San Fernando Valley pet-sitting, nor my Encino-area law office. Worse, I'd have to deal with the hunky guy, once my lover, as he tried to convince me, yet again, to give him another chance. But, hey, it'd be worth the hassle if Althea, using her amazing Internet skills — and hacking abilities — got me the info I sought.

"Okay, I'll check with him and let you know," she said. She added, in a kinder tone, "It'll be great to see you again, Kendra, and to catch up with what's going on in your life."

"Besides my still being a murder magnet?" I asked, attempting to punctuate it with a laugh.

"Yes," she said. "Besides that."

It was midmorning by the time I'd cared for and played with my remaining pet-sitting charges. I jotted the last info into my pet-sitting journal. I felt both exhausted and exhilarated. I loved this part of my life!

But maybe I was schizophrenic, since I also loved my other major career: lawyering. I happily headed my Escape toward Encino and my law office.

Mignon was, as usual, at the large front desk to greet me. The law offices were located in a building that had once been a restaurant, so the reception area was essentially where hostesses once hung out to seat guests.

Mignon could have fit that role, too, with as much ease as she did that of receptionist for a small law firm. She was the perkiest person I'd ever met. Almost always cheerful. Incredibly cute, with her bobbing auburn curls and constantly waving fingers. "Hi, Kendra," she chirped as I walked in the door. "You're not nearly as late as I thought you'd be. That's a good thing. Borden said he really needs to talk to you as soon as you get in, but didn't want me to call and bother you."

"It's never a bother to talk to him," I chided, but she lifted her hand into the air.

"I know that. But that's what he said."

"Got it. Please let him know I'm here, and if it's convenient, I'll come right over, soon as I drop my purse in my office."

It must have been convenient for Borden to see me immediately, since he was waiting at my office door when I got there. I'd strode through what had once been the restaurant's elongated dining room, hustling along the open corridor between doors to attorneys' offices along the outer walls, and secretary and paralegal cubicles in the center. Hustle? Heck! I had given as many greetings as I got, so my dash to my office had been on the slow side.

"Hi, Kendra," our senior partner said in his high-pitched voice, with one of his characteristically lopsided smiles on his long face. His hair was silver, and he wore one of his usual bright aloha shirts, orange and gray today. "I hear you have yet another murder under your microscope."

"Yes, I'm looking into it," I said as I led him into my perpetually messy office. Well, maybe it was just lived-in — with paperwork piled here and there on my desk and credenza. Borden had, bless him, furnished it with an ergonomically correct chair, so it was absolutely comfortable, easily my second home. I had a window overlooking the parking lot and a high-tech computer at my side on the desk. Who could ask for more?

I sat in that pleasingly comfy desk chair, and Borden took a seat facing me. "So," he said, looking slightly ill at ease, "do you by any chance have time to take over a senior law case for me? I know you're busy with your pet-sitting, and that missing wolf, and now another murder, so I really hate to —"

I practically pole-vaulted over my desk toward him, and stooped to give him a huge hug. He smelled like sweetened tea. "Borden, of course I have time. I'll *make* the time. You made me a partner here, even with the stigma still swimming around me from those bogus ethics violation accusations. You've been so understanding of all the extra stuff I get myself into. But you know I intend always to practice law, too, and I'll drop everything" — well, I might have to rebalance instead, since dropping pet-sat doggies wasn't exactly an option — "to take on anything you need me to."

I moved back and aimed what I intended

to be an utterly sincere smile at him. He grinned back, and I knew he'd intentionally teased me into making such a groveling statement. Maybe. "I figured," he said softly.

"So what's the case you want to toss my way?" I said, bracing myself for a bombshell.

"Do you remember Alice Corcorian?"

"Ellis Corcorian's mother? Sure." Ellis had been of-counsel at the law firm of Marden, Sergement & Yurick, the high-powered firm where I'd been employed before those awful ethics issues forced me to resign. Borden was that Yurick, and he'd left the firm at the same time, after traveling the world and deciding he'd had enough of huge firm nonsense and stress.

An "of-counsel" attorney was one who was generally too experienced to be a simple associate, yet not on partnership track at a firm. Ellis had specialized in entertainment law. He'd been single, so he'd brought his mama, Alice, who'd acted in films in the seventies and eighties, to a lot of the firm's affairs like parties and retreats.

"Well, she's been in our conference room all morning, waiting for you. She remembered you, too, and all you went through. She figured you'd understand, so she asked if you'd represent her."

Sounded like I'd been set up . . . kinda.

Borden had already decided I'd take this case. So had Alice Corcorian, apparently.

Only . . .

"What kind of legal problem does she have, Borden?"

"She says that her son is attempting to obtain a conservancy over her and all her assets. She wants us — you — to make sure he's the one to go to hell."

CHAPTER EIGHT

Alice Corcorian looked older than when I'd last seen her. Even so, she was one sensational middle-aged mama. She was probably my height. Her wavy hair skimmed her shoulders, a sleek, sensuous auburn that, at her age — maybe mid-sixties — might emanate from a darn good beautician's bottle.

"Kendra, my dear, how good to see you," she said as I entered the firm's conference room that was the restaurant's former bar. She rose from her seat at the elongated table in the room's center — between the big wooden bar still along the inside wall and the booths beneath the windows — and glided in my direction. She was clad in a red wraparound dress and matching shoes with slight heels.

I could only hope I'd look as good at her age. Sure, a few wrinkles edged her eyes, and parentheses-like divots emphasized her mouth, but she was still a great-looking example of the human race.

"Great to see you, too, Ms. Corcorian."

"Oh, I'm Alice, dear. You and I are friends, and I think — I hope — we're going to get even closer." Her voice was warm and husky, not a hint of middle age sneaking into it. "Did Borden tell you my dilemma?"

"He hinted at it, but why don't you explain?" Her son sought conservatorship of a woman as together as this one? On what basis? She certainly wasn't *that* old.

"Let me make a phone call first." She headed back to where she'd been sitting at the table, and I noticed the magazine she must have been reading: *Modern Bride.*

Hmmm. That provided a hint.

She spoke low into the cell phone she'd pulled from her purse. I couldn't quite hear what she said. She hung up quickly and motioned for me to sit at the opposite side of the table.

"I assume this won't be any conflict of interest for you," she began. "You know my son Ellis, of course, but you don't work at his law firm any longer."

I nodded. "I doubt that'll be a problem, even though your matter apparently concerns Ellis."

"It definitely does," she said grimly as the

conference room door opened.

Mignon stood there with a tall, good-looking guy about her age — early twenties. "Can Mr. Guildon come in?" she asked.

Mr. Guildon didn't wait for my answer. He strode right to Alice, who'd stood again. In an instant, she was in his arms and the recipient of one hell of a sexy kiss.

And I'd no doubt about why Ellis Corcorian wanted conservatorship over his mom.

When they broke away, they still regarded each other like they were lovers who'd been separated for ages. I'd little doubt about the first part. But I suspected they hadn't been apart for more than the part of the morning Alice spent at the law firm.

"Kendra, this is Roberto," Alice finally said, sounding, unsurprisingly, a bit breathless. "Roberto, this is the wonderful attorney I told you about, Kendra Ballantyne. I'm sure she'll be able to teach my son Ellis to mind his own business, and not mine."

"How do you do, Roberto." I shook the hand he held out to me. He'd gallantly come around beside the table, away from his apparent lady love — who was nearly old enough to be his grandma. "Please sit down, both of you, and tell me what's going on." As if I hadn't already guessed.

Alice took the lead in the conversation.

Sure enough, what I'd surmised was their reality. They'd told Ellis Corcorian that they intended to marry. He had gone ballistic, calling his mother all kinds of names, not the least offensive of which was "you senile old bag." He'd tried to convince her that Roberto was simply after her money — a substantial fortune, since she had invested her money wisely after a shining silver screen career.

Roberto's turn to talk. "I'm not dumb, Ms. Ballantyne," he said.

"Kendra," I corrected him, as Alice had done with me. I had a feeling we'd be working together for a while, assuming I agreed to take what appeared to be a difficult, emotional case.

"Kendra. Anyhow, I know how this looks. I'm a graduate of the USC School of Cinematic Arts. I do some acting, hope someday to get starring roles. But the thing is, I love films, especially some of the older ones. I think I fell in love with Alice long before I met her. And when she came to our school to talk about her films . . . well, I had to introduce myself. Now, I can't imagine life without her."

She rose and was back in his arms instantaneously. Apparently, the feeling was mutual.

After the latest kiss, and once they sat down, Alice said, "I'm not dumb, either, Kendra. You know that. But Ellis thinks I'm an aging, gullible fogy who's been taken in by a young cad who just wants my money. He wants to protect me from myself."

More likely, he wanted to protect his potential inheritance from the likes of this young star-struck stud.

But if Alice was sane and unsenile, then Ellis Corcorian should have no recourse even if she chose to convey every cent she owned to saving the cats of the world.

Or to supporting this youthful stud muffin into his twilight years.

"I see," I said. "Well, you seem pretty much with it to me. Let's chat a bit, and we'll see if we need to take any preemptive legal action to prevent Ellis from doing anything rash."

Our conference went on for another hour. I saw nothing in Alice's demeanor to suggest she had any mental impairment, and sixties weren't an especially advanced age.

If she chose to be a cougar and fall in love with someone so much her junior, more power to her, in my puny opinion. But I might have to convince a judge not to change her legal status under the law, so we discussed ways of proving she remained of sound mind.

"I'll do some further research," I said as they stood to leave. "But for now, don't do anything rash that could ultimately hurt your position."

"Like elope?" Alice said with a laugh. "I've thought about it, but figured Ellis could use that against me somehow."

"Exactly," I said. "I'll get back to you soon, Alice, with how I suggest handling this. Be sure to get in touch with me if Ellis tries anything. You can talk to him as usual, of course, mother to son. Just don't discuss Roberto or Ellis's possible claims against you."

We'd already discussed my rates and entered into a contract of representation, and I made sure Alice had an original as they left.

Then I went to see Borden. Of course, the firm's sweet senior partner had the biggest office. He'd bought this building, after all. Its walls were paneled in oak, and he was surrounded by shelves of law books. He had a charming antique desk, but his chairs were so oddly assorted that I'd concluded a while back that they'd been bought with the restaurant.

"What an interesting situation," I told him

as I sat in one of his desk-facing chairs. "Alice is absolutely as sharp as a tack, and she's not really at an advanced age. I suppose it's just greed that made Ellis say he'd try to get conservatorship over her."

"Maybe," he said, "and maybe not. I wanted you on this, Kendra, since Alice asked for you and you, as the youngest lawyer at this firm, should be best suited to represent her."

I soon left Borden's office with my mind swimming around thoughts of the lovely, aging film star and her handsome young stud. Interesting scenario. Would I someday want something similar in my life? I doubted it. I had too much trouble with slightly older men.

I'd barely sat down at my desk when I heard my cell phone ring. It was deep in a drawer, at the bottom of my large purse, and I had to dig for it.

For the longest time, I'd had a self-selected ring tone, the Bon Jovi song "It's My Life." I'd recently gotten a new phone. I'd settled in and become more complacent with my life since the time I'd chosen that song, and figured I needed a new tone, too. But I hadn't had time to choose one. As a result, my cell just sang in a generic tune that still caught my attention.

I finally found the phone and flipped it open eagerly, after seeing Dante's number on the ID screen. My heart flipped as it did so often when this man was on my mind.

"Kendra? Hi. Look, I have a legal problem I'd like to talk to you about."

That sank an ugly dagger into my suddenly fragile bubble of a mood. He wasn't calling the way he usually did, to tell me he missed me or something of the sort. He had business to discuss.

And so, I said in a most businesslike tone in response, "What kind of legal problem?"

"I'd rather tell you about it in person. Can you come here? There are others involved, too."

When he told me where "here" was, I became even more curious. Of course I promised to be there as soon as I could.

Chapter Nine

My curiosity climbing by the minute, I entered my Escape and headed north up the 405 Freeway, toward Granada Hills.

I'd never visited HotRescues before, but I'd read about it online. Of course. From the moment I'd met Dante, I'd looked up a lot about his interests and pet projects on the Internet.

I wasn't surprised, parking on Rinaldi, to see that the building bearing the organization's sign was large, clean, modern, and absolutely inviting. I assumed the idea was to invite everyone with a proper home to enter, check out the rescued pets, fall in love, and leave hugging a new friend.

I smiled as I pushed open the glass door and walked in. An older woman smiled back from the short, uncluttered reception desk. "Can I help you?"

I explained who I was and who'd invited me there.

"Oh, yes, Ms. Ballantyne. They're expecting you." She showed me to a hallway to her right — though I heard all the animal noises I'd anticipated to her left. I figured the administrative offices weren't in the middle of the sheltered pets, but I'd entered with an expectation of seeing some rescued pooches and kitties. *Later,* I promised myself.

For now, I entered the hall and made a nearly immediate right into the first office. It was sizable, with a conversation area where I walked in and the business part — desk, computer, and all — at the opposite end.

Dante sat on a sofa that appeared to have come from designer stock — beige upholstery on a deep brown leathery-looking frame, with matching brown and beige pillows, all resting on carved wooden legs. There was a matching table in the middle, too, and on it sat two coffee cups.

He rose as I came in, and so did the woman with him. No need to describe how Dante looked that day — well, not much, but of course I noticed. As always, he was one gorgeous, hot guy. He wore a yellow shirt and black slacks that suggested he'd donned a suit that day but forbore from wearing the tie and jacket, at least here and now.

The woman appeared to be in her forties, taller and thinner than me, with dark hair in a wispy bob that framed an attractive face. She had high cheekbones, and a wide mouth with a smile that revealed even white teeth. Her nose was a little long, and there was a hint of wrinkles at the edges of her large green eyes.

I wanted, immediately, to dislike her. She might be part of the reason for Dante's overnight withdrawal of avid attention from me. Or not. But someone so pretty, despite being older than me, was definitely worthy of some suspicion before I made up my mind about her.

"Kendra," Dante said, "this is Lauren Vancouver. She's the director here." In other words, his hand-picked honcho to run this place. The equivalent here of Megan Zurich at HotWildlife. I enjoyed Megan and her magnificent treatment of the wild animals in her charge at the sanctuary. Would I like Lauren Vancouver?

She approached with her hand outstretched, and I shook it. Her grip was firm, and her smile surprisingly genuine.

"Hi, Lauren," I said. "Good to meet you." Yes, I'm adept at polite lies when it suits me.

"As I suggested on the phone, Kendra," Dante said after we'd all sat down, "we may have a legal problem here, and there's no one better than you to handle it." I noticed with both relief and pleasure that he'd chosen to sit right beside me. Not Lauren. I started to chill out, at least a little.

"Tell me about it," I said, "so I can figure out if your flattery is because you're attempting to snow me." Our gazes locked, and I saw both amusement and smoldering sensuality in his eyes. Did my teasing turn him on?

Hell, I hoped so.

Lauren laid out the details of their dilemma. "Here's what happened, Kendra," she said. "I may have screwed up." Interesting, that although her words seemed apologetic, her green eyes glowed with what I read as self-satisfaction. I determined to listen even harder, try to discern the subtext as she spoke.

She briefly described HotRescues and how it operated. "We take in all kinds of pets — abandoned, abused, whatever. From wherever people find them. We clean them up, have our vets on call take care of their medical needs, and give them all the attention our staff and volunteers can provide. Mostly, what we want is to find each and

117

every one a good home. We of course have a no-kill policy, and there's always a danger of becoming overcrowded. Our main focus is to make sure that our charges are adopted, but only into the right situation."

"So you research the homes you place them into," I prompted when she slowed her speech a little. From what she'd said, I'd started wondering if her legal issue was an inappropriate adoption. Turned out I was right, but not for the reason I anticipated.

"Of course," she agreed. "And the little pup at issue — he looks like a cocker spaniel–Jack Russell terrier mix — seemed perfect for the couple who adopted him. They just moved in together, love animals, and work in the entertainment industry. They have a nice yard behind their townhouse, and we thought it a perfect match. They've named him Quincy."

"But?" I prompted, catching Dante's eye. He wasn't jumping in to comment, allowing Lauren to do all the talking. Which was probably fine, but when I'd heard her out, I'd want his insight on the situation, too.

"But I didn't think to ask the vet to check this particular pup for an identification chip. Turns out, a guy in Pacoima claims to own him. He's suing the new owners, HotRescues, Dante, and me to get him back, and for trumped-up damages like emotional distress and fraud." For the first time, she looked less than gorgeous as concern crinkled her face. "I suppose I actually was a little negligent, though I'll deny it if this thing gets to court. But other than this nasty fellow getting so upset, it was a win-win situation for the dog and his new people."

Seeing a glimmer of something I couldn't quite read on Dante's face, I decided to follow up on this strange comment. "Why do you say that? It obviously wasn't a winning situation for the guy who lost his dog. And didn't Quincy miss his real master?"

"Hell, no," Lauren all but exploded. "When one of our volunteers went to the park where Quincy had been spotted, she found him there, cringing every time anyone came close. He had open sores and bruising, and we definitely suspected all the damage hadn't been done after he'd fled his home."

Oh. Now I got it. The disappeared doggy had most likely left an abusive abode, and Lauren and staff might purposely have ignored any identifying assistance like a chip or tag. Better to get this puppy safely somewhere else.

Only, the original owner had somehow found this out. Learned of the connection to HotRescues. From that, it was only a short step to realize the connection to deep-pocketed Dante DeFrancisco.

"Okay, let's say that, hypothetically, Quincy was in an abusive home and you'd learned about him without his running away. What would you have done then?"

"There are resources. Local agencies, for example, that follow up on animal abuse situations. But you generally have to be able to prove the abuse before they can do much. That sometimes takes time."

"So you chose — er, forgot — to try to find Quincy's original owner in an effort to help him?"

"If I did that — *hypothetically* — it was to save his life." She glared angrily, as if daring me to dispute what she said.

"You get the gist of this, Kendra," Dante broke in smoothly. "The guy has only threatened to sue, so far. If I were to offer him a lot of money, he might never file a claim. But I hate to pay him off for what he did to that poor dog."

"This sounds like an interesting legal issue," I said. "And as you know, Dante, I do a lot of animal law. I prefer to use ADR instead of courtrooms to resolve things. That generally stands for alternative dispute resolution, but to me it's animal dispute

120

resolution. I'd be glad to look further into this and see what I can do." I was already pretty certain we could win some potential claims, but others were more troubling.

"Thanks, Kendra." Dante stood as I still sat on the sofa.

"Yes, thanks," Lauren echoed, sounding utterly relieved as she, too, rose.

I also got up, and Dante gently took my arm as we headed for the door. "We'll talk soon, Lauren," he said.

"And if you hear anything more about this claim," I told her, "don't say a word except to say you'll refer it to your lawyer."

"Got it," she said with a smile.

"Now, can I go see some of your rescued pets?"

"Absolutely!"

She took us on a tour of the other part of the rescue facility. Well, she took me on a tour. Dante had obviously been there before.

I have to say I was impressed. Dogs and cats were kept in separate areas, each in an individual enclosure, like at other shelters. All habitats had tile floors that looked easy to clean, with areas at the rear set up as potty places. The animals had comfortable-looking pillow-beds and generous water bowls.

The nice amenities didn't keep the poor creatures from obviously feeling lonely. Some slept, others lay on their beds looking morosely in my direction, and some came to the wire-mesh barrier where I stood, doggies wriggling eagerly and kitties appearing aloof as only felines can, yet needy nonetheless. A few dogs barked or whined for attention. The cats called out their meows.

I ached to adore all of them, right in my arms. I greeted them saying sweet things, happy at least that this was a no-kill shelter. All of them would eventually find homes . . . hopefully.

Dante took my hand somewhere along the line. I squeezed it hard, barely keeping my emotions in check.

Lauren stayed with us, too, and we soon turned and walked back along the other side of the enclosures. At the place where we'd begun, I turned to her. "This place is so wonderful, yet so sad. How do you stand it, day after day?"

"I keep thinking about all the excellent adoptions we've put together. It's hard to see how sad some of these guys get while they're here, and there are only so many of us who can give them attention. But it's exciting to bring them here when they're in bad shape, nurse them back to health, then make sure they're placed with the best people possible."

"You're the greatest," I exclaimed without thinking, tossing aside my earlier, ungenerous thoughts about Lauren and her possible relationship with Dante. "Do you ever have any pets here besides cats or dogs?" I asked her.

"They're in the majority, but we'll help any animal at all."

"Okay," I said. "I'll definitely be in touch. If you say you couldn't find Quincy's original owner and did your best for him by placing him in a loving home, who can argue with that?" Only that original owner and the lawyer he'd hired — in hopes of extorting lots of money from Dante — and maybe even some irascible judge. But I'd do my best to prevent Lauren, Dante, and HotRescues from losing this case.

"Thanks, Kendra." Lauren's hug seemed heartfelt. I admit I frowned a bit when she repeated the caring gesture with Dante — but, hey, hugging is an accepted means of showing gratitude.

In a short while, Dante and I stood together on the sidewalk as traffic slowly meandered along Rinaldi. "So," he said, looking down at me with one of those expressions that I'd come to anticipate and adore. A sexy look that suggested we spend the night together. Who said he was withholding his attention? "Have any plans for tonight?"

Damned awful time for my cell phone to ring, but that's what it did. "Hold that thought," I said, then saw who the caller was: Althea.

"Hi," I said eagerly as I answered. "Found anything interesting on Jon Doe?"

From the corner of my eye, I saw Dante's expression freeze. An intriguing response, I thought.

"I sure did," said Althea into my ear. "And I can tell you everything tonight, Kendra. Over dinner. With Jeff."

"That's the deal?"

"That's the price of his approval of my helping you."

"Got it." We quickly decided where and when, and then I hung up.

I looked at Dante, to find his face now utterly unreadable.

"You know me," I said. "I always try to get as much info as I can about the victim."

"I know." He didn't sound especially pleased.

"I don't suppose you could fill me in on Jon Doe's background?" I inquired sweetly.

"I could have Megan show you his employee file."

"That would be interesting," I agreed. "But do you know anything else about him?"

"Of course not," he said, his expression still so bland that I felt certain he was a great poker player.

"Anyway — about your question before, whether I have plans for tonight?"

"I gathered, from this end of the conversation, that you do now."

"You gather right," I said. "But after dinner, I might be available."

"Sorry, Kendra, but I've got plans then. Where'd you park? I'll walk you to your car. We'll talk tomorrow. You can let me know what you find out about Jon Doe."

"Sure," I said.

He wasn't the only fibber strolling the sidewalk toward my Escape.

CHAPTER TEN

We met at a restaurant in Westwood, a quiet Italian café, and they were already at a table in the corner. The hostess pointed me in their direction the instant I entered.

Checkered tablecloths and dim lighting added to the place's ambience, but the accoutrements did little to alleviate my nervousness. I really didn't want to see Jeff, not now, but I'd been left little choice.

They stood as I crossed the dark carpet. Althea was a geek, a techy wonder, and I'd always found it astounding that she was also a grandma. She was slim and youthful-looking, with longish blond hair and a fashion sense that seemed more teenage than middle age. Tonight, she wore a shiny print top over tight blue jeans.

But mostly my eyes lit on Jeff. I'd always considered him one hell of a sexy dude. He still was, with his face full of angles and his body absolutely buff — shown off now by a snug blue knit shirt. That, of course, brought out the beautiful blue of his eyes as he stared straight at me. And smiled.

"Hi, Kendra," he said in a deep, sexy tone that sent shivers through me even though I'd instructed my insides not to react to him at all. "Great to see you. Please, sit down."

I obeyed, gave my greeting to the obviously amused Althea, and immediately snatched up the menu. Not seeing anything on it, naturally. I figured it listed some kind of Italian salad. That's what I'd order.

Fortunately, this place served no Thai food, which had always served as an aphrodisiac for Jeff and me.

"Would you like some wine?" he asked. It sounded appealing, but I needed all my wits about me to stay soberly away from this sexy man whom I no longer wanted in my life as a lover.

Especially now that Dante was in it. Although . . .

Well, no reason to let myself wonder now about where that relationship was going. If it was going anywhere.

Or what Dante might have known about the now deceased Jon Doe and his untimely demise.

"No, thanks," I said. A server came over

and took our orders. And then I focused on the folder lying on the table between Jeff and Althea.

When we were alone once more, I asked, "Is that what you found about Jon Doe?" I gestured at the closed file.

"Some of it. What I printed out for you." Althea glanced at Jeff as if for permission, and he nodded.

Which he of course should have done. Hadn't I kept my end of this bargain — meeting them both for dinner?

Althea handed me the materials. "Let me give you a quick rundown," she said.

"Absolutely," I agreed in relief. That way, I could savor any delectable details later, but I'd have a better sense of what I was seeing.

"What I found about Jon Doe's history is that he grew up in Burbank, got his high school diploma, then went into the Army. He became an animal care specialist, worked on several bases, assisting veterinarians with treating patrol dogs and ceremonial horses. Honorable discharge. He then worked at two zoos, doing animal care, followed by a career at two independent wildlife sanctuaries. He recently wound up at HotWildlife. End of his story."

"Interesting," I said, not entirely meaning

it. Althea had said nothing that might lead to any clues about who offed the guy. An irate coyote who didn't like the way his food had been prepared? Not with the way Jon Doe had died — by a stab from a sharp knife, not bites.

His history in the Army could have been at a time he'd have run into Dante and Brody while they were in the covert ops stuff I'd come to suspect, but who knew?

As our dinners were served, I took the opportunity to thumb through the printed pages. A cursory look suggested they supported what Althea had said.

Not necessarily useful, but probably enough to justify my evening with my former boyfriend and his illustrious and knowledgeable computer geek.

I started eating my salad, noticing the aromas of the chicken cacciatore that Jeff had ordered, as well as Althea's cheese-smothered lasagna. Had I been too diligent in my calorie counting? I loved Italian food, after all.

Jeff noticed my gaze, and perhaps the watering of my mouth. "Want a taste?" His look suggested he remembered those days not long ago when we'd share Thai food as a prelude to some sexy alone time.

Still . . . I was too tempted to say no — to

Italian food, that is. "Sure. Want some salad?"

We all took samples of each other's food, which satisfied my palate a lot more than the green stuff.

When all that was done, Althea said, "So, Kendra, would you like to hear what I *didn't* find about Jon Doe?"

Talk about being tantalized. "Sure," I said, staring at her.

"Probably anything true," she responded with a grim grin.

"What!?" I exclaimed.

"The thing is," Jeff said, "Althea used resources on the Internet, plus some of our . . . less accessible usual sources. Sure, there were plenty of Jon Does for her to research, but she zeroed in on the one who worked at HotWildlife really fast. Well, you know how good Althea is."

As I nodded in utter acknowledgment, the object of our verbal adoration pinkened a little and took another bite of lasagna.

"She did some additional digging," said Jeff.

Althea's turn to talk. "Yes. Deeper than the surface. And what I found was that . . . I found very little. None of the ordinary things usually out there concerning most people, like more military information than who he was and where he'd been. High school classmates. Blogs and YouTube entries — although not everyone participates in that current-day stuff. Sure, Jon Doe was in his sixties, but there was nothing about his family, either. His military service was partly during the Vietnam era, but he didn't go overseas, or nothing indicated he had. There were no photos of him on Web sites or otherwise at the animal facilities where he'd worked. Nothing definitive, you understand, but even so —"

"What are you saying?" I demanded.

"If you want my opinion," Althea said, her young grandmother's face scrunched into a gloomy frown, "Jon Doe's background was entirely made up. A farce. Someone manufactured his history. And I didn't find out who he really is."

Surprisingly, that news didn't completely dim my appetite. We talked some more over the next hour or so, brainstorming where else Althea could look — and what I would do with the possibly useless information she'd gathered.

On the other hand, if Jon Doe — or whoever he was — had been so careful about manufacturing a fake identity, that said something about him.

I just had to figure out what.

And learn, if I could, how much Dante really did, or did not, know.

Could he truly have killed Jon Doe? No, my frantic insides called out, even as I feared it was true.

And this wasn't the first time I'd suspected him of murder. If he was innocent in this instance but stayed in my life, I might need to question what was it about him that made me think he was capable of such a crime.

When we finished eating, we wrangled over the check. I didn't feel right letting Jeff pay, especially when I hadn't contributed a penny toward the time and energy Althea put into finding out what was, and wasn't, there about Jon Doe.

"Next time, it's on you," he said. And smiled. Knowing full well I'd feel obligated to meet with him again for a meal to satisfy this damned new debt.

Well, I could choose the time, at least. Not too soon.

We picked our way through the crowded, dim restaurant. Outside, we turned our tickets over to the valet and awaited delivery of our cars.

"Thanks," I said. "To both of you. And if you happen to think of any other leads,

Althea, please let me know."

"I will, sweetie." Her car was the first to come out, so she gave me a hug, tipped the attendant, and departed.

"You know what I think this may mean, don't you, Kendra?" Jeff asked when she'd gone.

"No," I said, although I was afraid I knew what he was about to say.

"It's not just sour grapes," he said. "You know that I still care about you." *But you hadn't believed in my innocence in a nasty situation a while back,* I thought silently. "And I know you're now involved with Dante DeFrancisco. He's got everything — including a ton of money. But . . . well, he also founded HotWildlife. I understand he was around when this Jon Doe was killed. Not that I'm accusing him of anything." He lifted his hands in a gesture erasing any such accusation. "But . . . okay, I want him to be involved somehow. Like I did when your *Animal Auditions* judge Sebastian was killed. But this time feels different. He may not be someone you can trust. In any event, Kendra, be careful. And remember, I'm still around."

"Thanks, Jeff," I said, not revealing that I shared some of his concerns. I returned his quick kiss on the lips as my car was the next delivered.

I had a lot to think about as I drove toward the 405 Freeway and the San Fernando Valley.

And my mind continued to churn around our mutual questions about who Jon Doe really was and who might have killed him.

So, I decided to call the object of my concerns. I used my hands-free car device to place a call to Dante.

"Hi," I said perkily when he answered. "I learned some interesting things about Jon Doe this evening from a friend who does computer research. Will you have any time tomorrow for us to get together so I can fill you in?"

" 'Fraid not, Kendra." His voice sounded unusually grim, which got me all the more worried. But only a fraction as worried as I became at his next words. "I have to go back to HotWildlife. The sheriff's detectives are coming back to meet with me. Maybe even to arrest me. I have the feeling that I'm now their number one suspect in the murder."

CHAPTER ELEVEN

Though it was late, my next call from my car phone was to my dear friend and legal colleague, Esther Ickes.

Esther had represented me when I'd required a criminal law guru. Since then, I had referred her to my friends and acquaintances who'd become suspects in the killings I had investigated.

I'd mentioned her to Dante, and he seemed relieved at my potential referral. He had an attorney who represented him in business transactions, but no contacts in criminal defense. But one of the first things he'd asked me was "Is she discreet?"

Which led me to believe he'd have to confess some stuff to his counsel to get the best representation possible. That he'd actually committed the killing? Something more about the mysterious stuff in his past? Both?

And the lousy thing was that attorney-client privilege would prohibit Esther from telling all to me.

The last time I had suspected Dante capable of murder, hardly anyone else had — except Jeff, but he had motivation of his own. This time, the authorities appeared to agree. Did that make it true?

Not judging by my past investigation history, thank heavens. So maybe there was hope for Dante's innocence after all.

"Hi, Esther," I said when she answered. "Sorry to be calling outside business hours."

"All hours are business hours for lawyers. You know that. Or maybe that mostly applies to criminal attorneys." I could hear the grin in my good friend's voice.

Esther did not resemble the stereotype of a brilliant and nearly always successful criminal counsel. She was a gray-haired little old lady, the kind the opposition could easily dismiss as elderly, incompetent, or confused. Till they came up against her.

Or saw her at the helm of her sporty Jaguar convertible.

We chatted cheerily for a couple of minutes, then I asked, "So, are you up for taking on a new client?"

"Depends."

"Well, it's an interesting case. And I'm sure he can pay your most outrageous fees."

"Ah, I think I know what you're talking

about. I saw something on the news about a murder at HotWildlife. And I know that's a place your new sweetie supports. But . . . who's the potential client? Surely it's not him."

"Surely it is," I said with a sigh. I'd just finished my winding climb up residential roads in the Hollywood Hills, and my Escape sat waiting, as I remained in the driver's seat, for me to push the button to open the security gate.

"And the local authorities think that someone as astral as Dante DeFrancisco killed a lowly park employee? Why? Because the guy didn't feed the lions on time? Or didn't keep the place smelling clean enough?"

"That's the thing I don't know, Esther," I said after getting my finger on the right button. The gate swung open. "I've no idea — yet — why they're glomming on to Dante as a major suspect. I just talked to him, and he said he's cooperating, heading to Hot-Wildlife tomorrow to talk to them."

"Before hiring a lawyer and consulting with her?" Esther sounded mightily miffed. "Didn't you instruct him better?"

"I tried, but he's powerful enough to think he can handle everything himself. The only concession he made was that he'd not meet with them till the afternoon. I hate to ask, but do you have time to help on such short notice?"

A moment's silence, as I drove the Escape into my parking space beside my garage, and parked it.

"Okay," she said. "I'll make a couple of calls tonight and defer some meetings. Fortunately, I'm not scheduled for court tomorrow. But you can tell your friend Dante that my fees will include something for this inconvenience. Better yet, I'll tell him. Give him a call and tell him to phone me right back. Tonight. Okay?"

"Okay," I agreed, smiling. I adored Esther's attitude.

And I was sure there was no one better to represent Dante in this difficult situation.

I only hoped I wasn't doing Esther a disservice by getting her involved in a situation where I didn't think I had all the facts — and some truly important ones could be eluding me.

And I also felt really irritated that, maybe as soon as tomorrow, Esther would know more about Dante's undisclosed past than I did.

Fortunately, my clients' okays to substitute Rachel or Wanda as those who cared for their beloved pets had no time limit. Not the most professional thing to do, and I felt awful about it. But, hey, I hadn't counted on needing to travel to San Bernardino County so much.

Also fortunately — for me — Rachel was waiting for the result of her recent audition, so she had time available.

I cared about Dante and I wanted to be there for him during the sheriff's interrogation. I doubted they'd allow me to sit in, but at least I could hang out to provide some support.

And, just maybe, I might learn something new about Jon Doe and his murder. And about what Dante did or did not actually know about him.

So the next afternoon, after dressing in a nice pantsuit in case I had to appear professional, I headed toward the new Arrowhead View sheriff's substation.

It sat at the base of the mountains, not far from HotWildlife. It was blah beige in color, its stucco somewhat textured. At least a couple of odd angles gave it character. When I went inside, it looked similar to other law enforcement venues I'd visited. The reception area was staffed by a woman and man in uniform, and they had to buzz people through a locked gate before they could

139

enter the station.

I'd tried calling Dante on my way, but he hadn't answered. Was he already under interrogation? I wasn't sure, but his silver Mercedes was in the substation's parking lot.

I certainly hoped he hadn't been arrested.

I'd spotted Esther's unmistakable Jaguar convertible in the parking lot. Whatever was going on, Dante wasn't facing it alone.

I approached the facility's greeters. "Hello. I'm Kendra Ballantyne — a lawyer. May I see Sergeant Frank Hura?" It wouldn't do me any good to ask for Dante, but perhaps I could get to see his inquisitioner.

"Sorry, but he's in a meeting," said the lady deputy. No hesitation at all, which led me to believe that, in a substation as small as this, they all knew each other's business. Especially when that business involved brow-beating someone as well known as Dante DeFrancisco.

"Do you know how long he'll be?"

"Sorry, no. I'll leave word for him that you're here, though, if you'd like to wait."

I considered that, but only for a minute. "No, I don't think so," I said. I had a better place where I could hang out while waiting to hear what happened.

And so, a short while later, I headed my

Escape into the parking lot at HotWildlife.

Megan Zurich was in her roomy office when I knocked, then walked in. She appeared exhausted, her complexion even paler than I'd seen it before.

"Kendra! How good to see you," she said.

"How are the wolf pups?" I inquired without preamble, taking a seat facing her desk. I'd just strolled briskly through the sanctuary, peering at many inhabitants who appeared as calmly wild as always. But the infirmary was locked. For security after the murder? On sheriff's orders?

Whatever the reason, I'd missed out on visiting the baby wolves.

"They're doing well, though we've had to ask our staff and volunteers to put in lots of hours to help out — which isn't our usual policy for animal care. I just wish we knew what happened to their mother . . ." Her voice trailed off, and she stared out the office window behind me as if hoping to spot mama wolf walking around outside.

"Before I leave here today," I said, "I'd be more than happy to take a turn feeding them."

"That would be wonderful." Megan acted nervous as she ran fingers over her blond hair, pulled back in a barrette as always.

141

She gazed at me unhappily with her golden eyes. "Dante was here earlier. For a little while. He had someplace to go . . ."

"Yes, I know he's being questioned again by the local authorities. Do you think they suspect him in Jon Doe's death?"

"That's what he thought. He said his new lawyer was meeting him, and he had no problem going there. He had nothing to hide."

Right. If I believed that, I could also believe mama wolf would walk through the office door at any moment.

"Well, just in case, I'm hoping to get some answers myself. Anything you can tell me about Jon Doe that could help me figure out who might have killed him?"

"Oh, right — you have a sideline of solving murders, don't you? Er — I assume you don't kill people yourself to get the credit for supposedly solving the crimes?" Talk about nervous. Now she appeared downright agitated. Her hand moved somewhere below her desk. Seeking a button to call for some security — or to whip out a weapon?

"Nope," I assured her. "I was actually accused in only two related killings, and that was the first time I found the real culprit. Since then, I've become what I call a murder magnet. People around me . . . well, you get

142

it. And since I don't think Dante did it" —
I hoped — "and because I really like Hot-
Wildlife and all it stands for, I'd love to get
to the bottom of this murder, too. Fast.
Although —"

"What?" she asked as I broke off.

"You didn't do it, did you, Megan?"

She laughed uneasily. "The sheriff's detectives asked me that, too. The answer's no,
but I know I'll remain under suspicion till
the killer is caught. I hired Jon Doe. I was
his supervisor. I was around when he died.
I had no motive to kill him, but I guess the
authorities need to be sure of that before
eliminating me from their suspect list."

"I'll put in a good word for you if you
convince me." I smiled as if I were joking
— which I wasn't, not completely.

"How can I do that?"

For the next hour or so, I had her tell me
all she knew about Jon Doe and go over his
employee file. "I probably shouldn't let you
see this because of privacy laws," she said,
"but if you're acting sort of as the sanctuary's attorney . . ."

"Let's say that's so," I agreed. "At least
for the moment."

What I saw only confirmed the stuff I'd
already seen thanks to Althea. Jon Doe had
a wonderful employment history of being

hired to take care of wild animals at places like this.

Nothing to indicate it might all be an assumed identity.

Megan described Jon's work in glowing terms. He'd seemed to love what he did, thrived on caring for the animals. Was never tardy or irritable or anything out of the ordinary.

"And was he often around when Dante visited?" I asked casually, well into our conversation.

Megan pondered for a moment. "Maybe. Probably, at least recently. I can't say I remember them ever speaking to each other . . . at least I don't think so. Not until the last few times Dante was here, when you were along, too."

And noticed some . . . well, tension between Dante and Jon Doe that seemed exacerbated when Brody was about.

That didn't exactly exonerate Dante, or Brody, in my estimation. Nor did any of what she said or showed me seem to implicate Megan in the murder.

As we were finishing up, a knock sounded on the door. "Yes?" Megan called.

Krissy poked her head inside. Her smile froze as she saw me. I didn't exactly extend a welcoming hand to her, either. "Sorry to interrupt," she said, "but the greatest thing — we're going to be on *National News-Shakers* again. That cool reporter, Corina Carey? She's here with a photographer."

Corina had come here before, after I gave her the exclusive initial news of Jon Doe's death — only two days ago. I'd not been around when she'd arrived. Dante and I had already headed back to L.A. But I'd seen her report, and since she was a tabloid-type reporter, it had definitely been over-the-top.

There hadn't been a lot about Hot-Wildlife in her late-night story, other than as the locale of the latest killing I'd told her about — not that I, fortunately, was mentioned.

She had promised her audience, and me, that she would come back and focus on the wonderful facility. If nothing else, her presence might have the good result of bringing in additional visitors — and donations.

Megan and I hurried outside to greet her.

"Kendra! I didn't know you'd be here!" Her exuberant hug earned me a baleful gaze from Krissy, who stood off to the side.

Corina Carey always favored bright colors to set off the cute shagginess of her dark hair. Today, she wore a shocking pink dress. Her soft brown eyes tilted enough to suggest some Asian ancestry. She was taller than me, probably because she wore much higher heels. I wondered whether she'd stay on the occasionally uneven paved pathways at HotWildlife, but she'd covered so many different kinds of stories, she surely knew what she could handle.

"I didn't, either," I told her. I started to introduce her to Megan, then recalled they had met when Corina interviewed Megan on her news segment after the murder.

"So, have you figured out who killed Jon Doe?" she asked.

"No, but I'm working on it."

"So is the San Bernardino County Sheriff-Coroner's Department," said a deep, familiar voice from behind me. I turned to see Dante approaching from the area of the office. "I hope you do a better job of figuring it out than they seem to be doing."

"Well, Dante DeFrancisco!" exclaimed Corina. "I didn't figure on seeing you here, but I'd love to interview you about the terrible things that have happened at Hot-Wildlife. Did you just say you don't trust the local sheriff's department to get it right?"

I hadn't particularly focused on Corina's cameraman, but she always had one with her. The guy stepped out from behind her and aimed his equipment toward Dante, who said, "Hell, no," with so much fervor I almost figured he'd attack the shooter. "You want to interview me, Corina? Fine. But it'll be off the record. Off camera. Or I won't talk to you at all."

"Whatever you say, Dante," she responded.

They had met before, at *Animal Auditions* tapings. Dante had made it clear then that he did not like to be photographed.

Once again, I wondered why.

CHAPTER TWELVE

Getting Dante alone for a few seconds, I learned that Esther had headed home to L.A. Unfortunately, Corina stayed too close for me to ask any telling questions — like, did the deputies discuss placing him under arrest, and if so, what was their alleged evidence?

Since Dante clearly wanted nothing to do with Corina at this moment, Megan and I meandered with her and her camera guy all over HotWildlife — notwithstanding that Dante had, weeks ago, offered Corina a private tour. The tabloid reporter stopped often to ooh and aah over the animals, and lots of film clips about the inhabitants were the result.

So were some snippets of comments from the sanctuary's numerous visitors who often impeded our path as they, too, drank in the outstanding sights. Everyone gushed enthusiastically about how well the animals were treated. Espoused wildlife conservation. Applauded Megan and benefactor Dante DeFrancisco for their foresight in putting this place together.

Now and then the awful event of a couple of days earlier was mentioned, and I all but hugged Corina when she signaled her cameraman to turn off his equipment. Good thing I didn't. Her rationale wasn't as benevolent as I'd have liked. After the fourth time, she explained that it wouldn't make exciting news to get the opinions on who'd offed Jon Doe from people who hadn't even been around for the occasion.

I wondered, as I inhaled the growingly familiar scents of this animal sanctuary, whether Dante was still here or whether he had headed home. I hoped the former, since I'd come all this way to be supportive while he dealt with his summons to the sheriff's department.

And to see if I could satisfy even a tiny bit of my curiosity as to why said law enforcement types seemed to be settling on Dante as a suspect.

Sure, I might suspect him myself. But my reasons might not be the same as any official ones — and I wanted to know what the latter were.

We eventually returned to the office. Happily, Dante was still around. He'd apparently hung out in Megan's digs, and his cell phone was at his ear when I spotted him.

He wasn't alone, either. Brody Avilla sat in a nearby chair, also talking on his cell.

"Well, hello, Brody," Corina all but purred from behind me. She slipped around me and headed toward the film star. "Since you're here, could I interview you? I'd love your insight on HotWildlife. Today, I intend to do a short feature on what a wonderful place this is."

"Of course, Corina," Brody said. "But, before you ask, I came back here to cooperate with the county sheriff's office, and don't intend to talk about Jon Doe's death."

So he was a possible person of interest, too? I'd have to find out more about that later.

Corina's outside on-camera interview of Brody was charming but not especially eventful. And then Corina appeared to be done.

"Thanks again for the scoop the other day, Kendra," she said. "And this puff piece should go over well. I owe you."

"I'll remember that," I said sardonically. And as she left, shadowed by her silent camera guy, I slipped back inside the building.

Brody was conclaving with Dante and Megan, who had taken back her office. They all grew quiet and looked at me as I entered. I felt as if I'd interrupted something important — and wished I knew what it was.

"So, Brody, when do you talk to the sheriff?" I inquired, partly out of curiosity and partly because I hoped it was soon. I really wanted to find a way to get Dante alone — and not, this time, because I found him irresistibly sexy.

"I'm leaving in about a minute," Brody confirmed.

It was midafternoon. I wanted to leave, too. But first things first. "So what are your plans for the rest of the day, Dante?" I attempted to sound casual.

His gaze lit on me in an expression of amusement. "I assume you'd like to debrief me about what went on during my session with the sheriff's deputies," he surmised.

"That's right," I said.

"Well, I guess I'd better comply." He aimed a sexy smile that might have made me melt into a pile of oozing sugar if I hadn't seen through it.

I wouldn't be able to trust a thing he said.

Still, I smiled back. "I noticed a little lunchroom behind the food storage shed. There was even a filled coffee carafe a short time ago. How about if we head there?"

He agreed. Brody said goodbye, and Megan appeared relieved to have us all exit her office.

As we strolled through the crowd outside, on our way to the lunchroom, I spotted Krissy and Anthony, who were heading tour groups. They saw us, too, and Krissy came over to say hi. Not to me, of course, but to Dante. Clearly in a hurry to keep herd on her group, she didn't stay long.

In the lunchroom, which was empty this late in the afternoon, I poured us both some caffeine and sat down across from Dante at a small table.

"So, tell me what went on this morning," I said.

His eyes kept mine locked in a mutually heated gaze, which both stimulated and annoyed me. Even so, I made myself pay attention to his words.

"I still don't know why those Homicide Detail detectives think I had anything to do with Jon Doe's death," he said. "But the questions they asked seemed innocuous enough. Why had I started HotWildlife? How long ago? Was I involved in hiring its employees?"

"And were you?" I inquired.

"Along with Megan, of course, since I

152

founded the place and pay a lot toward its upkeep. But she has a lot of discretion in who works here and other administrative matters."

I nodded, sipping the strong brew and musing. Did Megan come to rue hiring Jon Doe for some reason, and decide to get rid of him the hard way?

Now, where had that thought come from? She'd seemed utterly cooperative when we'd gone through her files.

Too cooperative?

"What else did they ask?" I inquired.

Nothing sounded extraordinary. They wanted to know how long ago Dante had met Jon Doe. Whether he'd talked to him much. Spent much time in his company. Liked how he performed his work.

Had any reason *not* to like him.

"And that's it?" I asked when he was done. "It doesn't sound much different from the things they asked me after I found him — except for the stuff about how Hot-Wildlife is run."

"That's it," Dante confirmed. "I don't get it, either, but I want to cooperate." Like hell he did, but I knew he was savvy enough to do what was necessary to keep them from glomming onto him for lack of a better suspect. "I still have the sense I'm near the top of their suspect list, I but don't know why." His expression was so absolutely angelic that I almost expected a halo to appear above his gorgeous head. Which made my thoughts start circulating about how devilish this sexy man might really be. His name was Dante, after all, and that always brought infernos to mind.

"When are you heading back to L.A.?" I asked.

"Soon as we're done here," he said. "How about you?"

"Since I'm here, I'd love to feed a wolf pup before I go. After that, I'll drive home."

"Interested in grabbing dinner with me tonight?"

"Definitely interested one of these days, but I need to catch up on pet-sitting tonight, and expect I'll be exhausted. Tomorrow?"

"Done." He gave me such a torrid kiss that I wondered how I'd wait until tomorrow.

I walked Dante to the parking lot. Waved to the volunteer manning the entry booth.

Walked the perimeter of HotWildlife for the first time all by myself, wondering if I'd get any sudden insight about how mama wolf might have exited unseen.

Unfortunately, not.

154

Nor did it suddenly come to me who might have had it in for Jon Doe — or whoever he might have been. But since I was still here, I had time to ask some additional questions.

But Megan was busy with a group of visitors. Krissy was giving another tour.

When I stopped at the infirmary, Anthony and a guy I'd seen there before but didn't really remember were both heading inside. Anthony reintroduced me to Irwin. "He's become a volunteer," Anthony explained. "He's helping with the wolf pups. You, too?"

"Absolutely!" I affirmed.

A little while later, the three of us sat with the small pups on our laps as they nursed from the bottles we held.

An opportunity I couldn't waste.

"So, Irwin, didn't I see you here around the time poor Jon Doe died?"

Irwin was tall, wore glasses, and had large, round cheeks. "Yeah, I was at HotWildlife that day," he said in a slightly nasal tone. "I'll never forget it. I sat down later and started writing down everyone I'd seen here. Gave it to the cops, too. Not that I knew all the names, of course, but I jotted down descriptions as well."

"Awesome!" exclaimed Anthony. "I told them everything I knew, which wasn't much, but I never even thought of that." It still surprised me how gentle this big guy could be. The wolflet in his lap, though dwarfed, appeared well cared for.

"What did you think of Jon Doe?" I didn't address the question specifically to either one of them, but Anthony was first to answer.

"He seemed okay, I guess," he said. "I come here after school and on weekends a lot, and he was always here. He didn't say much to me except when he freaked out about me handling these little guys. I didn't really know him well."

"I didn't, either," Irwin piped up. "But he seemed — well, he yelled at me once when I put my hand too near one of the enclosures. I wasn't really trying to pat the tiger. I know they can attack without warning. But the way Jon Doe acted, I might as well have jumped in and tried to ride the thing." His tone had grown increasingly agitated, and he obviously realized what he was doing. "Not that I hated him enough to kill him, of course."

"Of course," I agreed.

But I'd learned, during my prior investigations, that the oddest things sometimes set people against others.

And the most innocent-seeming sorts

were occasionally the most lethal.

Consequently, since I didn't want Dante, or even Brody, to be guilty, I'd keep Anthony and Irwin on my own little list of people who had been at HotWildlife that day — and who might be murder suspects.

I soon got into my car to head home. My mind still buzzed with questions about why the local authorities had Dante in their sights. Brody, too.

Something similar to my own suspicions about whatever had brought them together in the past?

No one at the San Bernardino County Sheriff-Coroner's office would leap to answer my inquiries. I was a nonentity as far as they were concerned, other than being the person who discovered the body — and, perhaps on some level, a suspect. I had no credentials to convince them to co-operate with me.

But I knew another person with whom they might collaborate. Which was why I'd told Dante I was too busy to see him this evening, in the hopes I could schedule something with someone else.

Once more, I turned to my hands-free car phone to make a call.

"Hi, Ned," I said cheerfully when Detective Ned Noralles of the LAPD answered.

157

"How would you feel about meeting me for dinner tonight?"

CHAPTER THIRTEEN

I spent all the time I needed to take wonderful care of my evening's pet-sitting charges — I was so happy to see them again — plus feeding and coddling my own little Lexie before leaving her for the evening.

Then, after putting on a fresh change of clothes, I headed my Escape toward Hollywood and Highland, a nice upscale shopping center containing plenty of restaurants, and connected to Grauman's Chinese Theater — the one with all the stars' hand- and footprints.

I hadn't allowed Ned to think I simply wanted to see him socially — although I did enjoy spending time with this nice-looking African-American cop. We became friendly when I helped to clear him and his sister, Nita, from being murder suspects a few months ago.

And the fact that his pet, Porker, had wound up the second-place winner in the

Animal Auditions potbellied pig contest had kept his mood way high when it came to me. His sister's pig, Sty Guy, had come in first!

I thought about what a good guy Ned was, and how I seemed to have an affinity for latching onto the wrong men. First Jeff, and now possibly Dante. I pulled into a parking spot in the garage attached to Hollywood and Highland, then hurried to the restaurant where I was to meet Ned. He was already there, standing at the doorway.

"Good to see you, Kendra." A big smile lit up his great-looking face. He was clad in a non-cop outfit of blue shirt tucked into darker blue jeans. I'd dressed in similar casual attire.

We'd chosen to meet at an upscale American grill, and were immediately shown to a table. The place was crowded, the lights were bright, and the aromas suggested that the meats served there were, in fact, excellently grilled.

"So how's Nita?" I immediately asked. I had to raise my voice a little, since the acoustics turned other conversations into a hearty rumble around us. "And Porker and Sty Guy?"

"All fine," he said, smiling. "And you? Lexie? Dante?"

Which made my own smile fizzle slightly. "We're all doing well. At least I can speak for Lexie and me. I still see Dante, but . . . well, he's part of what I wanted to talk to you about."

A server came to take our drink orders. I thought of getting something absolutely alcoholic, since this conversation wouldn't exactly be easy. But, hey, I'd asked for it. And I asked Ned to do some digging on my behalf.

The least I could do was stay sane and sober.

We both settled on beer on tap — a good choice for imbibing at a grill. I studied the menu, made my decision, waited till Ned, too, put his menu down on the table.

And then I asked, "I know I haven't given you much time, but did you have any success extracting information from the San Bernardino County Sheriff-Coroner's Department?"

"A little." His grin appeared both amused and rueful. "You get right to the point, don't you, Kendra?"

"You always have, too," I said, smiling right back. "When you tried to get me to back off looking into murders you were assigned to solve."

"Touché. I'll fill you in on the little bit

161

I've learned so far — as long as we can talk about other things afterward."

"Absolutely."

"The main thing," he said — just as our server brought our beers. We toasted, then tasted them, and Ned soon continued. "There's of course a lot of professional courtesy among law enforcement agencies, especially in nearby areas. And you know I'm friends with Frank Hura. On the other hand, there are also things that are kept confidential. I had to promise the co-operation of the LAPD, which was a plus to them since some possible suspects live in our jurisdiction."

"Including Dante and Brody," I suggested.

"Right."

"And did Frank give any hints about why the two of them are favorite suspects?"

"Well, sort of. But here's the weird thing." He leaned over the table toward me, indicating he was about to lower his voice. "Frank suggested they'd learned some background info that linked the three of them — Dante, Brody, and Jon Doe — sometime in the past. Stuff that could possibly implicate Dante and Brody in the murder. He also made it sound like Jon Doe wasn't necessarily the victim's real name."

"No kidding!" I exclaimed absolutely in-
nocently. I wasn't about to tell him what I'd
learned — or hadn't learned — from Althea.
"But I can't imagine why anyone would
pretend to have a name that's so common.
Or at least supposedly common. I mean,
how many Jon Does are there, really?"

"Surprisingly, a lot," Ned responded. "I've
run into some in local investigations, although of course more are named John with
an h."

"Who'd purposely do that to their kid?" I
shook my head. "Especially if they had the
last name Doe. Anyway, go on. Who is Jon
Doe?"

"Frank didn't give me any real information after that. Only . . ."

"Only?" I pushed eagerly.

Which, unfortunately, was when the server
came to take our order. Of course, I ordered
something grilled — a small steak. Ned
asked for a sirloin.

When we were alone once more — assuming we could call ourselves alone in this
crowded café — I only had to look at Ned
to get his amused smile focused on me
again.

"I'll look into this further," he said, "since
I'm definitely intrigued. And I can't be sure
I interpreted what he said right. But —"

"But what?" I urged eagerly.

"He wasn't exactly forthcoming, nor clear on what he said, but he hinted that he'd learned Jon Doe's identity through his fingerprints — although there was something odd about that, too."

"Odd, how?"

"That's what I need to find out more about. I gathered that they were not in AFIS."

I knew what AFIS was: the Automated Fingerprint Identification System, a resource used throughout the United States to identify people via their prints. Of course, not everyone's prints were in the system; there had to be a reason, such as certain state driver's license requirements and criminal convictions.

"And that was the strange thing I didn't quite get," Ned said.

"What do you mean?"

"Well, if I understood the guy's hedging and hinting right, I think he suggested that whoever Jon Doe was, he had a criminal record."

I enjoyed the rest of my dinner with Ned, even as my mind sputtered and spun around his revelation. Or at least his suspicion.

Jon Doe, whoever he really was, had a

criminal record.

And yet his fingerprints were apparently not in the system.

Jon Doe might have had a past that somehow included both Dante and Brody.

But what? Where? How?

And how could I learn about it?

Ned was smiling after we'd finished our steaks. We sat sipping coffee for a while, talking about unimportant but enjoyable stuff like our favorite cop movies and TV shows.

"I really appreciate the info you got for me, Ned. And if you learn anything else about Jon Doe or what the San Bernardino sheriff's guys think about his murder, I'd love to hear it."

"You're welcome, Kendra. And if you happen to figure out who did it before those guys do, let me know. I'd enjoy thinking the LAPD's not the only outfit you show up with your oddball investigations."

I grinned right back into his dark, sparkling eyes.

"Well, if it turns out that Dante really is the guilty party, I've got shoulders big enough for you to cry on." He flexed his biceps, and turned in a manner that showed off said shoulders, even as his smile grew silly.

I laughed. "I'll remember that, Ned."

So okay. That night before bed, while sitting in a nightshirt in my living room, the TV on mute, I considered my phone options. Not that I'd call Jeff, even though ten had been his time to call me.

But should I get in touch with Dante? Let him know the little I'd learned from Ned?

Probably nothing Dante didn't already know.

If he had a history with Jon Doe, he might have known him under his previous name. But he didn't seem willing to discuss that with me . . . yet.

And how could a possible convict not have his fingerprints in AFIS?

Unless Ned or I had misunderstood. Or it was by official decree.

Dante might have some of the answers I craved. But how could I get him to share? He knew my history of resolving murder situations, but he hadn't let me in on anything about Jon Doe that would help me help him. Why?

Damn! No way was I going to get to sleep easily with my mind swirling around like this. "What should I do, Lexie?" I asked my clearly sleepy Cavalier, who lay beside me on the sofa. She wagged her tail in support, but offered no advice.

Okay. This might be a bad move, but I was miffed enough to do it anyway.

I called Dante's cell.

He answered so fast I wondered if he'd expected my call. Well, hell, how could he? I hadn't decided until an instant ago.

"Hi, Kendra." He sounded happy to hear from me.

Which nearly made me mess up on my resolve to stick it to him. Nearly, but not quite.

"Hi," I said sexily. "Lexie and I are here alone, Dante. We miss you. And, by the way — Ned Noralles said hi."

"Sure he did." Dante's tone resounded with ironic skepticism.

"He'd gotten some interesting information from his colleagues in the San Bernardino sheriff's department," I continued. "Shared some with me, but I had to promise to keep it confidential." Scrunching my head toward my shoulder to keep my phone at my ear, I reached down to my bare feet and crossed one toe over the other. Wasn't crossing toes similar to crossing fingers — to hide a lie?

Hmm. My toes' nail polish needed a little retouching. Something to think about.

"Anything that would help get them off

my case?" Dante inquired, sounding quite casual. Of course, he hadn't gotten so rich and powerful by acting all emotional, so I figured his offhand tone was assumed.

"Gee, I'm not sure. I guess it depends on when you really first met Jon Doe, and under what circumstances. Anyway, I'm really tired. Got to take Lexie out for her last evening constitutional, and then we'll head to bed. Good night, Dante."

I hoped that the steaming I thought I heard from the other end, before I hung up, wasn't just my imagination.

CHAPTER FOURTEEN

I didn't sleep well that night. Surprise!

Keeping my cell phone charging on the table beside my bed, I half expected Dante to ring me back and demand details. But then again, that rich-and-powerful attitude most likely made him feel above all things trivial, like being a potential murder suspect. Or information possibly leading to that conclusion.

Or even a potential girlfriend playing petty games with his psyche.

Okay, I admit it. I considered calling him back to apologize. To figuratively grovel at his feet for having hinted at things I wanted to know, rather than had any actual knowledge about.

But my phone didn't ring, and I made no calls.

Morning eventually arrived. I bounded out of bed and grabbed pen and paper.

I'm a listophile. A listoholic. My pet-sitting journals are full of lists of items I need to follow up on about my clients. My computer at the law office has multiple lists regarding upcoming issues about each case.

Right now, I jotted down a list of everything I knew about Jon Doe. And a separate list of things I needed to find out.

Guess which was longer.

At the end of the second one, I wrote at the bottom of the page — "Do I really want to do this?"

I mean, after all, in all my past adventures I'd known that my friend or acquaintance who'd been accused actually wanted, and needed, my assistance.

This time, the main suspects appeared to be Dante and Brody. And both seemed inclined to encourage me to butt out. Well, Dante at least. And Brody had barely spoken to me about the situation.

All this aroused my curiosity all the more.

Lexie had been utterly patient, but I saw my adorable pup prancing on the floor beside my bed.

Time to take her out and start my day.

Still no call from Dante a while later, after I'd checked in with Rachel, confirmed who was caring for which kitties and pups this morning — no exotic pets currently spiced up our agenda — then finished up my own AM pet-sitting.

I'd dropped Lexie off at Doggy Indulgence as atonement for ignoring her.

Right now, I sat at my cluttered desk at Yurick & Associates. My mind was on my research about conservatorship issues for my new client Alice Corcorian, and I'd brought up some interesting Web sites on my computer. In California, conservatorship required some degree of incapacity. To the contrary, I'd gathered that Alice had all her wits about her. The fact she'd found a young stud to marry? More power to her!

My desk phone rang. "Kendra Ballantyne," I answered.

And was immediately treated to one of life's interesting coincidences. "Hi, Kendra. This is Ellis Corcorian. How have you been?"

"Fine, Ellis," I said, going along with his politeness. "And you? And how are things at Marden & Sergement?" The firm had been Marden, Sergement & Yurick in the days I'd been an associate there, before Borden had formed his own firm.

"Everything here is going well," he said. "But I think you know why I'm calling."

"I take it your mother let you know that this firm is representing her." My voice assumed its professional tone. "Are you representing yourself, or have you hired another lawyer to help you with this matter?"

"Just me, for now. Did Mother tell you why I'm seeking a conservatorship?"

"Why, yes. She even brought that nice young fellow, Roberto Guildon, to meet me."

"He's a third of her age!" Ellis exploded. I pulled the phone away from my ear and rubbed it. My ear, I mean.

"That doesn't mean they don't love each other." I reached over to scroll down the computer page I'd been reading. "Basically, a conservatorship can be awarded only if the potential conservatee is too incapacitated to take care of herself. Your mother seemed entirely alive and capable to me."

"It's *res ipsa loquitur!*" he shouted, as if his loudness would somehow convince me. It didn't. Nor did his use of the Latin legal term that meant "the thing speaks for itself." "Just the fact that someone her age would fall for a young gigolo and not see through his wanting to get to her money is enough to show her incapacity."

That confirmed my suspicion that Ellis was in it to ensure his mother's money was there for him when she eventually passed away. But, hell, it was her money. And she and I hadn't yet discussed any estate planning she had done.

"I don't think so, Ellis," I said sweetly. "But I'll talk the situation over with my client. Maybe we can all meet soon and reach some kind of resolution that will save you both time and money. Okay?"

"Yeah, sure. I'll talk to her, and maybe if you're there, we'll be able to discuss this without yelling at each other." I doubted that, considering the tone Ellis had maintained in this conversation, but why not try?

"I'll call Alice, then get back to you with some possible times. Talk to you soon, Ellis. And say hi to the gang at the firm for me."

And be sure to tell them all how happy I am with my life without them. But maybe they already knew that. I'd stayed in touch with one of them, Avvie Milton — although I had to assume Avvie might have left the firm by now. She'd had an affair with Bill Sergement. Who hadn't? The thing was, he and I had come to a mutual parting of the ways long ago. Avvie and he hadn't, and then he'd gone back to his wife. Last I'd heard, Avvie was finally ready to move on.

Hey, what a perfect opportunity to find out how she was doing . . . and maybe get some insight into Ellis Corcorian, too! But when I called her number, I got voice mail.

I left a message, hoping to hear back from Avvie soon.

I got some times okayed by Alice Corcorian for a meeting sometime in the next few weeks. And back at my desk after lunch, I called another client: Lauren Vancouver, the head of HotRescues.

"Good to hear from you, Kendra," she said. "I was going to call you. I got an e-mail from Efram Kiley, the guy who supposedly owned Quincy before I rescued and re-homed him. He's probably just blowing smoke, but he insisted that I give his dog, Killer — that's what he called Quincy — back to him within a week or pay him a million dollars for his pain and suffering, or he'd make sure I regretted it. He's made claims before, but none with a time limit like this one."

"Have you responded?" I inquired, sitting forward in my seat. Were legal services suddenly required immediately?

"I did as you said, and told him I'd referred the situation to my lawyer and couldn't discuss it with him."

"Excellent!" Ah, a client who actually listened to legal advice. "Now, how about if I come back to HotRescues — maybe this afternoon — and we can strategize a bit?" *And I can subtly ask you some questions on everything you know about Dante DeFrancisco, including his history.*

"Sorry, but I have a women's club coming to look over our facilities and pets available for adoption. I'm hoping to place a few of our animals today, and that'll take up all my time. And I'd rather wait till I get Efram's answer, to give us a better idea how to respond. If he's got his own lawyer involved, he's clearly serious, and we'll need for you to jump in. Okay?"

"Okay," I said, keeping the disappointment inside myself and out of my voice.

"But thanks for calling to check on the situation," Lauren finished.

So . . . no chance to extract Dante info from Lauren. I looked on the computer for my list of stuff to do today at my law job. Nothing leaped out at me as requiring immediate attention. A good thing? Sure, but it didn't inspire me to dig into researching another brief or drafting a court pleading.

What did inspire me? Curiosity. I really wanted to figure out who'd killed Jon Doe, and why. Fast. Someone other than Dante. Or Brody. No matter what their connection, or not, had been to the guy in some prior life.

175

Talk about curiosity . . .

Anyway, I had some time to kill and wanted to get busy. I hadn't the skills of hacker Althea, but I was still pretty adept with the Internet.

I brought up another list I'd made — the one with everyone I'd recalled who had been at HotWildlife the day Jon Doe was killed: Dante. Brody. Me. Megan Zurich. The volunteers: Krissy Kollings and Anthony Pfalzer. The prior visitor who turned volunteer: Irwin Overland. Warren Beell, the hot-headed guy who'd brought the mama wolf there in the first place. And a few hundred visitors whose names I didn't know.

At least I'd gotten the last names of the few people with whom I was acquainted.

I could Google every name I had and see if anything exciting turned up — like whether Warren Beell blogged about how much he hated wolves.

Okay, I admit I spent an hour on the attempt. I didn't bother with Dante and Brody, but I found quite a bit about Megan and her championing of wildlife.

Krissy had been quoted in an article for a local college newspaper about how she didn't like the way some upperclassmen harassed incoming students and did what she could to stand up for them, even getting in their faces.

Anthony, a player on his high school football team, had gotten a few exciting scholarship offers. That was on a Web site for his school, and his reputation on the football field sounded a lot ornerier than he was at the sanctuary.

Irwin was apparently an accountant who commuted to a big CPA firm in L.A. I found nothing that indicated anything about his personality, but recalled the minor dispute he'd mentioned with Jon Doe.

And Warren worked for a car dealership and would be glad to assist any visitors to their lot to find the perfect deal. He apparently had an affinity for wild animals, since I found several articles quoting him regarding rescues. And he had come to Hot-Wildlife one day spoiling for a fight after being all but accused by Megan of stealing back mama wolf.

Any genuine suspects in this ragtag group? I doubted it.

I did learn addresses and phone numbers for nearly all of them. But none of the sites I found stated that any of them had a grudge against Jon Doe, nor that one of them had stabbed him.

Gee, what a surprise.

What else could I do from inside my cozy law office? Not solve the murder, apparently. But that didn't keep me from continuing to work on it.

I called Sergeant Frank Hura after bringing the San Bernardino County Sheriff-Coroner's Department Web site up on my computer. I looked at his photo as I spoke with him.

"Hi," I said, attempting to sound utterly ingenuous. "I was there the other day when you were questioning Dante again, and heard you talked to Brody another time, too. Do you need anything else from me?" Not that I hoped to suddenly head his suspect list, but if I was there being interrogated, I could ask a few additional questions.

"I know about you, Kendra." He sounded as if he smiled. "You've solved murders in the past for Ned. Or against Ned. I think my department had better handle this one ourselves."

"Then you won't even tell me who your major suspects are, and why?" I hoped I sounded flirtatious.

"I think you can guess the who. And the why I can't reveal till we're ready to make an arrest."

"I'm assuming you mean Dante or Brody,"

I guessed. "But, Frank, why on earth would someone of their stature pick on some little wildlife sanctuary handyman?"

"As I'm sure you know, Kendra, things aren't always what they seem." He sounded like he enjoyed taunting me a bit.

I pretended to be confused. "You can't mean that Dante isn't Dante DeFrancisco of HotPets. Or that Brody isn't Brody Avilla of film and *Animal Auditions* fame. So — oh, I get it. Jon Doe isn't Jon Doe? Or he didn't work at HotWildlife? Or he wasn't a handy-man?"

"Well, he did work at HotWildlife, Ken-dra. And he did use that name there."

"Then he wasn't Jon Doe? Do you know who he really is, Frank?" I asked excitedly, dropping any semblance of stupidity. Lack of knowledge, though — now that I could easily admit. "And if you do, how did you learn it?"

"We have a good idea," he responded vaguely. His image on my computer screen seemed to smile snidely at me, but I resisted slapping it away. "And how we learned what we did was by using general law enforce-ment resources."

But the guy's fingerprints apparently weren't in AFIS, I wanted to shout at him. *So what resources did you use?*

Well, hell. I didn't have to reveal my resources, either. But I could offer a guess. "So did the fact that Jon Doe's fingerprints weren't in the system suggest to you that he'd been an utter angel before, or was there some foul-up somewhere that kept his prints out?"

The imagined smile on my screen turned sour as seconds passed before Frank answered. "You're too smart for your own good, Kendra. But if you dig too deeply into this as a civilian, you're liable to wind up in big trouble. Stop your snooping now."

Chapter Fifteen

Okay, so I'd come across yet another irritable cop. There'd been times that Detective Ned Noralles of the LAPD had warned me off even more strongly. And that was generally without intriguing me with hints of stuff I absolutely intended to learn.

But for the moment, I said a meek goodbye as if I was buckling under, then hung up.

And stared at the phone while envisioning tossing epithets Frank's way.

Should I call Ned to tell him about this awful conversation? I decided to do so, but got his voice mail. I left an oblique message that suggested I'd done something he might not approve of, and asked him to call me back.

So what, then, should I do with the rest of my afternoon?

Call Dante, dared a little voice inside me.

Like hell, I told it back.

Instead, I attempted to concentrate on some further research into elder law conservatorships for the benefit of Alice Corcorian. Despite my good intentions, my mind kept wandering.

Who was Jon Doe? And why had he died?

"Damn!" I exclaimed softly to myself, as if that would get my mind back in gear. Not!

My office phone rang just then. Great! My sanity was suddenly saved by the bell.

"Hi, Kendra, it's Avvie," said the voice on the other end. "I just interviewed for a job in Calabasas and am on my way through the Valley, back toward town. Can you break away for a cup of coffee with me?"

Could I? Absolutely! "Just tell me where and when," I said.

Avvie Milton had been a new associate at the law firm of Marden, Sergement & Yurick when we first met. These days, we had much more in common — having both been screwed by senior partner Bill Sergement at different times.

She was also the proud owner of Pansy, a potbellied pig whom I'd pet-sat now and then. Pansy had also trained with some of the piggy cast of *Animal Auditions,* although she hadn't been an official contestant. She was so smart that she'd likely have out-shined all the others — or so Avvie had maintained.

Now, Avvie and I sat at a small, round table inside one of the large coffee shop franchises. I'd decided I needed to sweeten my day, so I'd ordered a café mocha. Avvie had gotten one of the concoctions of coffee, frothy milk, and who knew what else?

"So tell me, how are things going with Dante?" she asked, taking a sip of her hot brew.

Avvie looked utterly professional in a navy suit and white blouse. Her hair was short and highlighted, her hazel eyes somewhat shadowed. I knew it had taken a lot out of her to finally realize that Bill Sergement was an utter louse and had only been using her for fun. Not that I'd kept that opinion to myself even as the affair was going on.

"Okay, though we're taking things slowly." I took my own sip in punctuation.

"Really? I thought he was all hot and heavy over you."

I shrugged slightly in my own, less dressy suit jacket. "We'll see. Now, tell me about the job you just interviewed for."

Avvie was also a litigator. She'd taken on a lot of civil suits at the Marden firm, mostly for the defense. She'd excelled at it, as I

had. That's one reason we'd become buddies.

"It's a small boutique firm, but they take
on a lot of interesting cases," she said. Her
eyes began glowing, so I knew she was way
interested in the position. "They sought me
out, in fact, because of my success in the
Crader case."

I'd heard of it, of course. A wealthy local
businessman had been accused of breaking
into the home of a lovely film star he'd just
met, blindfolding her, and sexually assault-
ing her. There hadn't been enough evidence
to convict on criminal charges, but the star
had sued for civil damages.

Avvie had handled the businessman's
defense and had shown that the evidence
pointed in a different direction — even
though whoever had allegedly done it wasn't
ever identified.

"The case had been really high profile,
and the partners at this firm were impressed.
They tend to take on fairly well-positioned
clients in difficult cases, and they're highly
compensated for it. We're both still weigh-
ing whether I should work there, but I'm
definitely interested."

"Good luck with it," I told her sincerely.
"I think it sounds great. Oh, and I have a
question for you. Who do you think really

assaulted Ms. Crader?"

She leaned over the table toward me. "I don't imagine we'll ever know for sure. My client's fingerprints were in the apartment, but he'd been an invited guest the previous evening. And they weren't the only prints. My vote goes to a guy who remained unidentified."

"The prints were there, but the cops can't make an ID?" I asked. My interest in fingerprints had, unsurprisingly, spiked a bit lately.

She shrugged her shoulders. "I learned that the system is far from perfect. Only . . . well, in this instance it may have been someone in the system deciding to protect whoever had left those prints."

"Really? Does that happen a lot?" Now, my interest was absolutely piqued.

"I don't know," she said. "I doubt it. No one admitted it in this case, and it might have been a wrong impression on my part."

Or not. I had my own suspicions about some prints in the national system — Jon Doe's. Or whoever he actually was. But I figured I was heading toward a dead end. Even if there was such a thing as protecting someone's identity by not acknowledging whose prints were whose, I could probably never prove it.

Or who Jon Doe really was.

I asked Avvie about Ellis Corcorian. Other than suggesting he was as much of an ass as I recalled, she hadn't much to say about him.

We soon finished our coffees. "Great to see you," I said.

"Same here."

"And be sure to keep in touch. Let me know what happens with the job."

"Will do." She gave me a hug at the shop's door, and we each walked our own way — me to my office, and her to her car.

I felt disheartened over the subject of fingerprints after coffee with Avvie. I moped as I mused about it on my walk back to the Yurick firm's building.

I guess, inside, I'd held out a lot of hope that there was some deep and dirty government conspiracy that had obfuscated the genuine identity of Jon Doe except for a privileged few whom the system assumed truly needed to know.

On the other hand, Jon Doe might, in fact, never have had his prints taken. If he had, a mistake could have kept his identity secret, without anyone intending it. As with everything else in the legal system, a perfect process remained only as accurate as those who used or abused it. And whatever Frank

186

Hura had hinted to Ned — well, it could have come from professional discourtesy, pulling one another's law enforcement legs.

In any event, I needed to look in different directions.

After responding to phone messages, briefly chatting with Borden about the Corcorian case, and doing additional research into conservatorships, I decided to make one more call before leaving my office for the day.

"Hi, Ned," I said when he answered. "Forget, for the moment, what Frank Hura may have hinted about — or not. What's your opinion on how much police departments can rely on fingerprint IDs?"

I heard his snort from the other end of our connection. "Sorry I even brought up the idea of prints, Kendra. I got a call from Frank chewing me out for talking to you at all about his case, when I don't have jurisdiction. I promised him I'd butt out. Sorry. But I gather I was all wet about my interpretation of what he said. He said his guys had done some more digging. Jon Doe was exactly who he appeared to be. No problem with his prints. No record. Nothing. My opinion of fingerprint ID is that it works — very well. And Frank kept it close to his Kevlar vest who he thinks is now his top suspect — but I gather it's still Dante."

That sounded suspicious to me. Full of conflicting assumptions.

If Jon Doe was Jon Doe, then why would Dante have decided to kill him?

If he had a history under another identity, then why would the cops have determined he didn't?

My belief was that Sergeant Frank Hura had decided that the best way to encourage Detective Ned Noralles to keep his nose where it belonged, in L.A., was to make up his alleged facts as he went along.

But all this was getting me exactly nowhere.

Yet each time before, when I'd stuck my nose into a murder investigation, the parties under suspicion had needed me. Relied on me. Cared about my solving the killing.

And Dante only wanted me to butt out.

"What do you think about that?" I asked Beauty, the golden retriever, as I took her on a long walk in her northern San Fernando Valley neighborhood a while later. She was my first pet-sitting visit of the evening, before I picked up Lexie at Darryl's.

Beautiful Beauty did take the time away from sniffing some grass at the edge of a lawn to look at me sympathetically, as if sensing my angst, but she gave me no answers.

I next headed to Harold Reddingham's home. A long-term pet-sitting client, he had gone out of town for two days, so I had to peek in to ensure his kitties, Abra and Cadabra, were okay. When they deigned to show themselves as I checked their food and water supply, I considered asking them their opinion, but figured I'd only get their typical tail-in-the-air stares.

There was at least one human opinion I valued that might be given readily at my request: Darryl's.

When I was nearly done with my pet-sitting stuff for the evening, I called Doggy Indulgence to ensure that my dearest buddy was still indulging doggies. He was, and he promised to wait for me.

I soon parked and rushed inside the building, where some of his human staff members were still signing doggies out and into the custody of their owners. Lexie leaped toward me from where she had probably been sleeping — on one of the people-type furnishings at one side of the large play facility.

I picked her up and walked toward Darryl, who was just saying farewell to a cute cocker mix and her middle-aged owner. He lifted his hand in greeting, and in a moment motioned me to follow him to his office.

"You look awful, Kendra," he said without preamble, which made me feel even worse. "What's going on?"

Lexie lay down in my lap as I sat facing Darryl's desk and let him know how frustrated I'd become. "It's hard to look into a murder from an hour or more's ride away. And when the suspects I want to prove innocent remain uncooperative, it's even worse. Plus, what little info I've learned is likely to be inaccurate, but even if it's true, I'm not in the inner circle to be able to understand what it means." I explained the fingerprint fiasco.

My loving, lanky friend peered at me over his wire-rims. "I see two options, Kendra. Number one, go to HotWildlife for a week or so, do your investigation, and see if you can figure out who killed Jon Doe. For your own satisfaction, if not Dante's and Brody's. It's something you're good at, like it or not."

I let my mind swirl around that possibility, watching my friend for a sign of sarcasm. None. "But my law work. And my pet-sitting."

"You'll need to figure out if you can af-

190

ford the time from your attorneying. I'm sure Wanda would be glad to continue helping on the pet-sitting front. She's doing fine with her own clients, but she's always willing to help a friend." The sweet and sappy expression on Darryl's face confirmed how proud he was of her, and how much they were in love.

Which made me utterly happy for him . . . despite my ugly jostle of jealousy due to my current Dante-related predicament.

"And door number two?" I inquired.

"Just drop it," he said. "One way or another, the authorities will decide who killed Jon Doe, and why. They solve a lot of situations. And I gather Dante and you are currently not quite as close as you'd seemed, so even if they zero in on him, that might be the long-term answer for you."

"I can't say I like that alternative," I grumbled.

"I doubted you would — but you don't have to decide now. Think it over. And be sure to let me know the way you go."

I gently set Lexie on the floor, stood, and hugged Darryl. "Thanks for always being there for me," I said.

"Even if you don't like my advice," he responded with a grin.

■ ■ ■ ■

By the time Lexie and I Escaped to our home, I realized Darryl was right. There were only two possibilities: dig in and find the killer, or get out of it and stop stewing.

As if I could do the latter. Stop stewing, I mean. But the idea of butting out had started to sound pretty good.

Except . . . When I pushed the button to open the security gate outside my driveway, I felt my jaw drop nearly to the floor.

Dante's silver Mercedes was parked inside.

Not that it had never happened before. Rachel knew Dante, and had sometimes let him in so he could wait for me, but not for the past few weeks.

Probably because Dante hadn't shown up on my doorstep, except in my company.

But now . . . What was he doing here?

Guess I had to go in to find out.

I parked in my usual spot at the side of the garage. Dante was with Rachel, both of them watching Beggar and Wagner romp on the roomy lawn of my rented-out mansion. Lexie joined the pups as the humans both approached me.

"I hope it's okay that I let Dante in," Rachel said anxiously. "I saw him waiting outside."

"It's fine," I said, hoping it was true. My eyes were glued to Dante's chiseled features and his dark, unfathomable eyes. He had put an office-type white shirt on over his tight, casual jeans. Was this visit business or pleasure or both?

"See you both later." Rachel hastily made her getaway. Guess she had sensed the tension in the air.

She went into the main house with Beggar, while Lexie joined Wagner on the lawn.

"So, what brings you here, Dante?" I asked oh, so casually. Not that we'd actually been arguing, but the tension that had somehow grown between us seemed to be reaching a palpable crescendo at this moment. I considered clapping to see if the air would explode around us.

"I think you know, Kendra," Dante responded, his sexy voice in a quite canine growl. "We need to talk."

CHAPTER SIXTEEN

He'd brought the fixings for dinner! How could I refuse?

He had done that before, when he'd initially intended to impress me: acted as top chef right in my own kitchen, more than once. As if someone of his wealth, power — and sexiness — needed to do more to be impressive.

And he'd succeeded.

I helped him retrieve a couple of grocery bags from the trunk of his car and carry them upstairs. I unlocked my apartment door, and we all went in — Dante, our doggies, and me.

We put the stuff on the kitchen counter — what little there was of it in the small room in which I cooked and ate at a tiny round table.

"So what's on the menu?" I inquired.

"Entirely up to you," he said, and suddenly I was in his arms — and the subject of one really hot, sexy kiss.

"Oh," I eventually whispered. I wasn't sure I could say anything more.

"If you meant," he whispered against my lips, "what food we'll be eating tonight, I'm making beef stroganoff and a nice salad."

"Oh," I said again.

"And we'll talk over dinner, okay?"

I thought about saying "oh" again, but decided against it. "Sure," I said instead, attempting to put some nonchalance in my tone.

For a while, all we talked about was who was boiling the water for the pasta, who was stirring the stroganoff sauce, who was cutting which fresh veggies for the salad. Since this had been his idea, I suppose I could have adjourned to the living room and watched TV news while Dante did it all.

But staying in his company at this moment, with no nasty comments, innuendoes, or unanswered questions shouting between us . . . well, for now, it was bliss.

After checking with Dante, I fed Wagner along with Lexie — a whole lot more for the German shepherd than the sleek Cavalier. We both fed our babies nutritious stuff — from HotPets, of course, and I had plenty.

Dante had also brought wine — a nice

Chianti that didn't have to be refrigerated. And soon, we sat down at my tiny table, with our salad bowls and wineglasses before us, the scent of a potentially delicious dinner hovering in the air.

We looked at one another.

Lord, that man was one handsome dude! I still couldn't believe someone so suave and rich could seem so attracted to me.

And I still didn't know whether he'd murdered Jon Doe.

I suppose that reflection must have shown in my eyes. "Time for our discussion," Dante said, the suggestive sexiness in his gaze suddenly replaced by total shuttering.

He was good at that, too.

"Sure." I attempted to sound eager. "What are we talking about?"

He hesitated for an instant — not something Dante did often. "You know how I feel about you, Kendra," he began, sounding simmeringly angry about it.

"Maybe," I responded cautiously. He'd acted attracted to me since the instant we'd met, but was only sometimes happy about it. And the last few days, since the Jon Doe incident, he'd seemed withdrawn, perhaps because of my suspicions about him.

Although I hadn't exactly vocalized them.

"I care about you a lot!" he all but

shouted, as if he instead was chewing me out for some infraction of the man-woman rules. On the tiled floor below us, the dogs shifted and even cowered a bit. "Sorry," Dante finished, aiming his apology at me — or the dogs?

"I . . . care about you, too," I said in a much more subdued tone.

"I knew, during the last murder you investigated, that you thought for a while I could have killed our *Animal Auditions* judge Sebastian. But I didn't, and I also didn't take your suspicions very seriously. You kept them discreet, and didn't let them interfere in our relationship. But now —"

He stopped, and a slew of unspoken words seemed to swirl around my head.

He knew I suspected him in Jon Doe's death. What could I say to that — except, perhaps, to admit it?

"Now," I said softly, "there's another murder on my radar — someone else we were both acquainted with. You, perhaps, better than I . . . ?"

Okay, there was his opening, if he intended to confess all. Or even part.

"Because I care about you, Kendra, and because I don't want you getting hurt due to things you don't know about, I'm going to violate all sorts of oaths I took years ago and tell you a few things tonight — as long as you take an oath of your own, to me, that this will go no further. No matter what happens. Not even if I'm arrested for this murder. Or if Brody is. If that happens, we'll take care of it. Got it? And also, you absolutely may not discuss it with Ned Noralles, or even your buddy the private investigator."

He knew Jeff's name, but who cared? He was going to entrust me with some secret, which made my insides sing with pride.

"I promise," I told him. "I won't tell anyone anything you say."

"Good." He suddenly wasn't across the table from me, but right beside me, and once more I was in his arms. "This isn't easy to talk about now," he muttered into my ear. "And I'm not about to tell you all the details. It's all on a need-to-know basis. Okay?"

"Yes," I confirmed again, and then we kissed once more.

But in another moment, we were back at the table, eating stroganoff. And I was spellbound as Dante revealed what little he intended to say.

"Jon Doe wasn't his real name," he began. "I think you've figured that out. His initials were the same, though: J.D. Brody and I

198

both knew him many years ago. We worked with him until things went south at the government agency where we all were employed. J.D. was sent to federal prison. He must have gotten out recently, one way or another, and gone undercover to get revenge against us, or at least that's our speculation. His disguise was excellent. Neither of us recognized him, at least not at first, and we're still looking into the situation. We're pretty certain that the man you know as Jon Doe was determined to kill us."

I'd primed myself for a whole passel of information. Instead, as we finished eating, Dante only passed along tantalizing bits of data.

Which I remained unsure whether to believe. At least some of it.

Number one: Dante would not divulge Jon Doe's real name, only confirm he'd kept the same initials.

Number two: Dante, Brody, and the man recently known as Jon Doe did work together in the past, at a government agency, doing covert operations. Dante wouldn't name further names, including which agency, but he revealed that Brody and he had discovered some nasty stuff going on at the top. They'd gone to other government sources and ratted out their supervisors. Jon Doe had sided with the slimeballs in authority — and those same slimeballs had repaid him nastily, by making him their scapegoat. The result: the guys at the top cleaned up their act and stayed where they were. Jon Doe got sent to a federal penitentiary for quite a few years. And Dante and Brody had been warned they were toast.

Brody's way of dealing with it was to live his life in the public eye. That way, if anyone went after him, all he had to do was start talking to his adoring public.

Dante's was to go public a different way — with lots of money and authority behind him, but with his face remaining out of the news.

His former cronies — apparently highly placed government guys — probably knew who he was, but also recognized how powerful he had become. And didn't want to mess with him, at least not yet.

In any event, Jon Doe had recently weaseled his way into HotWildlife, probably seeking revenge. Had he finished serving his sentence first? Perhaps he was on parole, but Dante hadn't been able to ascertain that yet. If he wasn't, then he'd escaped from prison.

Either way, was he acting on his own or

on orders from his former higher-ups, who also wanted to avenge themselves on the men who'd caught and stopped them?

And had they been the ones to dispose of Doe? Or had someone else learned who and what he was, and decided on his expend-ability?

Either way, that fingerprint stuff was interesting, though it did not settle the issue of who and why. The federal prisoner's prints were clearly in the system, but the fact that his identity wasn't disclosed could simply be a mix-up somewhere along the line.

Or it could have been an intentional cover-up to assist the man then known as Doe infiltrate HotWildlife and deal with Dante and Brody.

Then again, the murder might not have had anything at all to do with their hidden pasts.

And didn't all these twists and turns sound like some kind of bizarre thriller novel instead of a murder mystery?

No matter. Dante and I soon finished eat-ing. We decided to take the dogs out for a short walk before bed.

That was when Dante finished with what he had intended to say — still not answer-ing any of my inquiries in depth.

"I want your help now, Kendra." He kissed me beneath a streetlight as the dogs stopped to do their nighttime doggy duty. "I know the sheriff's department thinks they have an exciting suspect or two, and they're wearing blinders about the truth. Can you get some time off from your pet-sitting and law obligations, and hang out around Hot-Wildlife with me till we solve Doe's killing?"

Okay, so he didn't mean immediately. And in actuality, he abhorred the idea. Which annoyed me.

But I believed he told the truth. At least a taste of it.

"I think I'm beginning to know you, Kendra," he told me the next morning, snuggled up against me in bed. "Sergeant Hura called to let me know about your latest questions — and made it clear that your interfering wouldn't sway him from arresting Brody or me if he felt like it . . . or at least if he thought he had adequate evidence, and he implied he was getting there. I'm sure my begging you to butt out won't get me anywhere. Plus, you're smart, and you're experienced in murder investigations. I've learned in business to always take advantage of whatever assets drop into my lap — and you're definitely one of those."

202

I didn't want to start my day being annoyed at this hunk — but it was time to tell him off, at least a little. "So you made those interesting but incomplete revelations last night, and invited me to save your butt — a really nice butt, by the way — just to keep me from contacting that cop again?"

His nod sent shivers through me.

"I'd also appreciate it if you'd tell Ned Noralles to back off. I'd do it myself, but he's more likely to listen to you."

"So what evidence do you think Frank Hura has against you? And against Brody?"

"Tell you what. This isn't exactly a time I want to get down to those cold non-facts. Let's get up and get dressed — much as I regret the idea — and we'll talk over breakfast. I'll take you out to a place we can bring the dogs."

But talk about regret — I had to pass on the idea of eating out. Our delightful activities had made me get out of bed later than I'd intended, and I had pet-sitting to do.

So, instead, after showering, dressing, and walking our pups, we grabbed a quick breakfast of cereal and coffee at home.

And all I learned from Dante about any evidence against him, as we sat once more at my small kitchen table with Lexie and Wagner watching our every move, was that he really didn't know.

"They seem to be aware that Jon Doe had a criminal record, despite their denial of learning of it through his fingerprints. You'd think they'd know his real identity now, but there's still apparently some confusion. They haven't found family or anyone else to claim Doe's body. I couldn't get from Hura why they're suspicious of Brody and me, but whatever they think they've discovered somehow involves us. That underscores my belief that Doe's being here was a setup, but I still don't have concrete information. If it's true, looking into Doe's death could be damned dangerous — and since I don't think I can convince you to stay out of it altogether" — he looked at me hopefully, but scowled when I shook my head — "I want you beside me every moment that you're sticking your nose into this situation. Got it?"

"I hear you," I said. And wanted to believe him. I really did. But all this talk of covert stuff and conspiracies made me wonder about this amazingly sexy guy's sanity. Even as it stoked my curiosity even more. "Did Frank Hura ask you whether you knew Jon Doe before?"

"Yes, but I said I wasn't sure. And that's mostly the truth. All I've actually got is suspicions — albeit strong ones — and your buddy Esther Ickes told me never to speculate. She's a great criminal attorney, by the way. I love the way her mind works — nice and devious for such an innocent-looking little old lady. Anyway, Jon Doe didn't really look much like the guy with the same initials I used to know. If it was him, he'd lost a lot of weight, grown a lot older, and his hair got really gray. And long. And that goatee — that was definitely not part of the fellow I thought he might be."

I moved my cereal around in my bowl with my spoon, looking for some that had stayed crunchy despite the generous helping of milk I'd poured on. "So did Frank Hura even give you a hint of what could possibly lead to arresting Brody and you?"

"No, but I'm afraid that time is coming soon, unless I solve Doe's murder myself." I must have made some kind of irritated sound that reflected my annoyance, since Dante caught my eye over the cup of coffee he'd lifted to his lips. "With your very able assistance. Or, more likely, the way things go with you, you'll solve the murder with my minor help." He moved his cup and grinned.

I couldn't help grinning back — confidently, of course.

I really wanted to believe in Dante's innocence. After all, I was sleeping with the guy.

I only hoped I'd be able to find the real killer — and that it really wasn't this man who had so gotten under my skin.

CHAPTER SEVENTEEN

Dante kept in close touch that day, which was Friday. He was reorganizing his extraordinarily busy schedule to be able to spend next week at his hideaway in the San Bernardino Mountains, checking into who had slain Jon Doe.

He expected I'd be doing the identical thing. Which I was. I lined up Rachel and Wanda and another couple of backups from the Pet-Sitters Club of SoCal, ran around introducing human clients who weren't yet away from our area to any sitters they might not have met, and tried to swallow my sorrow at not currently being as reliable as I'd like. But I'd fix that once this murder was solved.

I also met with Borden and other Yurick firm attorneys to ensure that any legal issues that might arise next week were well handled. Fortunately, Borden had hired a bunch of good people. I especially liked

Elaine Aames's attitude. She was a senior attorney who had inherited Gigi, the Blue and Gold Macaw who often hung around the office to speak her mind.

As part of Dante's preparations to get out of town for the next business week, I knew he was crowding a bunch of meetings into the weekend. With his money and authority, no supplier or store manager would dare to say no to spending their weekend that way.

Which meant, when Saturday morning rolled around, I had no plans to see Dante that day. Probably not Sunday, either, but I'd deal with one day at a time. We talked often, confirming our plans for the following week. And, gee, I never got around to divulging my designs on this weekend.

And so, without telling him, Lexie and I headed to HotWildlife right after completing our Saturday morning pet-sitting. I intended to return in time for the evening's duties, and, as usual these days, Rachel took over any midday dog walking — fortunately, there was only one taker at the moment.

I wasn't idle on the way there, either. Sure, I drove and talked to Lexie, who sat safely in the back seat, behind the divider I'd gotten along with my Escape. But she wasn't the only one I spoke with.

Hands free, as we sailed east along the

freeway, I used my electronic system to call Althea. Yes, I had her cell number. She wasn't always chained to her computer at Hubbard Security.

"Hi, Kendra," she answered immediately. "And the answer is no. I'd have called if I'd learned what you asked me yesterday — the name of an inmate who'd escaped or been released from the federal prison system recently whose initials were J.D. I still wish you hadn't been so closemouthed about it. I assume this is related to the murdered Jon Doe, but —"

"You're right, but I promised my source not to discuss it. And I haven't confirmed a thing — right? — in case you're asked."

"Correct. I'm intrigued, though, and will continue looking. But since I'm spending so much time, I'll have to tell Jeff."

"Sure, but no details, please." I rolled my eyes, but not too far — I had to keep them on the road.

"And as far as the rest of our deal . . . ?"

"Yes, I'll agree to see him again. But I'm really busy at the moment, and probably all of next week."

"Okay, as long as I can tell him you'll see him soon."

"Absolutely," I said as I hung up, wishing it weren't so. Jeff Hubbard was not a martyr sort, nor a glutton for punishment. I had to somehow discourage his futile hope of winning me back. I'd never consider him my guy again.

And not just because Dante was in my life. Especially since, at the moment, I wasn't sure how long that might be.

Not only was Dante a murder suspect, both in my estimation and in the San Bernardino County Sheriff-Coroner's Department's, but he was used to wielding absolute authority.

And at the moment, I was disobeying what amounted to a direct order from him. I was working on my own investigation of Jon Doe's death today without staying in Dante's presence. Yes, it was sweet of him to attempt to protect me. But he'd warned me, and I would be careful, and that would be enough.

Besides, if he asked, I could say that, today, I really wasn't working on the Jon Doe murder. I was after whoever had wolfnapped the missing mama.

Which meant that I intended to visit Warren Beell, who'd dumped her at Hot-Wildlife.

I'd Googled him further than I had before, confirmed the info on where he lived, and called to make sure he'd be home and not at the car dealership where he worked. I'd told him some of the truth — that I was still damned concerned about mama wolf's whereabouts, and wanted to see where he'd found her. Especially since I understood how much he cared about animals. I didn't tell him so, but that was the fruit of my earlier Internet search of his name.

I drove north of the 210 Freeway around the town of Muscoy and to the edge of the mountainous Angeles National Forest. Beell lived in a nice enough housing development, and I parked on a paved residential street.

He answered the door almost immediately when I rang the bell. "Hello, Kendra," he said, as pleasantly as if he had invited me. The short, stocky guy, dressed in a ratty T-shirt and jeans, looked down along the leash I held. "That's a cute dog. A Cavalier King Charles spaniel?"

I acknowledged that indeed was Lexie's breed. "I hope it's okay that I brought her. I didn't want to leave her home alone." Of course, I'd fretted about what to do with her here. What if Warren Beell had some kind of big dog around who ate little pups for lunch?

Or even a hungry mama wolf . . .

"No problem at all," he said. "We'll shut

211

her in the kitchen when we go outside. I have things to show you so you'll understand why I had the wolf here in the first place."

Interesting, I thought.

We went through his living room and into his kitchen, all of it messy. I supposed the guy might clean it now and then, but this was absolutely way past "then."

He moved newspapers from a couple of chairs around a crowded table and invited me to sit. "I was afraid, when you called, that this had something to do with poor Jon Doe. Rumor has it, around HotWildlife, that your hobby is investigating murders."

"Not exactly," I said with a rueful shake of my head. "But I've been around more than my share of that kind of nightmare." *And if you happen to want to confess to the killing, that would save me a potentially unpleasant time with Dante in this area next week.* But I didn't say that.

"Anyway, like it or not, I have a similar situation, where I don't exactly seek something out, but I'm still saddled with it. In a nice way."

"What's that?" I inquired, my curiosity piqued.

"It's why I had the wolf here. You know they're not native to California — at least

212

not this part."

"That's what I thought."

"And anyone who keeps a wild animal as a pet is supposed to have a license for it. But my suspicion, especially because the lady wolf was fairly calm around people, is that she was someone's pet, and whoever it was, dumped her when she got pregnant."

Which was what the speculation had been about Warren himself.

"Somehow, she knew to come here for help. And she was even tame enough to be coaxed easily into a crate so I could transport her. But the kinds of animals I generally care for — well, come on outside, and I'll show you."

Lexie looked dolefully after me as I walked through the door without her, but the instant I was in Warren's backyard, I was happy she'd stayed where she was.

There were small fenced-in enclosures all over the moderate-sized yard. And there were small animals inside each.

Raccoons. Opossums. A couple of foxes. Even some squirrels.

"I don't know how it happened, but whenever a creature around here is injured, it shows up on my doorstep. Maybe my neighbors help these days. I'm not sure. But of course I try to take care of them. And, no, before you ask, I'm not licensed, so I'm sort of throwing my life, and theirs, into your hands. If you turn me over and I get arrested or anything, no one will care for these guys. I could ask Megan, of course, but HotWildlife's full of other, more visible kinds of animals, more endangered than my little buddies."

I spent time oohing and aahing over nearly every enclosure. Warren hadn't seemed the nurturing type to me at HotWildlife, especially when he'd been so defensive about dropping mama wolf off there, and being questioned about her. But he appeared awfully caring now. He related stories about how each of his visitors had come for help, and what he had done.

And that's what they were, visitors. He said he always took care of them till they were healthy enough to release back into the wild.

"Thank heavens that's the case with all these guys here now," he said. He got a little teary-eyed. "Sometimes, though, I have to have one euthanized. I have a friendly vet who helps at reduced rates, and no questions asked."

These temporary visitors were apparently Warren's family. He looked a little dismayed, running his fingers through his gray hair when I asked if he was married, and, if so, how his wife felt about his avocation.

"No woman around here." He grinned. "None could live with me."

When I was done communing with Warren Beell's version of nature, we walked back inside the house. I felt fairly certain he indeed had nothing to do with mama wolf's disappearance. He clearly cared about animals, and wouldn't have done that to her or her pups. Plus, where would he have put her? He had a full house of animal charges.

But I still didn't feel I'd gotten answers to all I'd come here for.

As Lexie leaped in joy to have us back with her in the kitchen, I said to Warren, "You know, in a way you were right in the first place. I wanted to find out how you'd gotten charge of the mama wolf and confirm you didn't take her back. With all your charges here, well —"

"I didn't take her back!" He stood beside me, and his infuriated glare made me uneasy. "I wouldn't. I care too much about her offspring, let alone —"

"I get it," I said as I slipped a few feet sideways. I believed — maybe — that his indignation was genuine instead of a reflex of guilty defensiveness. In fact, he looked a little sheepish as he settled back down on a kitchen chair.

But I wasn't through with him. "And I also wanted your opinion of Jon Doe. And to learn all I could, so I could eliminate you from the list of possible suspects."

Warren rose again, slowly. "Thanks for being honest." His tone indicated that he struggled this time to maintain his cool. "I didn't really know him. Sure, with my interest in animals, I visit HotWildlife a lot. Even bought a membership, and I contribute what additional money I can — not, of course, on the scale of that Dante DeFrancisco. He's your friend, so I won't say anything against him. But the guy is a control freak."

I opened my mouth to point out the discrepancy.

But he clearly knew what I was about to say. The catch in his voice was replaced by a laugh. "Okay, I did say something against him. Anyway, I didn't know Jon Doe well, but I saw him around a lot during the past few months. Far as I could tell, he stayed in the background, caring for the animals. Seemed to do a good job. I had no reason to dislike him, let alone kill him."

Lexie and I left shortly thereafter. Was I certain about eliminating Warren Beell from my suspect list? No. But I sure liked the guy

216

more now than after the first couple of times I'd seen him at HotWildlife.

How could I not at least have some affinity for a man who clearly cared as much about animals as he did?

Only . . . well, what if he had, despite what he'd said, seen something indicating that Jon Doe wasn't as nice to the animals in the sanctuary as he should have been?

Warren Beell had shown a hint of temper when I'd suggested I'd considered him as mama wolf's abductor and, maybe, as having had something to do with Doe's death. He'd certainly shown his temper about Megan's earlier questioning of him. Had Doe done the same: Pressed him so he'd resorted to murder?

Maybe.

CHAPTER EIGHTEEN

So where did we head next? HotWildlife, of course.

On the way, my cell phone rang. Despite the hands-free stuff, I checked caller ID.

Dante.

Well, he wouldn't know I'd disobeyed his direct orders and come here without him, would he? I didn't imagine Warren Beell would have called about my visit. And unless he'd put some kind of tracking device in my Escape . . .

Heck, that whole concept about any covert government stuff he might have done in his early days was getting to me.

Even so, I decided to let him leave a message. That's not like me. I hate not to respond to a call that is coming in.

But at the moment, that simply seemed the best idea.

I soon pulled into the parking lot at the sanctuary. The volunteer at the gate recognized me, and I assured her that I'd leave Lexie in the front office if I went wandering.

But my real intent wasn't to enjoy myself by watching the animal inhabitants.

I intended to talk to Megan. Although, of course, I realized she might be unavailable. I purposely hadn't called to arrange a meeting, partly because she might mention it to Dante.

I also thought that making this conversation impromptu might be best. Responses to the topics I wanted to deal with would be less likely to be planned and more likely to be the truth.

"Kendra, hi," Megan said immediately as I walked through the door of the building where her office was located. "And Lexie. What brings you here?"

"Wolf pups, for one thing," I said. "And also I wanted to talk to you about a conversation I just had." Bringing up Warren Beell and his single-handed saving of a few wild animals would be a good way to segue into any inquiries about Megan's relationship with her staff . . . including Jon Doe. Or so I hoped.

"Sure. I was just about to take my late-morning stroll around the place. Would you like to come?"

I wanted to, as much to stay at Megan's side as to see the animals. However . . . "I'd love to, if it's okay to leave Lexie here."

"Of course. She can stay in my office, and I'll make sure one of my assistants checks on her every few minutes."

Lexie didn't seem to like the idea much, but we left her there anyway, after I gave her a reassuring hug and told her I'd be back soon.

We headed first toward the infirmary, where we peeked in on the wolflets. They were sleeping behind the glass of their airy enclosure, and didn't stir.

I waited till we were outside again before my usual oohing and aahing, since I didn't want to disturb the sleeping pups. "They're so adorable," I gushed, and Megan agreed. "It's such a good thing that they're here, so they can have constant care. I'm really glad that Warren didn't try to handle the pregnant wolf himself."

"Yeah, I've looked into the guy a little more," Megan said. "He visits here frequently, but I didn't know at first that he also does his own rescues of some wild animals." She sounded mightily displeased.

"I just learned that, too," I admitted. "I visited him at home to try to get a better feel for whether he might have taken back the mama and be hiding her."

We were outside the first outdoor habitat. Megan stopped dead in front of me and stared. Her golden brown eyes were huge, and she looked almost like a feral feline as she frowned. "You went to Warren Beell's place alone? Kendra, I'd gotten the impression that you're one smart and savvy lady. But you saw him here yelling at me. The guy's got a temper. He could have hurt you — or worse."

I felt justifiably chastised. Yes, I'd thought of that, and I'd told Rachel where I was going, so if anything had happened to me, word would have gotten out. But that could, of course, have been after the fact, which might not have done me a hell of a lot of good.

"You're right," I said solemnly. "It wasn't my smartest move. But he seemed much milder on his home turf — most of the time. And he genuinely seems to care about animals. He may have been mad at you out of fear for the missing wolf."

"Which we all feel," Megan said, out of my face and once more starting to stroll. "At least I'm fairly convinced Beell didn't take her back. Right?"

"I honestly don't think so. There wasn't room in his yard, and he convinced me pretty much of his concern for her."

"And what about . . . well, he was here the day Jon Doe was killed." Megan's tone was stony. "Did he know him?"

"Hey, that's exactly what I was going to ask you. He claimed he knew him mostly by sight, from his visits here. Do you recall anything that might suggest otherwise?"

Megan seemed to hesitate just as we got to the liger enclosure. The wonderful mix-breed feline, lying on the ground beyond the moat, stopped grooming her huge paw. She stared back at us with eyes that, from this distance, sure enough suggested that Megan was a relation.

The sanctuary director stared at her sort-of look-alike as she spoke. "I've thought long and hard about this, Kendra. I have some ideas about who might have hurt Jon, but they're mostly niggles brought about by feelings instead of any actual evidence I could give to the authorities."

"Me, too," I agreed. "Maybe we could share them and see if brainstorming helps solidify any suspicions." Not that I'd be entirely honest. But I sure hoped she would.

Especially since some of my suspicions centered on her.

But she started playing my game even before I passed the ball to her. "Who do you think did it, Kendra?" she asked, leaning on the concrete wall topped by a chainlink fence that surrounded the enclosure, and looking at me.

"I'm not really ready to point to any one person," I said cautiously. "For example, I haven't eliminated Warren Beell from the killing, only from the wolfnapping. How about you?"

"No, but I think you'd have a better idea than I do. How likely do you think it is that he did it, compared with anyone else?"

Was she fishing to see where she sat on my suspect list? I wasn't about to divulge that — especially since I wasn't exactly certain.

I shrugged. "I really haven't narrowed things down enough to determine who I think is the most likely culprit. Warren's not as high in my suspicions now as he was when I headed here this morning, though. So tell me something about your niggles. Who's your number-one suspect?"

Megan laughed, and we once more started walking through the sanctuary. The late September day was delightful, although the sun beating down could grow uncomfortable if we were outside too long. Our next stop was coyote heaven — with three pacing inhabitants. Once again, the enclosure

223

had a concrete wall around it topped with a tall wire fence. The animals were also safely ensconced behind a moat that kept them separated from visitors.

"I honestly don't have one person in mind, Kendra," Megan finally said. "And I have a feeling that what you're really trying to get from me is a sense of whether I might be the guilty party. The answer's no — although my saying so won't necessarily make you believe it."

My turn to laugh. "You're right, but your sense of humor just moved you a lot farther down on my little list."

She again turned to look at the closest animals who were her charges. Two coyotes ignored us, and the third didn't seem impressed by our presence. He looked in our direction, then snootily stared the other way.

"I hate that Jon was killed here, Kendra," Megan said seriously. "I hate that he was killed at all, in fact. He was fairly quiet, but he always did his job well and seemed to care a great deal about the animals. Only —"

"Only what?" I prompted, somehow seeing, in the wild and carnivorous coyotes, the specters of Dante, Brody, and whatever name Jon Doe went by in the old days working together, yet ready to tear each other apart if it suited them.

"I don't know," she finally said with a sigh. "There was something about him — watchful, I guess. He was so silent at times that I had a sense he was absorbing everything he saw and heard, to use it all later for some purpose of his own. But that's just pure fantasy on my part, I'm sure."

I wasn't so sure, though, and thought more highly of Megan for her apparently excellent perception.

I had to assume that what little Dante had revealed to me was right. Jon Doe could have been here seeking revenge. He might have been attempting to learn all he could from this place Dante funded so he could use it against the place's benefactor, who was less than his friend. He wouldn't learn much, if anything, about Brody here, but maybe that was next on his list.

"Anyway," Megan continued, "he never argued with me. If he seemed put out by any instructions, he sort of shot me a momentary glare, but it went away as quickly as it came, and he always did as I requested."

I wondered if that kind of response had been learned in the federal penitentiary . . .

"And though he occasionally criticized

other people, I never really saw him arguing with anyone else," she finished, saving me from asking her that question.

"So no other ideas about what happened to him?" I asked somewhat sadly. I hadn't gotten much from Megan, and was unlikely to get any more.

"Unfortunately, no. But I'm still thinking about it. I told Sergeant Hura I'd let him know if anything else came to mind, and I'll do the same with you. I Googled you, Kendra."

We were now closest to the mountain lion's den — a real cougar, not like my senior client Alice Corcorian. I'd been staring into her lair, but now looked back at Megan's somewhat smug face.

"I'd heard a lot about you from Dante," she continued, "but it was even more interesting reading online about how you stick your nose into so many murders. That reporter Corina Carey — she's on the TV a lot, and they pick up her stories on various Web sites as well. She seems very impressed by your murder-solving prowess. So . . . well, I figure you have some ideas by now of who killed Jon, but you're not ready to share them with someone you've barely met who's not in law enforcement. I get it. But once the culprit has been arrested, I'd love to hear your thought processes."

I was definitely taken aback by this, but didn't let it show — I hoped. With what aplomb I could muster, I said, "Let's see how it goes. If I actually do solve this case, of course. There are never any guarantees." But I certainly aspired to do it this time as well. And I also realized that it was entirely possible that Megan was indeed the killer, and had taken this tack to throw me off her track.

I considered asking for her opinion of Dante and how he appeared to get along with Jon Doe when I hadn't been around, but didn't want her to know that Dante remained on my list alongside her. And I'd seen Dante, Doe, and Brody all here to-gether, so I could probably gauge that myself — all utterly calm on the surface, but I'd seen something boiling beneath. Something, at the time, that had seemed somewhat inexplicable, but now I at least had some teensy yet undetailed understand-ing of why it might have existed.

We walked for a while more, and I again just soaked in all the sights and scents of the sanctuary. More visitors appeared and sauntered around us as well. I saw volun-teers Anthony and Krissy leading tours, as well as others I'd come to recognize. Even

Irwin Overland, who'd previously been a visitor himself, was now heading a tour group.

A few of the visitors seemed to be there more to walk than to see the inhabitants. A group of nicely dressed men just strolled slowly along the path, conversing quietly. There were also a couple of large guys in jeans who seemed more interested in rough-housing than in viewing animals, and Megan went over to ask them to save it for outside.

Eventually, I had to ask Megan, who absolutely agreed: I could once again cradle and feed a baby wolf. We headed in that direction. "I'm about to publicize the pup-naming contest," she said. "People will need to donate a couple of dollars for each name they submit. I'll send the information to our members and donors, and give them a short while to try, until someone submits names I can't resist."

"Sounds good," I said. "I'd rather call them by name than by 'hey, you wolf!' "

I soon checked to ensure Lexie was still doing okay without my ongoing presence.

I pondered possible names as I helped to feed the wolf pups. Krissy joined Megan and me, and the three of us smiled silently as the little ones took their formula from the bottles we held.

When they were done, so was I. "Thanks for letting me do this again," I told Megan. "And I'll be in touch." I aimed a pleasant glance her way, as if assuring her that I'd keep her informed about my investigation, which I of course wouldn't do.

Lexie and I soon headed out of the sanctuary toward where I'd parked the Escape. Time to head back to L.A.

Only . . . there was a piece of paper stuck into the well where my windshield wipers lay. I pulled it out before opening the car doors — and stared.

Damned if it wasn't a computer-generated warning: "Stay out of HotWildlife, and don't worry about who killed Jon Doe unless you want to join him."

CHAPTER NINETEEN

Okay, this had happened to me before. Was I becoming a threat-left-on-windshield woman?

The other time had been in a store's parking lot, and Lexie had been inside the car. Since I didn't speak Barklish, she hadn't been able to tell me who'd left it. I'd learned later that it was the killer.

Had the same happened this time? I held the piece of paper by the edges and carefully slipped it onto my Escape's floor on the passenger side. That way, no one could steal it back easily after I locked the door, and its evidence value wouldn't become more tainted, as it would if I folded it to slip into my purse.

"Come on, girl," I told Lexie, and we headed to the entrance booth. But the volunteer who staffed it only shook her head when I asked if she'd happened to notice who'd left something on my windshield.

"Sorry, but it's been really busy here." I noticed a fashion magazine on the floor beside her, and figured what besides visitors might be keeping her busy.

I could ask others who'd come to the sanctuary within the past hour or so, if I happened to know who they were, but the only log they kept at the entry was of people who were either members or wanted membership info. The young lady didn't hand me the list, but she waved it so I could see that she at least appeared diligent in ensuring it was kept up to date.

Next thing I knew I should do was call Sergeant Frank Hura. And I would call him . . . soon.

But there was someone I wanted to talk to first. I knew I'd get completely chewed out, but at least I might also be sent some sympathy over the cell phone connection. Standing just inside the sanctuary gate, not far from the building housing Megan's office, I pressed in the number I'd programmed in for Dante. Lexie lay at my feet, looking up as if in concern. I could see through the chain-link fence toward the parking lot and my car, in the unlikely event whoever left the note attempted to retrieve it. But none of the few people around even glanced in the direction of my Escape.

"Hi, Kendra." Dante's deep voice was warm, sexy, and welcoming. I mustn't have caught him in the middle of a meeting. "I assume you're returning my call from earlier." Oops. I'd forgotten about his message. Oh, well. "So how are your plans coming along for our . . . meeting next week?"

Meaning our trip to the area where I now was. "Well, that's one thing I called about. I had an idea and decided to follow through on it today." I inhaled the air from the near-mountain environment, getting only a faint whiff of animal aromas. "I'm standing in the parking lot at HotWildlife right now, and —"

"What! I thought I told you not to do anything on . . . this matter without my being with you."

"Yes, that's what you *told* me." Unlike him, I remained calm. "Only, I'm not one of your employees or in any other position where I have to follow your directions."

"Excuse me." That was muffled, so I figured he had his hand over his phone and was talking to whoever else was with him. And then he must have gone off by himself, since the next thing I heard was his angry voice in my ear. "I wasn't trying to control you, Kendra. Like I said, I'm concerned about your safety. I figured I could protect you when you dug into whoever killed Jon Doe if I was with you, and I knew I couldn't convince you to keep your nose out of it. Knowing something about Doe's background — well, that pretty nose of yours could be in real danger."

Gee. Despite his temper, he'd complimented me.

And . . . "In a way, that's why I called," I said, my tone subdued.

A silence. Then, "What happened, Kendra?" He spoke so softly now that I barely heard him, and all kinds of concern seemed to radiate from his voice.

I told him.

"Damn!" he whispered. And then, "Okay. Wait right there. My first meeting is about to start, but I'll reschedule. For now, stay with Megan. And make sure other people are around, too, in case she — no, I don't think it's her. Even so —"

"No, don't reschedule your meeting. I'm going to call the sheriff's department, and once they're through with me, I'll head back to L.A."

"Then I'll see you tonight," he said. "Call as soon as you're back. And drive carefully. Watch everyone around, and if you see anything that makes you uncomfortable —"

"I'll call 911 first, and then you," I assured him. And then we said our goodbyes and I hung up, a smile on my face.

Temporarily, since the next thing I did was call Sergeant Hura. "Hi, Frank." I attempted to sound friendly and at ease. "I'm at HotWildlife right now. Guess what happened to me here this afternoon."

"Twenty questions?" His sarcasm made me wince. Although we'd started out on affable terms thanks to our mutual friend Ned Noralles, that had obviously deteriorated, at least to some extent. "I assume," he continued, "that you weren't stabbed, like our victim."

I was becoming tired of irritable phone conversations, so I immediately told him what had happened.

"Stay right there," he commanded. I was receiving a lot of orders today, and I didn't like his any better than Dante's — although it made more sense. "I'll have someone there in a few minutes to check things out."

Megan came out to ask if everything was okay. I told her I'd had some car trouble and was waiting for someone to take a look — only partly a lie, since I was waiting for someone from the sheriff's department instead of the auto club. She went back inside the sanctuary.

A deputy more junior than Hura, not part

of the Homicide Detail, zipped into the parking lot in less than half an hour. Meanwhile, since I figured they'd want possession of the piece of paper, I photographed it with my cell phone.

Since I hadn't any information to impart about who might have left the note, other than to say it could be whoever killed Jon Doe, we hadn't a lot to talk about. The deputy indeed decided to keep the note, placing it into a plastic evidence bag and labeling it. He didn't seem inclined to send a crime team to check my vehicle for fingerprints or anything else.

As a result, Lexie and I were soon on the road back to L.A. — with me scrutinizing every other car on the road.

We got back in plenty of time for me to perform my pet-sitting perfectly after I dropped Lexie at home, behind the security gates. As I always liked to do, I spent a lot of time with each of my charges, ensuring that they ate their dinners. With the dogs, I enjoyed a walk or a game or both. The kitties were, of course, another issue — too adorably arrogant to enjoy playing with me.

Eventually, I headed back home. My intent was to call Dante from there.

But he'd already arrived and been let in

by Rachel. He sat in his Mercedes, his cell phone against his cheek. He looked so cute and official sitting there in a white shirt. I assumed he'd headed straight here after his meetings, rather than going home to change clothes.

I didn't intend to bother him, since he seemed to be talking to someone in his professional capacity as a megamogul, so I just smiled and waved. But Dante joined me nearly immediately.

Just inside my apartment door, he swept me into his arms and gave me one of his hottest Dante kisses as Lexie leaped around our feet. "Thank God you're really okay," he whispered against my lips. "At least —" He pulled away, and his gaze swept over my body. I'd worn a nice yellow blouse and beige slacks that day to look like a lawyer while confronting Warren Beell and Megan Zurich. His dark mahogany eyes started to smolder. "Yes, you're more than okay."

Need I say that we satisfied one appetite before we headed out to dinner?

Later, when we got back, Dante called Alfonse, his personal assistant at his Malibu house, to assure himself that Wagner would be well cared for that night before he allowed himself to fall asleep.

And as I lay in bed after some more

fantastic romance, I listened to his gentle breathing and considered putting myself in danger more often, if such excellence was a result.

Not. Especially since I felt a bit frustrated. Oh, not about my love life.

But with what I'd gone through that day, the couple of people I'd confronted. I still didn't feel much closer to solving who'd killed Jon Doe.

I eventually dozed off, and wakened with Dante still at my side. I snuggled up, but only for an instant. Didn't want to get too suggestive — not at this moment.

So what if it was Sunday? I had pet-sitting to do, and Dante needed to continue to clear his desk so he could head to Hot-Wildlife during the upcoming week. We separated soon after a quick breakfast. I left a sorrowful-looking Lexie at home and got on the road.

I wasn't surprised to receive a phone call while parked outside gorgeous golden retriever Beauty's northern Valley home. What did surprise me was where it came from — the Yurick law office.

"Kendra, it's Borden," said my boss's high voice when I answered. "Hope you don't mind my bothering you today."

"It's never a bother to talk to you, Borden," I said with a smile that soon disappeared. My planned week of investigating Jon Doe's death was about to become discombobulated.

I explained it to Dante later that day, when he called to arrange to pick me up early the next morning. I was again at home, this time preparing to take Lexie on a walk to make up for leaving her alone earlier. "I have a couple of law clients who really need to meet with me on Monday," I said, hoping I could schedule them on the same day. "Borden said they both had left him messages after our receptionist told them I'd be out of the office for a week."

"Business comes first," Dante said, spouting what was presumably his philosophy. "But I've been able to make arrangements to get away, so I'll head up to my place in the mountains and do a little snooping around HotWildlife, partly to look deeper into what happened to the mother wolf, and hopefully solve Doe's murder while I'm at it."

"But I won't be there to help you," I grumbled.

"Exactly," he said, making me sure that this was at least partly to pay me back for ignoring his orders. "But you can join me whenever you're able."

Sounded like a plan, or so I supposed.

But I also knew how much I'd hate it if Dante solved everything without me.

CHAPTER TWENTY

At least luck was on my side a little. I indeed was able to schedule both my meetings on Monday, one late morning and one early afternoon, so I could do my own pet-sitting that day without assistance. I dropped Lexie at Darryl's so she could enjoy the day.

I hadn't spent the night with Dante. He needed to get home to Wagner, and to prepare for his trip. But I hadn't liked how he rubbed it in that he was leaving without me.

My first meeting was with Ellis Corcorian. We'd agreed to get together this time sans his mother and her youthful fiancé, on the off chance we could come up with a solution without the main players.

He came to the Yurick firm's offices, and we met in the former bar, which was too big for a meeting of two. But it still seemed more official than my somewhat messy digs.

I got him some coffee, and we sat down at

one end of the conference table in the middle of the room.

I hadn't seen Ellis for over a year. He'd always seemed to try too hard to appear like the perfect film star's son — his hair, though mousy brown, was immaculately styled, without a hint of receding at his temples. His face, a bit too ordinary to hint of any genuine character, was always well shaved. The only thing exciting about him was the fuzziness of his straight brown brows. And of course he always wore a suit.

"So, Kendra," he began as we smiled confidently at each other in preparation to spar. "I'm not sure why we're meeting, but I'm always ready to attempt a compromise, even when it concerns my own mother's sanity."

"She's a cougar, Ellis," I informed him wryly. "That doesn't make her insane. It makes her one amazing older lady."

"But taking up with a guy a third her age, who's trying to become an actor, with no money of his own . . . doesn't that strike you more like he's a leech and she's an innocent, if confused, lamb? I assume this is all off the record, by the way."

"Settlement negotiations generally are," I confirmed. "And I won't tell Alice you said anything nice about her, I promise."

His smile widened.

"So tell me," I continued. "Since you're looking for a conservatorship over your mom's estate, I have to assume you're concerned as much about her assets as about her."

His sudden scowl suggested our moments of affability were about over. "I'm concerned about both," he confirmed coldly. "I don't want her hurt — either emotionally or financially. She needs to ensure she has enough to live on in her old age."

"And when she's gone, you want to ensure you get her estate." I could be equally cool, of course. I took a sip of coffee and continued to stare.

"I don't want some young punk to steal from her."

I leaned back and looked into his steely gaze. "What about a compromise?" I suggested. "Let your mother marry the guy she loves, perhaps even provide for him if she passes first, which is the most likely scenario. But she could also leave a substantial part of her estate to you. It would save your relationship with your mother, and you'd most likely inherit something eventually. If we go to court over this, you know your mother seems sane and possessed of all her marbles. You might lose everything."

He opened his mouth to protest, but then his brain apparently caught up with his need to assert control. "What do you propose?" he inquired.

"I'll have to talk to my client first, see if this kind of compromise works for her, and, if so, find out how she'd be willing to split things. I'll get back to you soon."

"I'm for resolving things outside of court when possible," he said slowly. "And it does sound somewhat logical." Which might be why he hadn't considered such an obvious solution before making his mother so mad. "So, yeah, let's see what she's willing to do."

He left soon afterward, and I headed for my office, where I called his mom. "Hi, Alice. I'd like to report the results of my meeting with Ellis." I described it and said her son would consider backing off if she'd allocate her estate in a way he'd accept. Which is what she and I had discussed earlier, as I was setting up the meeting. Of course, she was amenable. "Now, I'd suggest you speak with your accountant and come up with some kind of way to divide things so you'd feel comfortable about what you'd leave to both Roberto and your son, assuming you don't outlive them both — which you may just be ornery enough to do."

She laughed. "Great compromise, Kendra. I've already told Roberto this was a distinct possibility. And guess what?"

Since she didn't sound depressed, I assumed her guy was as sweet as he'd seemed. "He thought it would work."

"Exactly. Okay, I'll come up with some way to split things, probably halves, if that sounds all right to you."

"Perfect, Alice. Oh, and I'll probably be out of my office for the rest of the week, but I'll always get back to you if you leave a message."

I was feeling somewhat smug after that meeting. I might have resolved a potentially sticky situation with a win-win solution. It involved not animals but elder law, an interesting area and a part of my current practice that I was coming to love.

But I'm a lawyer. I knew I wasn't necessarily on a roll. The next situation on my agenda could be a whole lot stickier.

For that meeting, I would be off my home turf. I'd agreed to go to the offices of attorney James Remseyer, who represented Efram Kiley of Pacoima, the former owner of Killer. Or Quincy, depending on how one looked at it. Killer/Quincy was the Jack Russell terrier–cocker spaniel mix re-homed by Lauren Vancouver at HotRescues, possibly because she simply hadn't found his ID chip. More likely, because she hadn't looked, since she had believed the dog had been abused.

Fortunately, Remseyer's office, in Northridge, wasn't too far away. I'd scheduled this meeting with just attorneys since I didn't want to disturb Lauren for no reason, and I knew the other individual defendant and representative of defendant HotRescues, Dante, wasn't available today. But Remseyer had made it clear he wanted to talk about his case. Probably to threaten and attempt to intimidate, so we'd either come up with a high settlement number or go to trial on this potentially difficult case.

But, hell, as a litigator, I'd eaten worse challenges for lunch.

His office was in a commercial area, on the top floor of a three-story building. The penthouse, perhaps?

I introduced myself at the reception desk in an attractive suite that obviously housed several law firms, or perhaps they were all sole practitioners who'd officed together to economize. I was shown into a compact conference room and served a cup of strong coffee in a small disposable cup.

In a minute, a forty-something man with a shaved head and wearing a suit strode in and held out his hand. "Kendra? Hi, how are you?" He didn't really give a damn, and continued his monologue. "I'm James Remseyer. Thanks for coming on such short notice, but I'm sure it's in both our clients' best interests for us to get some of the formalities out of the way."

I opened my mouth to convey a qualified agreement, but he went on before I could continue.

"I mostly wanted to run some stuff by you so you'd know we have enough evidence to convince even the most skeptical jury of how your clients injured mine. The worst of emotional distress, for one thing. They stole his dog. Did it by fraud, too." Of course, he'd throw that in, since it permitted him to claim punitive damages, which were multiples of any actual damages awarded. But their award was unlikely in cases like this, though I wasn't about to say so just yet. "Not only HotRescues and its management, you understand, but even its board of directors and donors have some responsibility here. A lot of responsibility, in fact." Which was why he had threatened to drag Dante into his spurious suit — because he aimed for the deepest pockets in his contrived claim.

His mouth was still open to eject his next

unsubstantiated statement when I tersely shook his hand and took a seat. I motioned for him to join me at the small, rectangular table that fit snugly into the room. And simply sat there till he complied, not even attempting to interject a word.

"So here's the thing," he started to spout again, but I held up my hand and smiled.

"Whoa, James," I said right over his words. "Let's keep this simple. Your client, Efram Kiley, claims he misses his dog, Killer. My clients say they didn't know the dog they adopted out was Killer. They found an abused animal and got him a good new home. Period. Your client doesn't want the dog. He wants money. My clients may be willing to pay something reasonable to your client so they don't have to pay it to me. And you know courts generally consider pets to be property, so all those claims of emotional distress are spurious." I generally despised that position, but at this moment it worked to my advantage. Still, there were other claims that could have merit. "Let's try to settle this before you and I wind up with all the money and fun, shall we?"

He had amazingly stayed quiet. Not so surprisingly, he scowled now. "Maybe," he grumbled, when I knew he wanted to aim his fist at my face. Settle for something reasonable? That was probably not in his vocabulary. "My client denies abusing the dog, and I believe him." Of course. "They liked to roughhouse, and that dog was always running away and coming back with bruises. Got into fights with bigger dogs in the neighborhood. So, settle? Depends on what you consider reasonable." He smiled once more, so I knew multiple dollar signs paraded through his brain. "We were thinking in the neighborhood of" — he named a multimillion-dollar figure — "since your clients' acts were so egregious, and we'll still claim punies."

I laughed out loud. "Even assuming you could maintain your causes of action for trumped-up actual damages — which I seriously doubt — do you really believe a jury would award punitive damages once we skewer your client on the stand with all the evidence that Quincy — oh, right, your client called the poor little guy Killer — had been literally kicked around and probably starved?"

"That's not how it happened," he said. "I just told you —"

My turn to interrupt. "If you smear my clients with claims they stole a dog or committed fraud, or whatever, I'll smear yours. Simple as that. Not that we believe a jury would award any damages at all. But to save us time and more uncomfortable meetings, I did come here with a figure."

The jerk had the temerity to look me up and down in a sexually suggestive manner. "You sure do, sweetheart."

"Okay, that lowers the amount by a few thousand . . ." Like to near nothing, at least in comparison. "Here." I jotted a figure down on the pad of paper in front of me. "You'll get a substantial percentage of it — I assume you're working on contingency. I won't get much, since I'm on an hourly rate, but, hey, there's always value in keeping a client happy."

He looked at it and choked. "You can't be serious."

"Oh, but I am, *sweetheart*." He opened his mouth as if preparing to interrupt me, but I knew how to play his game, and pressed on. "Now, it's time for me to leave so you can run this by your client. Including how the media will adore this case, with the graphic before and after photos we have of a perfectly happy Quincy these days. And did I mention one of my dearest friends is a well-known TV tabloid reporter?" Okay, so I exaggerated a little. Corina Carey was becoming a good buddy, even if not exactly a bff — best friend forever, in online speak.

But she'd love a story with all the pathos of this one, though film stars weren't involved. Dante DeFrancisco was. Even if he refused to be interviewed on camera, he'd undoubtedly let Lauren spill her guts about the poor, persecuted pup she rescued.

But could James's assertions be true — that Killer hadn't actually been abused? That could shed a different light on this case — one that might not shine as brightly on my clients.

"You'll be hearing from me," he finally interjected. "I've already filed a complaint, and will have it served on your clients soon. And then —"

"Once you serve it, we'll start discovery, with our clients present. If yours doesn't have a really strong stomach, and friends and relations who'll stick with him through anything, you may wind up without a penny when he runs screaming from the situation. If you want to make it easiest on him and yourself, let's settle. If you're nice about negotiating, I may even suggest to my clients that they come up with a little more money — but if you delay, it'll be even less. See you soon, James." I picked up my purse and briefcase, and sauntered out.

And smiled. I wasn't a litigator for nothing. Confrontations like this amused me.

But I had to report to my clients, too. Starting with Dante. Which gave me a damned good excuse to call him at Hot-Wildlife — and make sure he hadn't received any threats there, as I had.

But when I'd returned to my office and was about to make some calls, I received one first, on my cell.

It was Althea. "Got something for you," she said, "although I'm only speculating that it'll be useful."

"What's that?" I grabbed for a notepad and pen. If Althea surmised something would be useful, it undoubtedly would be.

"Some stuff on guys in federal penitentiaries with the initials J.D. who've been released lately. And one who escaped."

"Did any —" I had to be careful how I phrased this, since I'd promised Dante not to divulge what he'd said. Even though there hadn't been much substance to it. "Did any come from an interesting background, not what you'd anticipate of a guy who went bad?"

I heard her laugh. "If you mean, did any come from places other than gang ghettos, the answer is yes. You can't always generalize where crooks come from, Kendra. Many come from where you'd expect — hard childhoods, broken homes, the wrong kinds of cronies. But sometimes people just want to find an easy way to get rich and think they can pull it off. Or they have hot tempers, and attack or kill someone else. Whatever. Anyway, I'll e-mail you what I found — sanitized a bit, of course."

Which meant I wouldn't be able to tell which Web sites she had hacked into. Not that I cared. Her form of redacting didn't generally erase anything of importance to me.

"Thanks, Althea," I said, and absolutely meant it.

In this day of instant communication, I wasn't disappointed. An e-mail from her appeared almost as soon as we'd hung up. I downloaded it onto my computer and started sifting through it.

There was a Jerry Davis who had been sentenced to a year for getting mad and destroying a public mailbox. I assumed there was more to the crime than that, but in any event he had recently been released.

Juan Dorez had been sentenced for helping his cousin sneak into the U.S. without appropriate immigration papers. He, too, was out now.

Jack Daniels — gee, another common name like Jon Doe's — had been convicted of counterfeiting money. He was a definite maybe, since something like that could be trumped up by those in authority, but somehow that didn't sound like *it.*

But then I got to two who sounded like actual possibilities. Jamison Dubbs was convicted of conspiracy in a federal racketeering matter, sentenced to seven years in the low-security Federal Correctional Institution at Lompoc, California, and recently placed on parole. And Jesse Dryler had been convicted of tax evasion and had escaped from the Federal Correctional Institution in Terminal Island, California.

These were two guys I had to research further. Could one have created the new identity of Jon Doe, along with a scheme to get back at Dante and Brody for snitching to federal government superiors who monitored the agency for which they worked? That was what Dante had suggested.

I stared at the names on my computer. I'd Google these guys, see if I could find anything more about them.

Like what agency they might have worked for, and whether it was the kind for which Dante and Brody might have worked as well. And whether the agency still existed, and if anyone else had been outed for illicit activities, and —

Hold it, Kendra.

Oh, yeah, I'd follow these strings to see if I could tie anything up. Only I absolutely hoped I'd be wasting my time on a useless dead end.

Since if one of these was truly Jon Doe — an alumnus of a government agency that had once employed Dante and Brody — and had come after them in retaliation for a perceived wrong, that could mean one or both of them could be guilty of murder.

I decided to do a little digging at home tonight — then hurry out to HotWildlife as soon as I could the next day, to help Dante dig into other possible suspects.

And hope we were immediately successful in solving the murder. Together.

With an as yet unidentified third party the person of absolute interest in this case.

CHAPTER
TWENTY-ONE

Maybe I should have backed off and gone to bed. But I spent another hour attempting to learn anything else useful about the two J.D.s on my radar: Jamison Dubbs and Jesse Dryler.

And found nearly nothing.

I wanted to zero in on Jesse Dryler. First of all, tax evasion could have been trumped up by agency apes he worked for. Plus, he'd escaped.

But then again, the conspiracy theory circling Jamison Dubbs gave me pause. His path into and out of prison sounded potentially less controversial than Dryler's, so if he was his higher-ups' scapegoat, they'd been somewhat gentler with him.

A con who'd escaped seemed more likely to me to go after those he blamed for sending him to prison — like Dante and Brody.

But whichever one it was, the guy was now as dead as — well, Jon Doe.

I felt a shiver go through me. So who had warned me off with a note on my windshield? Not Dante or Brody. They'd both know that attempting to scare me wouldn't get me to back off.

But what if one of their previous employers had decided to eradicate the guy who'd been their scapegoat? Maybe they'd attempted to get him to back off from seeking revenge against his prior coworkers, he'd told them to go to hell, and they'd made sure he went there instead. And then they didn't want someone like me to butt in and find out who they were. If so, that warning could mean that Jon Doe's fate awaited me, too . . .

Beside me on the floor, beside my tiny home desk, Lexie started to stir. "Time for our last constitutional of the night?" I asked, needing to get my mind off this nasty stuff.

She barked her assent, so we went out for a walk. On my property. I have to admit, with all this research, and after the note on my windshield, I felt rather spooked.

But did that stop me from continuing my investigation the next day? No way! I'd simply have to stay alert.

First, though, before Lexie and I started our trek to HotWildlife and our escapade to watch Dante's back, I made some calls. The first was to Rachel, right next door. She bounded onto the lawn with Beggar a minute later. "You could have just rung the bell," she said. "My dad's out of town, as usual."

"I just wanted to confirm again, before I leave, that you can handle all my pet-sitting this week, starting in the morning. With Wanda, of course." She was next on my list to call.

"I told you yesterday I'd do it." My young friend's pretty face started to pout. "And, no, I don't have any auditions scheduled for this week. The last one I went on, well, the producers are still thinking about who they want. And of course the next *Animal Auditions* season won't start for a few weeks — and I love the doggy scenario we decided on. So, yes, I'm on board. You can trust me."

"You know I do." I gave her a hard hug, then smiled at her. "But you also know I'm nervous and even a little compulsive when it comes to ensuring that my pet charges are taken care of."

"I know." She was also smiling now. "That's what makes you such a great sitter, Kendra. But it'll be okay. Go ahead and find that mama wolf, and whoever killed Jon Doe. Then you can come back and take over everything — because I'm convinced I'm going to land a great TV or film role really soon."

Her huge-eyed optimism was nearly contagious, and I felt a whole lot better about everything, especially when Wanda, too, reassured me about all the pet-sitting she'd do for me this week.

I was in an amazingly great mood when Lexie and I got on the road fairly soon after that. I was on a week's vacation. With Dante. Sort of.

The quicker we figured out where mama wolf had gone and who had killed Jon Doe, the sooner I'd be able to relax. Or at least I'd be able to, once the proper parties were arrested.

I speeded up and set my cruise control, still carefully checking the road around me to ensure I was driving safely.

Lexie was blocked in the back seat for her safety. I was in good shape to get to Hot-Wildlife and Dante without incident.

But . . . I could only hope that the answers would be easily ascertained first thing. It wasn't like they'd popped out at me the last couple of times I'd been there.

And I still needed more specifics on the two Jon Doe suspects — preferably without pointing to Dante or Brody. But maybe I could get Dante to be more disclosing about

258

J.D.'s identity and his own past if I showed that my sources could get to the bottom of who he was and what he'd done if I worked on them enough.

And so, I called another of those sources as we got on the freeway. "Hi, Ned," I said. "How's it going?"

"I wondered when you'd call, Kendra," he said, not sounding especially happy to hear from me. "Did you hear from Frank Hura? I'm a little surprised that he'd talk to you about this, but I'm beginning to think the guy'll gloat to everyone he can think of when it suits him."

"Gloat? About what?"

Ned paused, then said, "So you haven't heard from him?"

" 'Fraid not. But I'd love to hear what he told you."

A loud sigh, one I heard plainly. And then, "Well, it's about the real identity of Jon Doe."

"No kidding?" Heck, here I was, working so hard to figure it out, and the best I'd done so far was narrow it down to two guys who'd served time in federal prisons.

On the other hand, it wasn't as if I worked in law enforcement and had easy access to all pertinent databases.

"So who was he really?" I attempted to

sound nonchalant, even though Ned would know otherwise.

"Well, he didn't exactly tell me." Damn! Or maybe good. Maybe this was simply a ploy between cop types to annoy one another. "But he did give me some interesting background."

Ned proceeded to fill me in on some stuff that sounded like the little that Dante had already revealed: Jon Doe was actually a guy Dante and Brody had worked with at some government agency before they had blown the whistle on the whole lawbreaking group. Doe was the scapegoat and went to prison, et cetera.

Only . . . well, the upshot was a whole lot different than what I wanted to hear.

"Hura believes that Doe, or whoever he was, planned his revenge on Dante for a long time. Maybe he hoped to get Brody with it, too. He found out what Dante was up to these days, got himself some successive jobs with wildlife sanctuaries, and waited for his opportunity to get Dante — probably kill him. Only, his disguise wasn't as good as he hoped. Dante recognized him, and killed him first. End of Doe and of the story, except for what'll now happen to Dante."

I slammed on the brake pedal reflexively,

wanting to stop the direction of this ugly flow of information. Not that causing an accident would do that, of course. I glanced into my rearview mirror. Fortunately, the driver behind me was smart enough not to be tailgating. Even so, I no longer felt as if I was driving safely. I carefully pulled into the slow lane and started crawling along with the flow of traffic there.

"But, Ned," I soon said, glad I was still speaking hands-free. "Even if that is the situation and Dante did kill the guy, it was self-defense."

"Not necessarily." I already knew what Ned was about to say. "If Doe had attacked Dante and Dante fought him off, sure. If Dante simply figured out who he was and killed him before Doe got to him first . . . well, that defense isn't likely to work. Anyway, I'm fairly sure that Hura is just lining his ducks in a row and is about to arrest your buddy Dante."

I got off the freeway soon thereafter for a potty break at a fast food restaurant. A cup of coffee. And a few minutes to stop shaking. Maybe.

Poor Lexie, in the back of my Escape, obviously sensed my mood. I tried to calm her, too, by taking her for a nice walk.

261

While I was stopped, I tried calling Dante. I wanted to check up on him. Warn him.

Hear his voice before he was incarcerated.

But although I did hear his voice, it was only in a voice mail message. I left a brief, cheerful request for him to call me . . . as I wondered where the heck he was.

I called Megan Zurich to see if he happened to be with her, but he wasn't. I told her I would see her soon, since I would be in the area.

I didn't hear back from Dante for the rest of the drive. As I pulled into the Hot-Wildlife parking lot, though, my cell phone resounded in its hands-free incarnation.

I pushed the appropriate button to respond, not even glancing to see if the caller ID said it was him. "Hi," I said, knowing I sounded relieved. "Look, I have some things to talk to you about, and —"

But it wasn't Dante's voice that suddenly sounded. I didn't recognize it at all, possibly because it sounded metallic and disguised.

"You don't listen to warnings, Ms. Ballantyne," it said. "That means I'll have to take action. One more chance to get your nose out of the matters going on at HotWildlife, or you're going to be in the same condition as Jon Doe. Soon."

Chapter
Twenty-Two

Well, hell. I especially hate menacing communications. Threats. They remind me of just how vulnerable I really am.

Sure, somehow I seem fated to investigate deaths happening all around me. But I'm not like all those plucky women you see on TV or in films who know every aspect of self-defense, and can use their skills to kick weapons out of an assailant's hand on a moment's notice.

I can aim an appropriate kick at a guy's most sensitive areas when I have to. But here, with notes on my windshield and anonymous intimidating phone calls . . . I admit it, I was scared.

Still sitting in my Escape, doors locked and Lexie unhappily attempting to get attention in the back seat, I called Dante again. He looked as if he could fight off angry hordes. If not, he could pay someone else to do it. But once again, I got his voice mail.

Where was he?

I wasn't going to accomplish anything out here except additional stewing, so I snapped Lexie onto her leash and we headed swiftly for the gate into HotWildlife. The parking lot was far from full on this Tuesday morning, and no other person was out there but me. I kept looking everywhere, on full alert.

I didn't recognize the volunteer at the entrance. She didn't recognize me, either, and had to call Megan to get me through without paying.

That meant additional time in the open, which I didn't like at all.

But Megan gave the go-ahead almost immediately, and Lexie and I dashed through the gate. We went to Megan's office to see what she knew about Dante's whereabouts.

The pretty blond sanctuary administrator appeared awfully tired. She wore one of her standard safari outfits, and barely rose from behind her desk as we walked in. "Hi, Kendra," she said. "Are you here to help follow up on the lead on our missing wolf?"

I felt myself blink at her in astonishment. "You have a lead?"

"Guess you aren't," she said, a wry smile on her face. "I assumed Dante would have told you."

"Then that's where he is?" I sank onto one of the chairs facing her. Lexie sat down at my feet, looking up anxiously. Guess my tone told her I was confused, which confused her, too.

"That's what I understand."

"What was the clue?" Maybe I should dash off to find Dante, and help.

"That's the thing," she said. "I don't know. No one bothered to tell me, but half the staff took off to look for her . . . again. I don't suppose you'd be interested in helping me feed the pups, would you?" She eyed me pleadingly.

"I sure would!" But first . . . "Only, please give me a few minutes. I need to make a couple of phone calls."

Not that I harbored any hope that calling in the cavalry would help with my latest threat, but I nevertheless took Lexie into an unused office near Megan's, sat behind the empty desk, and phoned Sergeant Frank Hura. "And you're back at HotWildlife, prying into official business again?" he demanded.

"I am back at HotWildlife," I confirmed, ignoring the rest of his question. "If I come to your station with my cell phone, can you trace who placed the last call to me? There was no caller ID number, and it said 'blocked.' "

"Then, gee, it must have been blocked. And I don't think it's necessary for us to waste our time trying to figure out how to get around that. So let me give you some advice, Kendra. Go back to L.A. and tell Ned your troubles. Maybe he'll try the trace for you. But you seem to get your threats here, in San Bernardino County. That should tell you something — like, stay home."

"Thanks for the suggestions, Frank," I said sarcastically, unhappy that our initial amiability had deteriorated this badly. "And for all your hard work attempting to protect a citizen who's visiting your community. I'm sure we'll talk again soon." I hung up.

And looked down toward Lexie, who attempted to cheer me by standing on her hind legs, front paws on me and tail wagging eagerly. "You're right, girl," I said. "I won't let that dratted detective get to me."

I did, however, take an iota of his advice. I called Ned. "We didn't even get into the Jon Doe–J.D. stuff specifically," I said after informing him I'd just spoken to Sergeant Hura. "I only told him of the latest threat I received, also in the parking lot of Hot-Wildlife, but this one was by phone. He

266

wouldn't even try to trace it for me, since the number was blocked. Can your tech guys do that if I give you my number?"

"Whoa," Ned said. "Let's go back to those threats." Oops. Hadn't I mentioned the first to him? I'd informed Sergeant Hura, which had gotten me exactly nowhere. And in between, I knew Ned had also spoken with Frank Hura. But their topics of conversation, although related, hadn't officially included me. I didn't recall expressly letting Ned know. So perhaps this was the first time he'd heard of the note. It certainly was, regarding the call. "So someone is warning you not to poke your nose in where it doesn't belong? I hope you got the message, Kendra. I'm not sure what's going on, but there are obviously complications in this situation — of a kind where I probably couldn't help you even if I wanted to. That means the answer's no, by the way. I'm not even going to attempt to get someone to find out that call's origination. Why don't you just do as Frank said, and return to L.A. like a good girl?"

Talk about condescension! I thought Ned and I were better buddies than that by now.

"Thanks for the advice, Ned." I didn't even attempt to insert cheerfulness into my tone. "See ya." I ended the call.

So now what should I do? I felt somewhat stuck.

A knock sounded on the office door. "Kendra?" asked a male voice — which moved me to the edge of my seat, but only for an instant; it wasn't Dante.

It was, however, Brody.

"Come in," I called, as if this were truly my office.

He pushed open the door and entered. Was it the mountain-vicinity air that made people seem so tired and stressed today? Looking at this handsome guy, and seeing how his firm jaw seemed slack and his flashing gold eyes appeared dull, I wondered what he was thinking.

I intended to find out.

"Any idea where Dante is?" I asked immediately.

"Some ideas." He took a seat as Lexie leaped to greet him. "But nothing specific."

Which made me feel no better. But I was always one to avail myself of an opportunity — which Brody's presence presented. I pulled no punches, hoping to get him to open up. "So, are you under imminent threat of being arrested for Jamison Dubbs's murder? Er, I mean Jesse Dryler. Oh, wait. That's Jon Doe. Sorry." I didn't regret a word, especially as I read the shock on Brody's face.

"What are you talking about, Kendra?" he demanded, obviously getting hold of himself in an instant.

"I think you know," I said. "Dante gave me a sketchy background when I pushed him on it, and my research" — well, Althea's followed by my own — "has netted me the rest." Such as it was. It certainly had a lot of gaps. "But I'm still not entirely clear on who Jon Doe originally was, although I think I'm getting close. And —"

"Don't you get it, Kendra?" he exploded, standing so suddenly that Lexie barked and I cringed in my chair. I had never seen the always affable, usually on-screen personality Brody go berserk. "Megan told me about the threats you've been getting."

She did? But who told *her?*

My confusion must have shown in my expression, since he continued, "She just got a call from Frank Hura, who said you'd been in touch with him. I walked in then, and eavesdropped on her end of the conversation. She filled me in on what I couldn't hear. I'm not sure who's making the threats, Kendra, but Hura seems to like Megan, and was warning her . . . about Dante. That's who he suspects. We know better, of course."

He added that as I attempted to insert a protest.

"But — well," he continued, "I gather you know at least a little more now about my background with Dante. I'm not going to give you details. That's up to him, and may be foolish for him to do. But you might know enough to have figured that we blew the whistle on some nasty stuff years ago, and that Jon Doe — I'm not saying who he used to be — bore the brunt of it. His disguise wasn't bad, but Dante saw through it even before I did. He wouldn't have killed Doe unless he had to, and in that event he'd have told me. Which he didn't. But since he didn't, that could mean that . . . Doe's superiors are still, or back, in the act. If they're sending threats to you, that means you may be getting too close to finding them. And we're certain they'll do anything to keep from being found out. We suspect they finally got Doe, but we're using our own means to investigate that. In the meantime, the more you're in the middle, the more obvious it is to them that Dante's not just backing off now that the deed is done. So . . . do you understand what I'm saying?"

"Not exactly," I said as my head swam.

"The more threats you get from these

guys, assuming they're the source, the more danger Dante is in. And me, too."

A while later, I sat with a quiet baby wolf on my lap, holding his bottle and loving the soft puppy feel of him. At the same time, I mulled over what Brody had said, and watched Megan and a volunteer I hadn't met before fuss over the other two.

Brody had already left HotWildlife. And I admit it, I was confused by his circumlocution. But I sure didn't want to be the cause of imperiling either of them, even inadvertently.

But would I back off?

I'd ponder that, but my initial reaction was hell, no. Someone would pay for this guy's murder, whoever he was, and I wanted to continue to search for the culprit.

Preferably not Dante or Brody. And preferably someone who wouldn't be able to plead some kind of supersecret immunity.

But this was getting so damned complicated . . .

"I think we're done," Megan whispered, blessedly interrupting my train of thought.

I gently pulled the bottle away from my little canine charge, running my fingers over his small, gray, furry body. He and his siblings were a couple of weeks old and definitely growing. Soon, they'd become even livelier and carnivorous, and holding their wild little selves would become impossible.

But I loved it for now.

After we'd placed them back in their wolf nest, I followed Megan toward her office, where Lexie waited. I felt utterly drained and perplexed. Brody was angry with me. Dante wouldn't return my calls. Sergeant Hura wouldn't give me the time of day, and Ned Noralles had told me to butt out.

So why was I really here? Regardless of my prior experience, I certainly couldn't solve every killing that crossed my path — especially given their inexplicable volume.

And with those threats flaying my mind, if not my shoulders, I had every reason to head home.

In fact, I was preparing to tell Megan my choice when I heard some noise outside the infirmary. I exited the area where the glass permitted a view of the wolflets, and went into the main hall.

There was Dante, at last. Holding his hand was Krissy Kollings — or was he holding hers?

And did it matter?

With them were big, brawny Anthony Pfalzer, ecology-minded Warren Beell, and

Irwin Overland, former tourist and current HotWildlife volunteer.

At least they hadn't been alone together — had they?

"Hi, gang," I said preemptively, not wanting Dante to offer any excuse for their clasped hands.

"I understand you were off checking out a clue about the missing wolf mama," I continued. "Any luck?"

"Not really," Warren said sadly. "I'd heard from some people I know who also unofficially rescue wild animals. They live up near Big Bear, high in the mountains. Something supposedly attacked some dogs in a neighborhood up there, and a couple of residents said it looked like a wolf. But no one had captured it, so we decided to check it out. We hiked through the woods up there till we got a likely answer. Turned out it was probably a large local dog who'd gotten through a fence. Fortunately, none of the pets it attacked was badly hurt, and the owner promised to pay for vet bills."

"I see." I refused to meet Dante's gaze, though he seemed to attempt to capture mine. "I don't suppose anyone in that area had any ideas where mama wolf might be, did they?"

"We don't think so," Irwin said, "although

we had lunch there and did some brain-storming. I'll look at some other sites on my computer this afternoon."

"We've already done that," snapped Krissy. I glanced that way and saw that her hands were both free now, which probably had messed up her mood. Oh, well. And maybe Irwin would discover another clue that Krissy and Dante could scope out together. She would undoubtedly like that.

"Well, I was just leaving," I said. "If I get any other ideas, I'll let you know . . . from L.A."

"No," Dante said, suddenly at my side. "You and I have some strategizing to do before you go."

"Oh," I said airily, "we can do it by phone."

But then my hand was in his, and he was squeezing — gently enough, yet I read some kind of communication in it, even if I couldn't interpret the message.

"Sure," he said, "but one-on-one here is so much better. Come on. We'll take a little walk to get started."

CHAPTER
TWENTY-THREE

And so we strolled outside without my retrieving Lexie from Megan's office.

I inhaled the animal scent of the sanctuary as I sighed. We didn't hold hands, and I suspected Krissy was watching us. Oh, well.

The air was slightly nippy, now that it was the beginning of October. Of course, Southern California was always subject to Santa Ana winds, so today's chill could become tomorrow's heat.

And speaking of chill, our prolonged silence grew increasingly uncomfortable. I suppose I was expecting at least an explanation, and preferably an apology.

But, hey, we were free adults. Not in any kind of committed relationship. Dante could hold whoever's hand he wanted. Or not. Like he wasn't doing with me.

We passed the first few animal habitats as we walked along the paved path. It was a Tuesday, early afternoon, not a time that attracted a whole lot of visitors. A few people were peering into the enclosures and exclaiming over the awesome rescued inhabitants. Their excitement was contagious, and made me smile despite myself — especially as I eyed some indifferent coyotes inside.

"I'm glad you finally made it here," Dante eventually said.

Oh, ho. Apparently I wasn't the only one miffed. Maybe his hand-holding with Krissy was a kind of retaliation for my not dropping my entire life to head up here yesterday, on his command.

"I guess," I responded noncommittally. So far, this visit to HotWildlife had been fraught with stuff I could have done without, like that menacing telephone call, and the subsequent conversations with Frank Hura, Ned Noralles, and Brody Avilla. And I'd yet to have one on this subject with Dante. "Anyway, I'm really sorry that the possible clue about our missing wolf mama didn't amount to anything. I'd love to have had at least that mystery solved by now."

"Me, too." He stopped walking and started staring into the nearby home of the liger. "If you'd been here, Kendra, you'd have come along with us to look for the wolf."

I stood beside him and also regarded the fascinating large feline. I loved the leonine

276

look along with the soft stripes. But I also didn't completely see the lovely creature pacing in the habitat. "That's true," I said, wondering what Dante's point would be.

"But you weren't. That meant I didn't have your amazing insight and intuition along when I was in the presence of a lot of possible suspects in Jon Doe's death."

"Oh." Was that why he'd gone? "But I thought Warren was the one who'd gotten the supposed lead on an attack animal. How could you have made it up?"

"I didn't," he acknowledged. "I took advantage of it, though, and encouraged as many people as I could to join us. I wanted to observe them. Talk to them in a non-threatening situation. Get them to open up on their opinions, if possible."

"On the missing wolf?" I asked.

"On Jon Doe," he said, still without looking at me.

"Oh." I finally got it. He had come to this area to seek out other viable suspects in the murder, to help prevent his own arrest. And he had wanted me along as backup. Mostly, he'd wanted me here for my own protection, in his presence, if I intended to look into the murders. That way, he could keep his eyes open and keep me out of danger.

He didn't know about the latest threat I'd

received. This didn't seem the most opportune time to fill him in.

"So was it worthwhile?" I asked. "Did anyone say anything that suggested they'd hated Jon Doe? Or killed him?" This particular group of people were all on my suspect list, though none appeared especially murderous. Warren, Irwin, Krissy, and Anthony all seemed like nice enough animal lovers, not Jon Doe despisers. And I had no motive in mind for any of them.

"No one did or said anything at all suspicious," Dante said with a deep sigh. He finally looked toward me, his dear dark eyes suddenly bleak. "And Sergeant Hura can't say the same about me. He has enough information on my background to make it look like I had more than enough motive to kill Jon Doe."

"But it'd be self-defense, wouldn't it?" I tried that again, though I figured I knew the answer.

"Depends," Dante acknowledged, "on whether he was armed and attacked first."

"And did he?"

Dante didn't say anything for a long moment as he continued to regard me, his expression suddenly blank. "Then you *do* still suspect me, too, Kendra." It wasn't a question. "Are you here to try to hammer

278

another nail in my coffin?"

"I'm here, Dante, to find the truth."

I was suddenly clutched in his arms, and we engaged in one hell of a sexy kiss.

"So," he finally said as he broke away, "am I."

We did wind up holding hands as we ambled through the rest of the sanctuary. Didn't run into Krissy, though, even when we got back to the entry area, so I couldn't rub it in.

Heck, why was I even thinking that way? I still hadn't discussed the hand-holding thing with Dante, and chose to assume it was Krissy's doing. And in any event, I was the one heading to Dante's cabin that night.

We stopped into the office so I could get my sweet and patient Lexie back. My pup acted so exuberant to see me that you'd have thought I'd abandoned her for a week.

We also said goodbye to Megan. She looked up sadly from behind her desk. "I didn't really think that lead on the wolf would amount to much, but I couldn't help hoping."

"Yeah," Dante agreed. "And the more time that passes, the less likely we are to find out what happened to her. But we'll keep trying."

"Have you done any more with the wolf pup naming contest?" I inquired. "Maybe as part of that, you can charge a fee to enter, as you suggested, and at the same time put out the word that whoever provides the best lead to help find their missing mama will get an extra-generous prize."

"That's a great idea," Megan said. "We've thought about doing both, but this way the two contests — if you can call the search for clues on mama wolf a contest — will be combined."

"Exactly." I smiled. "We'll be around the area for a few more days, so when I stop in tomorrow, I can help brainstorm the details."

"Thanks." Megan rose and approached. She hugged us each in turn, even Lexie. "You two are really great," she said to the humans among us. "You, too, Lexie. See you tomorrow, then. And, Kendra, be really careful, okay?"

I assured her I would, and then we left.

"What was that about?" Dante asked as we left the building.

"Nothing much," I lied. "Tell you about it later."

We drove separately, in a mini-caravan, to Dante's mountain retreat. I did as I'd promised Megan — and myself — and kept

an eye on the road and the others everywhere around me, making sure I saw nothing, and no one, that appeared threatening.
At least I got no further phone calls. And I
felt slightly relieved as the big wrought-iron
gate closed behind us.

I hadn't realized that I'd felt some sense
of security while behind the chain-link fence
around HotWildlife, but I had, rightly or
wrongly.

Dante had brought Wagner along on this
visit to his cabin, and the adorable German
shepherd was obviously in ecstasy to see us
— Lexie included. The two romped through
the abbreviated yard and into the wooded
area within the perimeter fence, then came
back to join us almost immediately.

Dante didn't have a personal assistant
here, the way he did at his Malibu home
with the wonderful Alfonse, but his staff on
retainer kept his plush but rustic cabin clean
and well-stocked with wine and food. At
least one staff member showed up often
when Dante was in attendance. None was
around now, though. And we'd already
decided to go out to dinner. Brody was supposed to meet up with us at the restaurant.

And so, a short while later, we headed
back out through the gate. Lexie and Wagner had each other for company at the

house, and they'd already been fed.

I rode with Dante in his Mercedes. I didn't have to watch the road, but maintained my vigilance on everything else.

The restaurant was a nice steakhouse not far away. When we went inside, it was crowded and smelled great. Lots of people, white tablecloths, and wait staff in aprons over white shirts and black trousers. I loved it already.

Brody had booked a table, and sat there with a bottle of white wine in a chiller beside him. "Glad you could make it," he said. "Although I was a little surprised you wanted to eat out tonight, Dante. Or do you have some undercover security guys here? I couldn't tell."

Oops. Apparently Brody assumed I'd told Dante about the latest threat. Dante's initial confused expression, as he sat down after holding my chair out for me, turned thunderous. Toward me, although his response was to his longtime buddy Brody. "What are you talking about?"

Brody looked at me. "Didn't you tell him?"

"Well . . . no. I didn't think about it." Not entirely true, and Dante would know it if he'd observed my watchfulness in the car. I aimed a smile intended to be charming toward my host and said, "I got a rather nasty phone call as soon as I pulled into the HotWildlife parking lot this morning." I proceeded to tell him all about it, as briefly and lightly as possible.

Didn't fool him, though. "I assume you're taking this seriously, Kendra," he said. "And now there's even more reason for me to stay close. What time was it?"

I guessed as best I could. "To rule out possibilities, were all the people you were checking out from HotWildlife with you then?"

"Probably not. We split up sometimes to comb those woods, then met and exchanged notes. We can't rule any of them out. But I'm more likely to think . . ." His voice trailed off, and he exchanged a look with Brody before both of them took a sip of wine from their respective goblets in gestures that appeared awfully decisive — but I couldn't tell what they'd decided.

I was determined to find out.

Dante excused himself a short while later, just after we ordered our meals, to wash his hands.

"I wish you'd let me tell Dante about that call my own way," I said accusingly to Brody.

"And you'd have gotten around to it when?" he retorted. I felt almost like I was acting out a role across from this handsome movie star. Certainly being under a threat from an unknown source was surreal, not actually me.

But then again, my involvement in solving several murders never quite felt like reality to me, even though it was.

We all were absolutely charming to each other as we ate our meal. Brody followed us home to Dante's, and we all gathered, dogs included, in the log cabin's living room to watch Brody's *Rin Tin Tin* remake on one of the classic TV channels. As the star, he played a dog trainer and mentor to a young orphan adopted by an early American cavalry troop out west.

Dante left the room for a while after the film started. And I heard his raised voice from inside his office.

Fortunately, I'd seen before that Dante had no landline in this house. That meant he'd spoken on his cell phone.

I laughed along with Brody as he spat out commentary now and then about what had gone on behind the camera. Soon, Dante returned. His expression seemed a combo of smugness and rage. Interesting.

Despite my curiosity, I settled down and snuggled against him on the couch as the movie continued. When it was over, I gave

Brody a quick kiss on the cheek in congratulations for an absolutely entertaining classic film.

We all soon headed for bed. Dante and I were both either too exhausted or too irritated to even think of sex. I waited a long, long time till I heard his breathing turn deep and even, signifying sleep.

And even then I didn't move immediately.

But when I finally did, I sneaked to Dante's side of the bed and retrieved his cell phone. I hurried to the bathroom, where I'd already hidden paper and a pen. I looked down the caller ID list. No name on the most recent call, but I was able to jot down the number.

I flushed the toilet in case I'd been heard, but Dante was still sleeping when I returned to the bedroom. I quietly slipped my note into a pocket of my purse that was already filled with papers, hoping to obscure it from all eyes but my own.

And tomorrow, I would use a reverse phone directory, or resort to Althea, to learn whom Dante had talked to.

CHAPTER
TWENTY-FOUR

I wasn't surprised to learn that the person Dante had palavered with on the phone was with the U.S. Department of Justice. Not too surprised, anyway. That was the info that Althea exhumed from her online sources when I gave her the 202 phone number that was clearly in the area of Washington, D.C.

Yes, I'd resorted to relying on Althea, partly because I couldn't get a long enough time to hit the computer with Dante around. Plus, I was certain I'd get accurate info fast that way.

Dante, Brody, and I had discussed various plans of attack for the day, but no one had ome up with anything definitively designed discover who had killed Jon Doe. We had g out at Dante's home during the morn- and it had been one heck of a hard task t any private time. These guys were n most ways, including attempting to keep me safe. But it had been awfully hard to create time to contact Althea. And then to learn the results of her research and jot stuff down.

I'd even resorted to multiple potty breaks, which earned me curious looks from the guys, who obviously wondered whether I was well. Plus, Lexie and I went on a couple of extra outings for her, with Wagner along, too, even though she didn't really have to avail herself of the lawn that often. Of course, we stayed inside the fence, and I kept watch for any movement outside it.

Hanging around the house for a few waking hours drove me a bit batty. I was used to running around pet-sitting. Loved my extra vocation and all the animals I cared for. Even loved cleaning up after them when necessary.

Well, okay, that was an exaggeration.

And now it was early afternoon. We had just left Lexie and Wagner in the charge of one of Dante's local housekeepers and headed for HotWildlife, all of us piled in Dante's car.

"So we're going to just mingle among the remaining caretakers today and act like volunteers?" I confirmed as we pulled into the parking lot. "See if we can push any of them to give further info on Jon Doe and his friends and enemies?"

Though HotWildlife wasn't the largest local animal sanctuary, it employed at least half a dozen people to ensure the inhabitants were fed regularly and right, and that their enclosures were clean and secure. Then there was a team of groundskeepers who kept the areas outside the habitats in good condition. Not all were necessarily on duty at the same time.

"That's the plan," Dante agreed. "We'll meet up every hour or so to exchange what we've learned. I've already told Megan part of our plan, and she's okay with our poking our noses into areas that she wouldn't otherwise allow."

"Is she really able to dictate rules to you?" Brody inquired drolly, then opened the door behind the driver.

"I may be chief contributor here," Dante said, "but, like with my HotPets stores, I pretty well give my managers free rein, as long as things run smoothly. And as much as I like the animals here, Megan's much more experienced in their care, so I definitely listen to her."

And offer strong suggestions of your own, I thought. Suggestions that amounted to orders, even if not phrased that way. That was a major part of Dante's powerful personality — something I'd experienced myself. I thought it attractive and cute, most of the time. Especially when I simply followed the orders I agreed with and ignored the rest.

As always, I carried my large purse with me. Inside were my cell phone and a spiral bound notebook that contained my pet-sitting log. And other notes.

Including the name and phone number of the person whose identity Althea had found for me.

My habit had been to inhale the unusual animal odors of HotWildlife deeply as I entered the facility. No, I wasn't nuts. It just felt like an appropriate intro to the creatures I'd soon see.

As we entered, Dante's high-tech PDA sang out that he was receiving a call. He pulled it from his pocket and scowled at the caller ID. But his tone was level as he said, "Good morning, Sergeant Hura." As he listened to Frank's response, his expression grew even grimmer. "Of course, I'm willing to cooperate," he responded. "I'm at Hot-Wildlife right now. How about if I come by at around four thirty this afternoon? Yes, I can bring Brody with me."

In a moment, he ended the call. "They

have more questions because of some evidence he claims just came up. I'm going to call Esther Ickes to join us. Hopefully, she can make it. You should call your criminal lawyer, too, Brody. I had the impression that we might not be leaving for a very long time — or at least until we post bail."

I wasn't completely shocked, but even so . . . "They're arresting you?" I asked.

"He didn't exactly say that, but I wouldn't be surprised."

That made our planned outing here more critical. But would we actually learn anything helpful? I didn't really think so.

I felt utterly depressed as we stopped in to give our greetings to Megan. What could I do to instantaneously assist Dante and Brody? I suspected that the call I intended to make might work the other way.

Next, I headed to the infirmary to peek in at the wolf pups. They were growing. I wasn't sure at what age they needed to be fed regurgitated food, but figured that time was fast approaching.

The guys went on their ways without me, a good thing. One caretaker was in the back room of the infirmary, and I used the opportunity to question him about his opinion of Jon Doe. His name was Paul, and he didn't seem excited about the interruption or interrogation. "I told everything I could to the cops," he said, giving me the evil eye. "I didn't know Jon well. He kept to himself. He did his work, and that was all the rest of us cared about." He turned his back and hefted a big bag of food, obviously signaling that our discussion was over.

Not that such a thing ever deterred me. "Did anyone ever come here to see him? Did he talk much on the phone?"

But all I got was a shrug, so I gave up.

Besides, I had better things to accomplish. Like make the phone call I'd been dying to make.

I went outside to the rear of the infirmary and looked around. It was chilly here, and I stood on the dirt between the concrete building and the beginning of the lush sanctuary landscaping. I saw no one else. And of course I'd stay alert, just in case whoever had threatened me was present behind the facility's fence.

I pulled my notebook from my purse and pushed in the number I'd stolen from Dante, armed with the information about its source that Althea had given me. I waited nervously for someone to answer.

"This is Gibson Callaway," said a voice.

I took a deep breath before plunging in. I'd been pondering exactly what to say and how to say it, and all I'd been considering seemed to have evaporated. But I certainly knew the gist of it. "How are things at the Department of Justice today?"

"Who is this?" he growled, and his tone made me look around yet again. All I saw moving was a beautiful hawk circling overhead. I knew I wasn't his prey, and I certainly hoped I was no one else's, either.

"My name is Kendra Ballantyne, Mr. Callaway," I began. "I think you may have heard of me, but in case you haven't, I'm an attorney in Los Angeles. I'm also a good friend of Dante DeFrancisco's and Brody Avilla's."

A pause. "So you can drop names well. What do you want?"

"Well, I'm unofficially looking into the murder of a man who went by the name of Jon Doe. I know you knew him under both that name and another. I'm still trying to confirm his former identity, and have narrowed it down to Jamison Dubbs and Jesse Dryler. Do they all sound familiar?"

"No. Not at all. What the hell do you want? Make it fast, or I'll hang up."

If none of this had rung a bell with him, I felt sure he'd have terminated the call immediately. I'd been careful to press numbers in to block his ability to use caller ID, but wasn't sure how well it worked with a cell phone, or whether the government system overrode it. In any event, I'd felt it necessary to give my name, and he'd undoubtedly be able to find me.

Something else to worry about.

Even so, I pressed on.

"So here's the thing, Mr. Callaway. I know you've worked your way up to be an assistant to the director of one of the bureaus within the Office of Justice Procedures. Sounds impressive. But I'm aware of your work some years ago within the DOJ with Dante, Brody, and Jon Doe." Well, okay, I was guessing here. "In the investigation of Jon Doe's death, Dante and Brody have been the subject of some interrogation. I'm certain of their innocence" — I hoped — "and I want to rule out any possible connection with their employment all those years ago. Can you help me?"

"No," he spit into my ear. Good thing he was so far away. "I can't. Goodbye, Ms. . . . Ballantyne, was it?"

"Yes, it was. And I just want to warn you, then, that if I don't get cooperation from you, I have a very good friend who'll cooperate with me. She's a TV tabloid reporter, and quite excellent at digging out details of anything juicy she gets her claws into. Researching Jon Doe's background, with the information I'll be able to give her, should make her salivate. I'll put her in touch with you soon. Goodbye, Mr. Callaway."

"Wait!" he all but shouted, which told me volumes. He wasn't exactly acknowledging that what I'd implied was true, but he clearly wasn't denying it, either. "Look, Ms. Ballantyne. You're correct. I do work for the Department of Justice, and I stress the 'justice' part of that. If you believe that Mr. DeFrancisco and Mr. Avilla — both of whom are well-known people — are being unjustly accused of something, I'm willing to help. As it turns out, I have a trip scheduled to Los Angeles tomorrow. Is that where you're calling from?"

So he did have caller ID. My 818 phone number was a giveaway.

"Nearby," I said. I resisted a dig about what a coincidence this was, since I was certain it was anything but. He had good reason to talk to me in person.

Which meant I'd better bring along a bodyguard or two.

"Fine, then. Can we meet at about . . . say, two o'clock in the afternoon? I'll find us an office to meet in at the federal court-house there."

"Sounds good," I said. "See you tomorrow." Assuming I lived that long.

CHAPTER
TWENTY-FIVE

I made a couple of additional quick calls. Then I ran to find Dante.

I located Brody and him near the mountain lion lair, both talking to a couple of the groundskeepers. I gathered from body language that the discussion wasn't especially productive. I motioned Dante aside, then told him I'd been on the phone.

Oh, no, I wasn't about to tell him whom I'd been talking to, or why. I acted admirably frantic when I asserted a pet-sitting emergency. I asked that he drop me back at the cabin so I could get my car as soon as possible. I had to head back to L.A. immediately with Lexie.

With everything going on around him, and the concern he must be feeling about having to face the cops again this afternoon, I nearly melted at the look of absolute concern on his gorgeously sexy face as he stared into mine. "Anything I can do, Kendra? Is everyone okay? What kind of pet-sitting problem?"

I put my arms around him and held him tight so he wouldn't see my regretful expression as I lied. "It'll be okay once I'm there. I just have a scheduling problem without enough backup, so I need to do it myself."

"Oh. Okay." I felt his mouth moving my hair, and sighed.

"I wish I could be here as moral support, at least, when you see Frank Hura again," I said, "but I called Esther to make sure she's on her way. Martin Skull, too, for Brody." Martin Skull was another excellent criminal attorney whom I often recommended when there were two murder suspects I was attempting to help who had interests that could diverge. I'd mentioned him to Brody, who'd gone ahead and hired him.

"I'll let you know how it goes," he told me. "Unless I'm in custody and can't use a phone. If so, I'll tell Esther to keep in touch about me."

"Oh, Dante," I said sadly. "I wish I could do something to make this all go away for you." And as it stood, what I *was* doing might only increase my own suspicions about him. But if all went well, I'd wind up with others I could point at with actual evidence. That's absolutely what I hoped.

■ ■ ■ ■

Several hours later, Lexie and I were back in L.A. Dante had taken me to get my car, and my pup and I got on the road immediately. I kept a close eye on everything around me, considering the threats I'd received, but saw nothing at all untoward. And maybe, by leaving the area of Hot-Wildlife, I was easing someone's concerns about me enough to take away the danger.

I wasn't counting on that, though.

It was late afternoon by the time we arrived. I'd spoken with Rachel and Wanda on the way, and we'd arranged for me to take back about half of my usual pet-sitting contingent that evening. That way, I wouldn't have been entirely lying to Dante.

At my office, Lexie on a leash at my side, I was greeted eagerly, as always, by perky Mignon at the reception desk. "Oh, Kendra, I'm so glad you're here," she chirped in her shrill voice, her head bobbing a nod that bounced her curly hair. "You've gotten phone messages from Alice Corcorian. I knew you were really busy, so I passed them on to Borden. I hope that's okay."

"Perfect," I reassured her. The place hummed with activity as Lexie and I headed down the corridor to my office. I left her in there with a bowl of water, then went to the biggest corner office — Borden's.

I knocked on his open door, and my dear, thin partner grinned as he looked up. "Kendra! I didn't expect you. But it's wonderful to see you, and such great timing. I'm off to meet with Alice Corcorian and Ellis. Care to come?"

Of course, I did. I got Mignon to mind Lexie, whom I left in my office. And I knew Borden meant business, since his usual aloha shirt was white on white today, and he wore a navy jacket over it.

Ellis Corcorian still practiced law with my former firm, which was now just Marden & Sergement. It was located in downtown L.A., and I felt as if I was coming home — not.

Even so, there were plenty of people around whom I remembered as being nice to me. I popped my head into Avvie Milton's office and gave her a brief hello. We couldn't talk then, but her smile and wink suggested she'd been offered the job she'd interviewed for. I gave her a high five and exited to say hi to both Marden and Sergement. But I didn't have time to fuss around with them. Neither did Borden. He was welcomed back with less exuberance, since he had walked off with a lot of the firm's clients when he had opened a practice of his own.

We were told that our clients had just arrived, so we headed back to the reception area, where Alice Corcorian and her young fiancé, Roberto Guildon, were waiting.

"We did as you told us, since we're here on official business," Alice said after hugging Borden and me. "We refused to go into Ellis's office until you accompanied us as our legal representatives." The lovely middle-aged lady looked affluent and elegant in her tailored silver suit. Roberto was clad more conservatively in black, with a red tie.

I'd asked Borden, on the way there, what the meeting was about. And when he conveyed what our client intended, I'd been full of grins. Alice had absolutely heeded my advice — and how!

Even so, I took all three of them aside so the receptionist and others in the area couldn't hear us. "Here's what Borden said you want to propose to get Ellis to back down from his opposition to your marriage." And then I laid it out as I understood it.

"Exactly," Roberto said. He was the one who'd be most affected by the answer, and

I smiled at him.

Even so . . . "You should have your own lawyer to represent your rights at this kind of a meeting," I admonished. "Borden and I were both hired by your fiancée."

"No way," he said. "I know what I'm doing. And what it means to my future. But my intent was never to go after Alice's money — only Alice." The look that passed between them was so loving that I sighed and smiled all over again.

Which was when Ellis Corcorian appeared in a doorway. "Come on in," he said, and gave his mother a kiss on the cheek before leading us down the hall.

His office was pretty much as I remembered — standard smooth and successful attorney. We settled down in a pleasant conversation area and a secretary brought us each coffee. Then Ellis said, "You called this meeting, Mother. What's up?" Despite speaking to Alice, he aimed a suspicious glare toward Roberto from beneath his mousy brown brows.

"If I could treat you like the child you were, the way you're treating me," Alice began, utterly calmly despite her son's pursed lips, "I'd do that. But I'm perfectly sane, and my mind is as sound as it ever was — although I admit to having occasional senior moments. Then again," she said, keeping her son from speaking through his now open mouth, "I've seen you forget a word you're looking for now and then. But we're having this meeting because Kendra told me about your discussion with her a few days ago. She confirmed, as I suspected, that one of the reasons you're so concerned about my marrying Roberto is that you think he's only out for my money. And maybe that's a bit selfish on your part, if you're thinking way ahead about what you might wind up not inheriting."

Ellis shot an irritated glare around, not singling anyone out, not even me. "That's not the point. I'm successful in my own right, and your money is yours to squander or will away. But I'm concerned about you, and —"

"No need to worry," Alice said, "but here's the deal. I'm going to keep control of all my assets while I'm alive, but I'm willing to hire a business manager who can keep track and ensure I'm not squandering it, as you put it. One thing I intend is to produce a film in which Roberto will star, but we'll get other backers as well, once we find the right property. My monetary input will have a cap. And Roberto is insisting that we have a prenup that ensures he walks away with very little if we divorce — which won't happen — and an estate plan that expressly limits his inheritance."

"I'm marrying your mom for love," Roberto explained to a dubious-faced Ellis. "And I intend to be a successful actor. That's the only way I intend to rely on her at all — for instructing me and introducing me to appropriate film industry big shots. And her believing in me enough to produce that film she's talking about — awesome! I intend for it to be a huge success. One day soon I want to support her, instead of the other way around."

"You lawyers can come up with the paperwork." Alice gestured gracefully toward her son, Borden, and me. "Do we now have an understanding, Ellis? I'd love to invite you to our wedding, after all."

Ellis rose. I couldn't quite read the expression on his face as he approached his mother, but I watched with interest as he bent down and hugged her. "Guess we have a deal in concept, at least, Mom. As long as that film and its expenses aren't over the top. And as long as you let me walk you down the aisle. Roberto, I'll reserve judgment about you till I see how this works out . . . but I'm not going to stand in the way of your marriage." He held out his hand, and the two men shook.

A while later, in the car on the way to our law office, Borden was all smiles. "Guess you really have the hang of elder law," he said, "not just animal-related things. Alice told me that this solution was based on your suggestion that she determine how to divvy things up. This time your ADR was truly human alternative dispute resolution, and I'm proud of you."

I beamed. But I also wondered how the next meeting I anticipated would go . . . and I was certain it wouldn't be either so cordial or so smooth.

I was absolutely delighted, that evening, to have the opportunity to do my own pet-sitting. Sure, I still liked the practice of law and was mightily pleased with the results I'd helped to achieve earlier that day.

But there was nothing like popping into a house where there was a lonely pet, playing with an exuberant dog and taking him for a walk, or laughing at the sometimes friendly foibles of an arrogant cat or two.

The latter was what I faced at Harold Reddingham's house when his kitties, Abra and Cadabra, came nearly to the door to see who was there, then waved their tails airily as I followed them to the kitchen to change their litter box and feed them. And talk to them. We were old buddies by now.

And then I visited Piglet, Fran Korwald's adorable pug, who wanted all kinds of attention with her mama out of town.

Then there was Beauty, the beautiful — of course — golden retriever who eagerly took me for a brisk walk. And Widget, the terrier mix, who took me for a brisk run.

Loved 'em all. And also loved that Lexie was waiting for me at home in the company of Beggar, my assistant Rachel's dog, while Rachel herself was finishing up her own evening's sitting.

This ended up being a pretty good day.

Until I got a call from Dante at its end, nearly ten o'clock — which should, in other circumstances, have made it end even better.

"We're still in San Bernardino," he said softly. His throat was clearly sore. "Back at my place. Not under arrest, at least not yet, but we have to go back tomorrow. Esther and Martin are staying here overnight in my guest rooms. How was your pet-sitting emergency?"

"Under control for now," I said, even sorrier now that I was lying to him. And I had no real idea how tomorrow would go for either of us, as I wished him as good a night

305

as possible and held the phone in my hand for a minute longer than I needed to before hanging up.

CHAPTER
TWENTY-SIX

I'd have loved to have Dante and Brody along as bodyguards at my meeting the next afternoon. But I'd checked, and they were still being detained by Sergeant Frank Hura in San Bernardino.

So, I had to resort to another, perhaps even better, resource: Jeff Hubbard. Jeff was officially in the security business, unlike Dante and Brody, who might have been in something similar in their earlier days, but who knew? Plus, since Jeff wanted me back, he was more than cooperative — although I still made it clear I wasn't interested in renewing our relationship. Instead, I'd arranged to pay him to be my bodyguard for the day.

Which oughtn't to be needed anyway, since my meeting with Gibson Callaway of the Department of Justice was to be held in a conference room in the Roybal Federal Building in downtown L.A. There would be plenty of people around.

I'd been in the tall building before, since it also included federal courtrooms. The room number given to me by Callaway required an elevator ride. Jeff and I bickered the entire way up. Fortunately, we were alone.

"I don't want you out of my sight," he said. He had donned a dark suit for the occasion, and his dusty blond hair was neatly combed. Tall and hunky, he looked pretty hot, though I'd never admit that to him. Or even, really, to myself anymore. Except that I just had.

"But confidential information will come out at the meeting," I responded. I had dressed up all lawyerly, also in a nicely fitting suit — blue. I hadn't had time to have my hair styled lately, so it lay loosely around my shoulders. I carried a briefcase containing some notes and a pad of paper. I was definitely looking official, even if that wasn't truly the case. "And Callaway wouldn't attack me himself — not physically — even if there is some danger here."

"You're a lawyer. You've hired me. We're both bound by attorney-client privilege, so I couldn't reveal anything I hear."

"But I'm not exactly acting as Dante's, or anyone's, attorney here."

We reached the floor with no resolution. And I really didn't want to let him in, since the stuff I hoped to hear about Dante's past shouldn't go any farther than my ears — unless it was to Dante's and my advantage otherwise.

Outside the door, I looked way up into Jeff's blue eyes and said, "Stay. Here. I mean it. I'm paying you." And at his scowl I reached up, pulled his head down, and gave him a quick kiss. "Please. See you later." And then, before giving him time to respond, I ducked inside and closed the door behind me.

It was a compact conference room. I didn't know what it might usually be used for, but I didn't see a lot of law firm-like amenities. A long set of windows, a small table, a phone, and several chairs.

One was occupied by a sixty-something man, or so I guessed. His face was thin and pouchy, his forehead high and framed by short white hair. He had taken his suit jacket off and draped it over the back of his seat, revealing a slightly wrinkled white shirt and black striped tie.

"Mr. Callaway?" I inquired.

"Yes. Call me Gibson, Kendra." He stood and held his hand out. Of course, I shook it, although I didn't exactly want to. It was limp and chilly and rather disgusting. Ugh! Or maybe my mind exaggerated the uglies, since I anticipated despising the guy. But I smiled as he motioned me to a seat.

He had a cup of coffee in front of him from one of the major chains. I hadn't brought one, nor did I anticipate anyone would come in and offer me a refreshment.

This would be one stark sort of meeting.

I decided to take as much control over it as I could. "I really appreciate your meeting with me, Gibson," I said. "I want to tell you right up front that my client, Dante De-Francisco" — okay, so I exaggerated the attorney-client thing to him, but I needed to appear as if I had more of a reason to inquire than being nosy — "hasn't told me much about his early employment by the DOJ. Here's the little that I do know, and I'd appreciate it if you'd correct any mistakes. What I believe is that Dante, Brody Avilla, and the man most currently known as Jon Doe all worked there together on a task force, and I believe you were in charge of it. Dante's now being looked at as the possible killer of Jon Doe, who recently got out of federal prison. That's about it. Please give me some of the details."

"You've got the gist of it right," Gibson began smoothly. "Many years ago, I headed a minor task force that helped to confiscate stolen property and return or dispose of it. The man who later took the name of Jon Doe did his own form of confiscating, and when he was found out — thanks to information supplied by Dante and Brody — he was prosecuted. His identity then was Jamison Dubbs. To protect our confidentiality, the case made against him was basically a racketeering charge. He was convicted, served his time, and was paroled from Lompoc a couple of years ago."

I'd removed my notes from my briefcase. So far, what he said tracked what I'd learned about one of the possible Jon Doe identities. I looked up. "So when he got out, he sought revenge against Dante and Brody? That's why he started working in wildlife sanctuaries, eventually aiming for Hot-Wildlife, which is largely funded by Dante?"

"Exactly."

"And he was acting alone?" I shot an oh-so-innocent look toward Gibson Callaway.

He got the underlying question. "Do you mean, did I encourage him?" His frown looked almost ferocious. I considered calling Jeff in, but simply sat still . . . for now.

"Well," I said sweetly, "let me posit a hypothetical to you, okay? We lawyers like to do things like that. What if, when Dante and Brody blew the whistle on the missing confiscated goods, they let it be known that it wasn't only underlings on the task force who were involved? Maybe one or more of those in charge of the task force were in charge of stealing, too." And were there any others in charge besides Callaway? "What if the deal worked out was that Jamison Dubbs would take the fall?" I was reaching a bit here, but not too far — thanks to some of the stuff Althea had suggested from her findings.

"Interesting idea," Callaway said icily, "even if totally untrue."

"Totally? I don't think so. I won't name any sources, but I've found enough to suggest some of this while conducting research into possible Jon Doe identities. Anyway, here's some more speculation. Dubbs agreed to stay silent in exchange for being paid well when he got out. And the opportunity to get revenge, with the encouragement and backup of those whose scapegoat he had become. Now, what if those others saw a whole different kind of opportunity — like disposing of Dubbs altogether, and pinning his murder on the guys Dubbs, and they, had wanted to avenge themselves against? That looks a lot like what's happening now, don't you think?"

He had half risen from his seat, and his formerly pale, wrinkled face was now florid. "I don't think you have it entirely correct, Ms. Ballantyne." And here I'd thought we were on a first-name basis.

"Well, fill me in," I urged.

"It's like this." His side of the story suggested that he was actually one of several guys with authority over the task force. He'd been properly appalled when Dante and Brody had come to him with evidence of Dubbs's lucrative thefts and resales — stuff like cars and jewelry and more. He had helped in Dubbs's prosecution. And if any of the DOJ higher-ups were involved, it wasn't him.

So why did he look so shifty-eyed? Or was that merely my interpretation?

"And now?" I inquired when he was through. "Do you know of anyone from the task force or otherwise who'd have killed Dubbs to protect his or her reputation — one that's probably unsullied thanks to Dubbs taking the fall?" I looked straight into his face, and though he looked slightly discomfited, he didn't blink.

"I'll look into it further, but my belief is that Dubbs acted alone in seeking revenge."

"And now that he's dead, who's trying so hard to frame Dante and Brody?" I'd kept my voice even and calm until now, but this question came out as an accusation.

"I'll look into it from the DOJ's perspective," he said, "and if I find out anything, I'll make sure it stops. If those men are guilty, that's one thing. But to the extent I can prevent it, I'll make sure no one is framing them."

"Good." I relaxed back into my seat once more. We had an understanding, even though it was only alluded to. "I might even be able to get my reporter friend to make you out as a hero when the true killer is brought to justice. Anonymously, of course, if you prefer it."

Ah, yes. I'd reminded him of the reason he'd decided to be so cooperative yesterday.

As if he'd ever forgotten it.

And also suggested what could happen if he reneged on his word.

"That sounds good, Kendra." He rose. "But now I have to excuse myself. I have another meeting coming up soon."

"Thanks for getting together with me," I said, figuring his next meeting might be with a bottle of scotch. But what did I care? "Oh, but before I leave, is there anything else helpful you could suggest about my investigation into Jon Doe—Jamison Dubbs's murder?"

"Not really," he said, "although I've been trying to keep up with the situation since I realized who he was. And there is one suggestion I can make as a sign of my good faith here — and to make sure you understand what I've said is true."

Interesting, even if not entirely credible. "What's that?"

"That missing wolf from the HotWildlife sanctuary? Here's a possible tip about where she's gone."

Wow! How could he know that? *Why* would he know it? Could it be true?

Of course, what he told me didn't exactly divulge mama wolf's whereabouts, but it was absolutely worth looking into next time I visited HotWildlife, which would be as soon as tomorrow.

I also felt sure that there'd be some stuff dropped tacitly by the feds at the San Bernardino County Sheriff-Coroner's Department to get them to back off from Dante and Brody, unless they came up with evidence far more than circumstantial. And that evidence was not likely to have been manufactured by the feds. At least not the fed I'd just met with.

I thanked him and prepared to leave. But I had a parting shot to deliver at the door. "By the way, Gibson, I gave the information

I told you earlier, along with my related surmises, to my reporter friend on a confidential basis. She's to use it only if something happens to me. And since you explained that what I understood was full of half-truths, I imagine you'll want to ensure, as much as possible, that I stay safe and healthy. I'll definitely check out what you've told me, Gibson. Thanks."

I exited the room to face a steaming Jeff — whose ear, no doubt, had been pressed to the conference room door the entire time. Or maybe, since he was in the security business, he'd brought a portable electronic device he'd somehow gotten through the security system downstairs, and had used it both to listen and to record what had gone on.

And maybe I'd thank him for it . . . later.

CHAPTER TWENTY-SEVEN

As I'd half anticipated, Jeff took his assignment way seriously — as an excuse to hang close to me that afternoon, and even the evening.

I admit I let him — to a point. I certainly appreciated his presence as we strode from the building and into the parking lot. He held my arm, and we both kept a close watch on everything around us.

Even though I'd reached a sort of understanding with Gibson Callaway, and even though I'd threatened him with a very public tabloid story of potential untruths — or not — if anything happened to me, I didn't exactly trust the guy. I mean, he worked for the Department of Justice, yet had apparently gotten away with some pretty unjust stuff years ago, making Jamison Dubbs take the fall. And that guy J.D. took an even heavier fall as Jon Doe, possibly thanks to Callaway.

Was I accusing him of murder? Maybe. But I walked away with nothing that looked like evidence against him.

We'd come in Jeff's Escalade, and I was happy to allow him to drive me home. Only when we were on the Hollywood Freeway heading north did I ask him about his eavesdropping and recording. With a grin, he handed over a small device and started playing back our conversation.

I grinned, too.

We went pet-sitting together, and my animal charges all seemed excited about the extra attention from two of us. We even had Thai food for dinner — my treat, as previously promised. I made sure he knew he wouldn't be spending the night, though. "You're the one who installed my latest security system. I trust it, and I trust you."

"So . . . what next? Are you still going to put yourself in danger following up with that guy, and what he told you?"

"I'll be following up," I said, "and I'll definitely call if I need your bodyguard or other services again. I appreciate all you've done, but, really, don't worry about me. I won't do anything stupid . . . without calling you first if I need help."

His scowl was cute, but it didn't convince me to let him stick around. "Goodnight,

Jeff," I said, and gave him a quick, nonsexy kiss and went up the stairs to my apartment while Jeff exited back to the street. I knew he was irritated, because he kicked the gate.

Inside, Lexie waited eagerly for me, and I just as eagerly hugged her and told her what a good girl she was. We went outside for her evening constitutional, and then I settled down and tried calling Dante.

No answer. Was he in jail?

Well, I'd find out tomorrow. I was heading back to the San Bernardino area after my early pet-sitting.

I got a call while enjoying my early walk with Beauty, the golden retriever, the next morning. I hoped it was Dante.

Instead, it was Lauren Vancouver of HotRescues. "Anything new on the claim by Efram Kiley?" she inquired.

"No," I said, just as glad I had nothing to report. I hadn't yet come up with the perfect solution. I'd often used my animal dispute resolution skills to find a way to soothe ruffled egos by finding the complainer a new and similar pet. That wouldn't work this time. None of us on our side would want to see Kiley, who'd allegedly abused the pup in question, wind up with another dog if he'd harm it, and there was no good way to confirm his story that the energetic pup had injured himself. "These things sometimes take a long time." A good thing. "I'll certainly let you know if I hear anything — or come up with something substantial — and you do the same. Okay?"

"Okay. And . . . by the way, how's Dante?"

"Okay, I think," I said lightly. "I hope to see him later today to make sure."

"That murder investigation that's been on the news . . . ?"

"Yeah, it's a bit of a mess, isn't it? The cops on the case don't have a good suspect yet, or that's what I think. Oops. Gotta go. I'm walking a dog right now, and *she*'s gotta go. And I'll need to clean up after her. Talk to you soon." I ended the connection, not really wanting to talk anymore to Lauren, or anyone else, about the Jon Doe death investigation that so far had gotten me nowhere.

Soon, Lexie and I were Escaping east toward HotWildlife and beyond. I had already run a reverse directory search on the address Gibson had given me, where he claimed mama wolf had been taken. It seemed awfully odd. The place was on the way to Lake Arrowhead — and it was the location of a petting zoo. Actually, it was a place that maintained animals to bring to parties and such for kiddies to pet them.

They'd have a wolf there? Mama wolf wouldn't be pettable. And with all the stuff in the news about HotWildlife, the missing wolf, and the murder, surely the owners would have known to contact authorities if a strange wolf had somehow shown up on their doorstep.

More likely, if they saw a strange wolf like that, they'd have killed her to prevent her from eating their petting charges.

I shuddered at that idea, and prayed that if mama wolf happened to be there, she was hale, hearty, and ready to go home to her babies. Maybe a place where animals were nurtured wouldn't harm any creatures . . . I hoped.

I soon reached the address. It started with a gated driveway along the road, which was otherwise lined with shrubbery, alongside a chain-link fence. A sign proclaimed it was the Amazing Animal Farm, as I'd found on the Internet. I stopped and pressed the security button. On the way, I'd come up with my cover story to see the place — and look for mama wolf.

"Yes?" said a female voice over the inter-com.

"Hi, my name is Kendra, and I'm a teacher. I'm hoping you can bring some animals to my school to help educate the children. May I come in and talk to you?"

"Well, sure, although it would have been better if you called first. Just a second."

The gate swung open, and I drove up a gravel driveway that was lined with fenced-in areas filled with dirt and — what else? — animals. I saw several ponies, a potbellied pig — love 'em! — some goats, and even a pair of llamas. How fun!

But I didn't see a wolf.

At the end of the drive was a small ranch house with a paved parking area beside it. I pulled into the lot, beneath a big tree that would provide shade, and left Lexie in the car with the windows cracked open for air.

Air that Lexie, who enjoyed all sorts of scents, would go wild over. It smelled like — what else? — multiple animals.

A lady in jeans and a plaid work shirt waited on the front porch. She looked mid-forties, and her mid-brown hair was plaited into braids. I approached her.

"Hi," she said. "My name is Esta. Come on, and I'll show you around. My husband's not here right now, or he could talk to you, too." Were there other people present? I didn't see any, which was a good thing, considering all I wanted to accomplish. "What school do you teach at?"

"Ford Elementary School in Fontana," I said, hoping there really wasn't such a place. "I'm planning an assembly to help teach kids about unusual animals."

"Ours are not especially unusual, although they mostly aren't kinds used as house pets." She pointed out the llamas, who sauntered curiously toward us within their enclosure. They seemed rather bored by the whole experience. "Lately, a lot more people in the U.S. are raising llamas, but you still don't see many in Southern California."

"Perfect," I proclaimed. What I really wanted to do was demand that she take me to see mama wolf, but instead I continued, "Not only farm-type animals, but those will be great, too. But do you have any even more unusual sorts? Wild animals, for example, that aren't generally seen around here?"

We began walking along a path that wove between the various enclosures. "Not many," Esta said. "We're not a wildlife sanctuary or anything like that, though if we come across anything needing help, we try to call in the right assistance."

"That's wonderful," I said. But if it was true, why did she sound somewhat defensive?

I didn't feel as if I was really getting

323

anywhere, and so, instead of following Esta, I headed in a different direction along the paths, up toward the side of the house.

"Oh, this way," she called to me. "I want to show you our ponies."

I ignored her and hurried forward. Okay, I was kind of trespassing. I'd been invited onto the property, but not to dash off my own way. Even so, I figured that if mama wolf was there, she wasn't in an area where Esta was willing to show me around.

I saw several small sheds behind the main house. I couldn't really get too far ahead of Esta, so I headed for the closest shed. It was gray weathered wood, looked like it needed lots of maintenance, and the door was open. I looked in. There were all kinds of relatively small cages, stacked one on top of another. I wasn't happy to see that. Were the animals inside being treated well enough? Or was their abuse the reason Esta hadn't invited me here immediately?

"What's in there?" I asked brightly, as if I was simply a curious teacher wanting to see more animals.

"We have some raccoons and rabbits and such that we keep in here. All the smaller crates are empty. We use them when we have to transport animals to places like schools, but we don't want to confine the animals in

324

them too long."

"Oh. That's good. And what other creatures do you have here?" I edged around her and headed for the next shed.

"What's going on?" Esta demanded, attempting to block my path. "Who are you, really?"

Uh-oh. Busted.

"I'm here representing HotWildlife," I responded with chilly accusation in my tone. "And I recently learned that you have our stolen wolf here."

Esta visibly paled. "Who told you that?"

"It's confidential. Now, please take me to see the wolf."

"But I don't . . . I can't . . ."

I pulled my cell phone from the bottom of my large purse. "Then I'll call the authorities to come here and retrieve her."

Esta reached toward me, and I stepped back. I wasn't sure how well I'd do in a fight against her, and didn't especially want to find out. I decided I'd do exactly as I said, and started pressing in 911. Better safe than sorry, I figured.

But she stopped moving and started crying. "I'm so sorry. I didn't realize at first, and then when I did, I was afraid we'd lose our licenses, and — I shouldn't have agreed. Go ahead. Take her back."

And somehow, miraculously, Esta led me not into any of the sheds, but behind one where a large enclosed area had been fenced in, including a covering over the top.

Inside lay a large gray wolf who looked familiar. The canine looked dejected until we approached.

Too bad no one had named her yet, so I couldn't gauge who she was by her reaction to a word. Even so, she stood up alertly and started pacing in her enclosure as we approached.

"Do you miss your babies, mama?" I asked softly. She stared at me as if she understood, and stopped walking. "I think it's time you get to see them again."

I immediately called Megan Zurich, watching Esta's eyes the entire time. They were wet but watchful, and I felt somewhat unnerved. At least now someone knew where I was. And why.

I wished it had been Dante, too, but he had never returned my phone call, and I suspected he was still with the sheriff's department. Poor guy.

Yet I wasn't sure this tidbit of extra information would do much to resolve that, even though it had come from Gibson Callaway. What else had he intended to relate to me by this discovery? I suspected, from what he actually had said, that he'd also intended some subliminal message.

I asked the obvious. "Who brought her here? Who got you to agree to keep her?"

She stayed silent.

"You're going to have to tell the authorities anyway. Why not start with me?"

"I can't," she wailed. "I promised."

"Was it Warren Beell, the man who brought her to HotWildlife in the first place?"

"He is so nice to take in injured animals," she responded obliquely, without actually answering. Since it wasn't an absolute yes, I decided to see her reaction to others I named.

"Then is it someone connected with Hot-Wildlife . . . like the director, Megan Zurich?"

Her expression seemed somewhat surprised through her tears, so I surmised her answer was negative. Maybe. But at least for now I'd try to trust Megan.

"One of the caretakers? Like the dead one, Jon Doe?"

She shuddered and asserted, "Heavens, no."

That would have been too easy, I supposed.

"Another caretaker?" No response but a

stubborn set to her chin despite her tears. "Some other employee?" Still nothing. "A volunteer?" I asked in growing irritation. And still nothing. Well, I did have an idea how to find out.

I called Megan again, quickly, telling her not to bring the cops, but a way of transporting mama wolf. And not to mention to anyone but Dante, if he happened to show up in the interim, where she was going, and why.

Jon Doe's murderer could have killed him because Doe had seen that person abscond with the wolf, though that seemed like a slim motive. Maybe blackmail or something worse was involved.

But the fact that Gibson Callaway knew where mama wolf had gone supported my current assumption that the incidents were related. Sure, he could have learned incidentally about the wolfnapping as he poked his nose into Doe's death — or even caused it to occur. Yet I'd had a sense that the tidbit he had thrown me, the place where I could find the missing wolf, also contained other clues. He knew I wanted to protect Dante, and simply helping me find the wolf, without more, wouldn't help with that — or necessarily keep me from spilling my guts to the news media about Gibson's own possible involvement. Helping me learn other answers was his best means of self-protection.

He could have learned mama wolf's whereabouts as part of his investigation into Doe's death. Or in his assistance with Doe's intended revenge against Dante and Brody.

Or simply because, as a DOJ director, he was officially omniscient — or at least had unlimited resources.

I felt sure he'd never tell me the truth about his info source . . . at least not directly. But if I was correct in these assumptions, the way I now intended to learn the identity of the wolfnapper might also assist me in figuring out who the murderer was.

If not, I'd keep on with my own kind of investigation.

I really hoped to point an accurate finger at the killer before Dante was sent to prison.

CHAPTER
TWENTY-EIGHT

Of course, it took a while for Megan to arrive. I checked on Lexie now and then, and otherwise sat on the front porch of the house with Esta without getting any more info from her. I nevertheless sometimes shot a name at her — Dante's and Brody's included, even though they had nothing to do with mama wolf's abduction. Her eyes widened at their august names, but she still said nothing to admit or deny who could have had a hand in what had gone on there.

I kept watching the driveway, hoping Esta's husband didn't get there before Megan. I hadn't allowed her to slip into the house, even when she claimed she needed to pee, so she hadn't been able to call him. I gathered she didn't have a cell phone in her pocket.

In a while, I heard a buzz from somewhere in the house. "That's the security gate," she said irritably. "Are you going to let me open it?"

"Depends," I said cheerfully. "Let's go find out who it is." The voice was Megan's. And I was absolutely relieved and delighted to see that she hadn't come alone.

Dante was with her in her enclosed pickup truck.

Dante got out first and dashed in my direction. He grabbed me by the shoulders with his large hands. He was clad in nice slacks and a button-down shirt, so I figured he'd come straight from his interrogation, or was heading there again. "Are you all right, Kendra?" he demanded, glaring at me angrily with his dark, sparking eyes, as if he dared me to say no.

"Of course," I said. "What about you? I take it you're not under arrest."

"Not yet. We'll talk about that later. Let's get the wolf home first. And then there's a lot you'd better tell me."

"Ditto," I said, then caught Megan's amused smile as she stood off to the side.

Her smile disappeared immediately, and I turned to see Esta on the move.

"Great," I said. "I'm sure you were on your way to show these nice people from Hot-Wildlife where they could retrieve the wolf stolen from there, weren't you, Esta?"

She looked stricken and scared. "Well . . . sure," she said, then motioned halfheartedly. "This way."

It was only a short while until mama wolf was crated in the back of Megan's truck, and we were convoying back to Hot-Wildlife.

We'd left Esta at home. She seemed to care enough about her animals that I doubted she'd abandon them to run away. And at this point, I still wasn't ready to call in the authorities.

Plus, I'd reminded Dante that he had offered a reward for info leading to the safe return of mama wolf. I certainly wasn't about to suggest he pay anything to the source of my knowledge of where mama was. I did get him to tempt Esta with the reward if she revealed who'd brought mama wolf there, but she declined, and we departed.

Since Dante was driving the pickup, and I followed in my Escape with Lexie, I didn't get to ask him anything about his latest ordeal with the sheriff's investigation. He might already have conveyed some or all of it to Megan, who rode with him. But I simply drove along, my mind humming.

When we got near HotWildlife, I called Dante on my hands-free phone. "Stop here!" I said. "I have a better idea how to find out who wolfnapped our passenger." And perhaps even get a substantial suspect in Jon Doe's murder as well, in the event I was correct and Gibson Callaway's hint had a broader scope than who had absconded with mama wolf.

Dante definitely obeyed, pulling into the parking lot of a nearby convenience store and parking. We exited our vehicles, and he aimed a perfectly luscious, sexy smile in my direction and said, "I can see those wheels turning in your head. I don't suppose your idea would be broad enough to encompass catching a murderer, too, would it?"

"I wouldn't be entirely surprised," I said with a smile of my own.

Fortunately, Megan was on board with my odd idea. That was a good thing, since it involved closing down HotWildlife the next day — Saturday, a busy day for visitors — and telling all the staff to stay home till called. We'd accompany her back to the sanctuary a little later to assist her with the calls. We would give everyone the excuse that the sheriff's investigators were going to be around in the morning, and we'd let people know when things were back to normal and they could report in.

I drove to Dante's to leave Lexie and my car in charge of the household help he had called in for the occasion.

Then, since we hadn't wanted to have mama wolf restrained overnight in the back of the truck, we contacted Warren Beell without explaining why. I wanted to see his reaction when we pulled up at his mini rescue facility with the wolf he purported to have saved. We ascertained he was home and not at the car dealership where he worked.

First, though, we took mama wolf to the closest all-hours emergency veterinary clinic to check her health and ensure she wouldn't bring some contagious sickness back to her babies. She came out with a clean bill of health — and a hefty bill for Dante to pay.

We pulled onto Warren Beell's residential street, with the Angeles National Forest forming an appealing background, about an hour later. Dante parked in the driveway, and we all got out. I was the one to go up to his door.

I didn't need to ring the bell. He was waiting for us, and opened the door. "What's going on, Kendra?" the stocky guy demanded, once again his belligerent self. His uniform at home appeared to be casual unchic, ratty jeans and an even rattier T-shirt.

"We need to board a friend with you for a few hours," I said. Our plan was to bring mama wolf back to the sanctuary in the wee hours of the morning, once all the usual staff had departed.

"Who's that?" he asked.

"Come here and see." I beckoned him to follow me to the enclosed bed of the pickup truck. Dante waited there, standing beside the window. I led Warren to the window, too, and watched him while he looked inside. His reaction, whatever it might be, could tell me whether he did steal mama back and drop her at the Amazing Animal Farm for a while.

"You found her!" His exclamation was full of excitement. "Where was she? Is she okay? Hey, this is great! Of course, I'll watch her for a few hours. But why aren't you bringing her right back to her babies?" At the last, he turned to glare at me as if I was mistreating mama wolf even more. Which, sad to say, I might be doing, but there was a good reason for it, and the additional delay would amount to only a short while.

"Have you ever heard of the Amazing Animal Farm?" I asked without exactly answering his question directly.

"I think so. Don't they provide a petting zoo of sorts for local events?" His puzzled

335

expression could be feigned, of course, but I didn't believe it was.

"That's it. Anyway, mama wolf has been there all this time." I had no answers to his demands about whether the owners were alive, hadn't they listened to the news about the missing wolf, and the same kinds of questions that I had tried to obtain answers to from Esta at the farm. And what little I did know, or suspect, I wasn't about to enlighten him with.

Instead, I encouraged him to prepare a place for mama for a little while. Dante and Warren carried the crate, and we used the same kind of treats we had used previously to lure this suspicious, wild canine out of the crate and into her fenced temporary motel.

And then, after again thanking Warren profusely, Dante, Megan, and I headed to HotWildlife.

We made our calls quickly and calmly, waking up nearly everyone except the staff already onsite. And then I made an extra call.

Brody, who'd gone back to Dante's to rest after their grueling session with the sheriff's department, soon showed up at HotWildlife to help us see to the animals' needs without the people who were usually there.

Just before dawn, Dante and Megan headed back to Warren Beell's place for our newfound rescue wolf. When they returned, we immediately put her in the infirmary enclosure with her babies, who'd only recently been fed.

"Is she likely to have any milk to feed them?" I asked Megan.

"Doubtful, after all this time not having them nurse. And we need to keep them under strict observation to ensure she isn't going to harm them. She may not relate to them as hers anymore."

But, thankfully, that did not turn out to be the case. Mama looked suspicious when the little ones squeaked their ways over to her. Their eyes were open now, but they would recognize their mother by her scent instead of by sight.

She sniffed them, too. Nuzzled at them. Growled a little as they nipped at her.

And then she lay down and started licking one after the other.

"That's so beautiful," I said with a sigh.

"And a big relief, too," Megan agreed.

The first employees we summoned back to HotWildlife were some of Jon Doe's closest coworkers — the other caretakers. On their entry into the sanctuary, Megan sent them to the infirmary, saying there was some work to do there, transporting some food for the sometimes ailing inhabitants.

Three of them arrived at the same time. More would come later. The only one I'd talked to directly was Paul, but Dante and Brody, who were also present, had spoken with the other two about their opinions of Jon Doe.

The men entered the outer area of the infirmary in their work clothes, chatting quietly among themselves, obviously uneasy and a little curious about what was going on. I motioned them to the glass outside the baby wolf habitat.

All three looked inside. "Hey!" Paul said. "She's back! Where was she?" A familiar question, and it was repeated by the rest. "She looks good. Did someone take care of her?"

"We think so," I said, without answering the rest.

I watched them all carefully for any sign of discomfort or knowledge or fear, but everything appeared aboveboard in their re-actions. Each seemed pleased to see mama, and all were eager to get back to helping care for her.

"Nothing there that I could see," I said to

Dante and Brody after they'd left.

"Not exactly the most scientific or legally admissible evidence," Brody said dryly, "but I have to concur."

Dante just nodded. "Who's next?"

A few of the off-and-on employees were asked to come in, and their reactions turned out to be similar.

Which left the entire roster of frequent sanctuary visitors — and the volunteers. Of course we'd start with the latter, since they were easiest to identify and contact.

We had confirmed that mama had no milk to feed her babies, so I happily stepped in to assist in that task.

They were furrier now, and squirmier, too. Sitting in the back room, I hugged my sweet puppy charge. I knew she would not be handled so much by people as soon as she was weaned. She'd revert to wildness. But for now, I basked in her playful puppy warmth.

It was midafternoon by the time the regular volunteers started trickling in. The first to arrive was Irwin Overland. As a visitor-turned-volunteer, had he developed a belief that he knew more about how to care for the animals than the real staff did?

But his delighted reaction on seeing mama reunited with pups took him off the top of

339

my list. And this sweet, gangly guy didn't seem the type to have offed Jon Doe for any reason, even considering their minor disagreement. Once again, not exactly the most useful opinion for exoneration, but that was how my instincts led me.

Anthony Pfalzer, the guy with the football player physique, came in along with Krissy Kollings. He could have wrestled a wolf into a crate to take her to the Amazing Animal Farm. He'd already been questioned in depth by the sheriff's department, who seemed not to consider him a significant suspect in the slaying — even though he, too, had engaged in a minor verbal disagreement with Doe. Even so, the two crimes could actually be unrelated, despite what I had assumed from Gibson Callaway's otherwise useful clue.

And Krissy? She bugged me, but mostly because of the way she hung on Dante's every word, not to mention his hand. I didn't think she'd have either the interest or the stamina to steal a wolf, let alone kill a man. She looked like a pretty airhead, even carried a bigger purse than mine, probably full of makeup instead of stuff to care for pets and take notes with (like me).

But I watched them both as Dante motioned them to look inside the glass-fronted enclosure. I edged closer to him, considering taking his hand to irk Krissy.

"Is that the missing wolf?" Anthony asked. "Awesome!" was his response when I confirmed it. He put his nose to the glass and observed the ongoing reunion inside.

But Krissy . . . Her pretty twenty-something face froze. "Where was she?" she demanded, obviously attempting to get her expression under control. But as I watched, she seemed to melt. Even her curls seemed to come unglued.

"Why don't you tell me?" I asked, oh, so casually. I darted a glance at Dante and Brody. Had they gotten it, too?

This was our wolfnapper. Could she be a killer, too? Guess we'd have to figure that out.

"How would I know?" she asked with a shrug. And then, edging past me, she slinked her curvy body, clad in tight jeans and an even tighter yellow knit shirt, toward Dante's. "Isn't it wonderful that she's back? I can't wait to watch her play more with the pups. We could watch her together, Dante."

"Oh, I doubt it," he said. "I suspect that Sergeant Hura will be talking with you for a while about her disappearance." Dante's smile toward her held absolutely no warmth.

"What do you mean?" Krissy demanded,

all defensive huffiness all of a sudden. "Why would he want to talk to me?"

"I think you know that, too," I said. "Since you're the one who got the wolf away from here in the first place. I'd love to know how you did it. And why, as well. Oh, and did Jon Doe happen to see you? Was he trying to blackmail you, or —"

"You've got it all wrong!" she screamed. "I only wanted Dante to notice me, and I thought that he and I could 'find' the wolf together. Only, you were so pushy, Kendra, and he couldn't see past you. And then I learned that Jon Doe was here for all sorts of underhanded reasons, so I had to protect Dante." She had reached his side, and looked up at him beseechingly. "I did it all for you."

"You should have asked me if I wanted you to," he said calmly, shaking his head. "You could have saved yourself a lot of trouble."

"You bastard!" she screamed. "You only wanted her! That's why I decided to make it look like you killed Doe." And before any of us realized what she was doing, she extracted a wicked-looking knife from her purse and drove it into Dante's chest.

CHAPTER
TWENTY-NINE

"No!" I screamed.

"Hell, no," shouted Brody, bounding toward us, aiming a gun.

My scream must have sounded outside as well, since Jeff, too, lunged in with a weapon pointed. Yes, my extra phone call had been to him, requesting his assistance with the animals, if needed — he's an all-purpose handy sort, in addition to his security expertise.

Good thing they were both armed, since Krissy next seemed interested in stabbing me. I tried to ignore her as much as possible, though, as I sank to the floor beside Dante. The two armed guys immediately got her under control, facedown on the floor, as she shrieked obscenities and attempted to roll away.

"I'm calling 911!" shouted Anthony, bless him.

And beside us, from inside the glass

enclosure, came a series of eerie wolf howls.

Dante was bleeding, but his eyes were open, and he smiled at me as I started unbuttoning his shirt. "Keep going," he said. "Oh, and by the way, she just grazed me. I anticipated who we were after and what she might do, so I moved just enough to prevent being badly hurt."

I blinked at him. "You knew who it was, and didn't tell me?" Well, hell. There was a lot that he'd known that he'd chosen to keep to himself. But why this?

"I didn't know, but I did suspect." His voice was weaker now, and I saw he was fighting to stay conscious. The brave S.O.B.! Maybe he didn't think he was *badly* hurt, but that term was definitely relative.

"Why?" I demanded. "And how?" I was no longer watching his face, though. Instead, I bared the big slash along his side — how deep was it? — and peeled his shirt further away. I grabbed onto the only thing I could think of to stem his bleeding. No time to find something sterile, but I'd put on my white T-shirt only that morning. I lifted it quickly over my head, and held it against Dante's wound.

"Keep going," he whispered, then slipped into unconsciousness.

■ ■ ■ ■

No sense going any further into the emotions of the next few hours. Suffice it to say that I was a wreck.

I almost welcomed the inquisition Sergeant Frank Hura laid on me much later, at the hospital, after Krissy was taken into custody. By then, I'd already ascertained that Dante's wound was, in fact, not life-threatening, like he'd said. No major organs had been punctured, although he'd lost even more blood by the time the EMTs arrived, despite my stanching efforts.

Brody had given me his shirt to wear. He and I had followed the ambulance to the local hospital, and we did all we could to ensure Dante was treated well. Jeff met us there. I had to admit that he had been not only an excellent backup, but also utterly emotionally supportive. He was really there for me, even as he had to realize he was helping me cope with an injury to his rival for my affections.

But Jeff wasn't stupid. He left as soon as the doctors assured us that Dante would be okay. "I'll call you, Kendra," he said.

Brody was there till Frank Hura arrived. Frank took him aside first for his statement.

And then he asked for mine.

We sat in the lobby area outside the emergency room; Dante was in a small room for treatment.

"So you did it again, Kendra," Frank said with a frown. The large Homicide Detail detective appeared a bit deflated. "Ned Noralles warned me it would happen — that you'd solve this murder case before I did."

"I'm just lucky that way, I guess," I answered with irony I hoped was obvious.

"I've gotten a little about what went on from the others who were there — Megan Zurich, Anthony Pfalzer, and Brody Avilla." He glanced down at a pad of paper in his lap, as if to assure himself he had gotten their names right. "They've all said that you were instrumental in getting Ms. Kollings to show her hand that way." He aimed an angry glare at me. "Foolish, you know. You could have gotten killed. As it is, Mr. De-Francisco was wounded."

I noticed that he had spoken Dante's name formally and with obvious deference, now that the megamillionaire was no longer a murder suspect. I kept myself from smiling at that. I didn't need to antagonize this cop, even now.

"I'm not sure I was instrumental in anything," I said, not trying to be modest —

just diplomatic. And careful. I obviously couldn't reveal the entire story, since it could give up the identity of someone I'd promised to protect from the news media, at least as much as I could. And he'd earned my compliance. "I simply was fortunate enough to find our missing wolf. I didn't know for certain that the person who had taken her away without authorization had also murdered Jon Doe, but by not revealing her return to the sanctuary ahead of time, I was hoping to get a reaction from the thief that would give him or her away. And that worked."

"Did you know who it was in advance?" Frank asked, making notes.

"Not really, although I had my suspicions."

"So how did you know where the wolf was, so you could go retrieve her?"

Now I was in delicate territory. "I got an anonymous tip, in a phone call." Okay, so I lied to a cop. And I knew he'd have ways to check calls that had come in to any and all of my phones.

Sure enough, he asked, "On which phone? Was caller ID blocked?"

I told him it came in on a landline at my law office, and, yes, there was no way I could see who it was or where it had come from. And, no, I didn't really know why anyone would call me at all, let alone there, with the information. Shouldn't it have come in to the sanctuary itself?

Anyway, I explained how I'd followed up, found mama wolf, then come up with this way of getting the perpetrator to react in a way that gave away her guilt, which had happened.

"And you're right," I remarked remorsefully. "It was foolish, in a way, even though I had a P.I. friend outside for security. I feel responsible for Dante's getting stabbed."

I must have looked as guilty as I honestly did feel, since the sergeant said soothingly, "It's not entirely your fault. Dante's going to be fine. And you did manage to get our suspect to confess, and not just to stealing a wolf."

I nodded. "As much as I like that mama wolf, I'm even prouder of helping to unearth the murderer."

"You're everything Ned said, Kendra," said Sergeant Hura. "I have to chew you out for your interference of course, and for not keeping us fully informed, but unofficially, I want to thank you."

"You're welcome," I said, purposely not tossing out the common response of "any time."

348

"Oh, and by the way," he said, "we're looking into it further, but we understand that the owners of the Amazing Animal Farm, where the wolf was stashed, are distant relatives of Ms. Kollings. So far, they're not cooperating much in our investigation, but hopefully that will change."

Interesting. No wonder Esta didn't cooperate much with me, either. I'd imagine, though, that the worst she thought she had gotten herself into was wolfnapping, not being an accessory to murder.

Frank left soon afterward, and I assured him I'd be available whenever he needed more official statements, or testimony at Krissy Kollings' trial, whenever that might be.

I had a sense that the sergeant was satisfied with what he had found out from me, at least for now.

But I still had a lot of questions I intended to lob at Dante as soon as he felt better.

In a way, he owed me a whole slew of answers.

But not now. Taking a deep breath, I headed back to the emergency room, afraid of what I might find there.

Was Dante really okay? Surely someone would have come to get me if there'd been any change in his condition. Brody, at least. I wasn't a relative, so the hospital staff wouldn't especially care whether I was worried about the man who'd been stabbed.

I recognized then how worried I actually was. Like it or not, Dante had become damned important to me. He could have died when Krissy stabbed him. And then what would I have done?

Thank heavens, I didn't have to think about that. He was still propped up in the same tiny examining room's bed, and he grinned broadly when I burst in. Brody sat in a chair beside him.

"Kendra! You're back. I thought you might have left."

"Only to answer Frank Hura's questions," I said. Dante's color was good, and he looked essentially okay, if I ignored the white hospital gown and the IV stuff stuck into him. He had a sheet up around him, so I couldn't see the bandage on his side. "So, what's next? Are they going to admit you to the hospital, or release you?"

"I'm staying at least overnight for observation," he said, not looking particularly pleased about it. "They want to make sure there's no infection, and all that."

"Good idea." I considered bombarding him with some of the questions I still had about the situation, but figured they'd wait till he was out of there.

"You ready to leave, Kendra, and let this malingerer rest?" Brody asked, his face as expressionless as if he was serious. But, hey, he was an actor.

"Yeah, let's let this big baby play his crying games with the hospital staff. See you tomorrow, Dante."

And only when I was in the car with Brody did I let loose and cry.

That night, in Dante's classy cabin near the mountains, Lexie hovered near me as if she knew exactly how upset I was, sweet pup that she is.

I was so exhausted that I actually got a little sleep. Brody and I headed back to the hospital fairly early, and I saw that Dante was in pain despite his meds. I hung around to give him moral support, and decided my questions could still wait.

In the afternoon, he was doing much better — so well, that relief made me feel like pirouetting in pleasure.

I even decided I could run by Dante the ADR idea my brain had begun to ponder. I wanted to resolve the situation at HotRescues before the lawsuit was actually served by Efram Kiley's lawyer, James Remseyer.

And now that mama wolf had been found and Jon Doe's murder had been solved — even though I still hadn't all the background details I intended to demand — my subconscious had returned to the other main unfinished matter on my mind.

Brody had already headed back to L.A., and I had driven to the hospital, again leaving Lexie with Dante's household staff. I sat on the chair beside his bed and pressed the button on the remote to mute the business news on the TV.

I told him what I wanted to talk about, and he agreed — probably relieved that I wasn't pressing for the missing details about Jon Doe. Yet.

"It'll take a bit more settlement money," I told him, "and more effort from Lauren Vancouver, but I suspect she'll consider it a win–win situation."

When I'd explained, Dante was on board — even to the tune of expanding on the funds he would commit to make the case go away. Together, using the speaker function on Dante's spiffy super-techno phone, we spoke to Lauren. I wasn't sure whether she worked at HotRescues twenty-four/seven, but with her commitment, I wouldn't have been surprised. She sounded pleased by the settlement possibility we presented, if not extremely excited.

Next, as the lawyer for HotRescues, I called James Remseyer from my own cell, got his voice mail — it was Sunday, after all — but got a call back fairly soon. He agreed to meet the next day, as long as it was in his office.

"Your settlement offer better be a lot better than your last suggestion, Kendra," he asserted. "You know the last time —"

"It is, you'll see." I cut him off before the assertive attorney allowed his words to run rampant over the phone lines. "Just be sure to bring your client."

Lexie and I had headed back to L.A. that evening, too late for me to pet-sit, but I picked up keys from Rachel the next morning to hit a few of my favorite charges' homes.

And then I headed for Remseyer's Northridge office.

Lauren was already in the suite's reception area. Efram Kiley was waiting with Remseyer in the same small conference room where I'd convened with the attorney the last time.

I hadn't met Kiley before. Couldn't say he looked especially abusive, but his snide glances from Lauren to his lawyer suggested he was visualizing lots of dollar signs. He looked to be in his early twenties, perhaps an exercise addict, with lots of brawn outlined by his sleeveless T-shirt.

My idea might be an ideal use of all those muscles, I thought.

"Glad you could join us, Ms. Ballantyne, Ms. Vancouver," Remseyer began. "Now, you know, we've been holding off serving the complaint in our action only to give you another chance to propose an acceptable settlement offer. I hope this one is better than the last one. Of course —"

"Of course," I interrupted. This guy, with his perfectly tailored suit and shaved head, still attempted to assert control over the meeting by never shutting up. I wondered how he fared in court, if he tried the same kind of manipulation with judges as well as opposing counsel — and hoped I wouldn't have to find out. "And here it is."

I laid out the proposal, in which Kiley could earn a heck of a lot of money without worrying about the iffy nature of a lawsuit — but, yes, he would have to earn it by working at HotRescues and being tutored in animal care and kindness by the staff. He had claimed a misunderstanding, after all. Not cruelty to his dog, but failure to keep him from injuring himself. Efram would commit to a minimum number of hours over an agreed-on time period — an amount that allowed him to keep whatever other job he might have. From what I'd gathered, he was an air-conditioning repairman, and this idea was not incompatible with his schedule.

He would help in all aspects of animal care, and if at any time he did anything that resembled cruelty, he would be kicked out and have to refund half of what he had earned.

His efforts would be monitored by a neutral third party — well, neutral as between HotRescues and Kiley, but an animal advocate who wouldn't put up with any nonsense or nastiness from him. At the end, assuming he never did anything wrong at the rescue facility, he would get a lump-sum bonus.

And, with luck and perseverance, Lauren would get some feel for, and assurance that, this guy would learn enough not to harm any hounds again.

"If you agree, we'll memorialize this in a settlement agreement, of course," I finished.

There was silence from their side of the table as I described all this. Yes, silence from Remseyer. I exchanged glances with Lauren. Maybe we'd need to go to trial on this case after all.

"Can I talk to you?" Kiley whined to his attorney. They rose and started talking in whispers near the window at the end of the conference room.

"What do you think?" Lauren asked. "I love the idea, especially if we can get some publicity for it."

"I'm sure we can," I said, thinking of my friend Corina Carey. I'd called her last night as soon as I was sure Dante agreed I could give her the down-and-dirty details — as far as they could be made public — about mama wolf and Jon Doe.

In about five minutes, the two men sat down across from us. "Depending on the details in the settlement agreement," Remseyer stated formally, "throw in another five thousand dollars and we have a deal."

I didn't tell him that Dante had authorized up to an additional ten thousand dollars.

CHAPTER THIRTY

Lauren and I called Dante from outside the office building. He sounded extremely pleased by our news. And then he asked, "Will you be back here soon, Kendra?"

"First thing after my pet-sitting tomorrow," I told him.

"There's some more news," he said. "Megan figures that, with all the less than stellar publicity HotWildlife is getting, it's a good time to announce the winners of the contest to name our wolves. She got some good entries right away — along with some contributions — and always made it clear that the contest wouldn't go on very long."

"Great!" I exclaimed. "What are they?"

"The winner based the names on the fact that the wolves were rescued by Hot-Wildlife. Mama's name is now Pepper — the epitome of hot. The male pup is Cal — for 'caliente,' 'hot' in Spanish. The girls are Sparkie and Flame. Perfect, in my opinion."

"And no wonder," I said, "in the opinion of the man who owns HotPets." The names were perhaps a little too cute for wild wolves, but, hey, they weren't likely to know their monikers or care about them.

No one, apparently, had claimed a reward for helping to find the missing mama wolf — certainly not Esta — and the only man eligible to ask for it certainly wasn't about to go public.

I soon said goodbye to an extremely pleased Lauren. She had started the day looking so stiff that I knew she was nervous. Now, her green eyes glowed, and she appeared to be a happy kid — even though I'd figured she was older than me. "I hope that neither HotRescues nor I ever need legal representation again," she said, "but if we do, you're at the top of our list."

As promised, I headed back to the San Bernardino Mountains the next day after my early pet-sitting rounds, bringing Lexie so she'd be able to hang out with her friend Wagner. I dropped her off at Dante's home and headed to the hospital, where he was just being released. They'd kept him a little longer to be sure he was healing okay.

After all, he was Dante DeFrancisco, and they wouldn't need the bad publicity if he took a turn for the worse after going home too soon.

He looked a whole lot better than he had yesterday, and even managed to appear sexy as an aide pushed him to the curb in a wheelchair.

Back at his luxurious cabin, Dante thanked his staff and asked them to return tomorrow. He probably would hang around for a few more days before chancing the long, bumpy road back to L.A.

And then, except for the dogs, we were alone.

I propped him up with pillows on his lush leather sofa, wanting him to be as comfy as possible. I'd taken a change of his clothes with me to the hospital, so he now wore jeans and a loose brown sweatshirt over his bandage.

It was Tuesday afternoon. I brought him a sandwich and coffee from the kitchen, courtesy of the staff before they left. Lexie and Wagner, on the floor nearby, were charmed by the smell and started begging, to no avail. Well, to little avail. We did give them some small treats.

When we were done, I let Dante finish watching an investment show on a business channel.

And then I dug into what I wanted to

know as the dogs went to sleep at our feet.

"I think I understand a lot of what started that whole Jon Doe situation, but I want you to tell me the rest."

His smile was both amused and rueful. I knew he'd rather go off on a tangent than follow the direction I'd set for him.

"I gather that you pretty well filled in the blanks in the story I told you," he said. "Especially with Callaway's help."

I stared at him in surprise. "How did you know I spoke with him?"

"Your favorite P.I., Jeff, told me — and also how you'd sneaked Callaway's number from my cell phone."

Oops. I guess I'd mentioned that tidbit to Jeff when he'd inquired. But why were Jeff and Dante discussing this situation? "So Jeff and you talked?"

"I called him from the hospital when you weren't around. Since you weren't being particularly forthcoming about how you'd gotten the clue that led to our missing wolf, I decided to ask him. He seemed okay with filling me in. Even said he figured I should know what you'd been up to, especially after you contacted the feds, since I might be in a better position than he is to take care of you."

"I'm glad Jeff and you are becoming buddies," I said sarcastically. At least it sounded as if Jeff was conceding that he and I weren't involved anymore. He still sounded concerned about me, though, which was sweet. Maybe. "Anyway, please continue."

Dante repositioned himself, hunkering down as if bracing for something less than pleasant. "Okay, here goes. But you still have to keep this utterly confidential."

"I will," I said. "That was part of my deal with Callaway, before he told me where to find . . . Pepper."

"You made a deal with him? Hubbard didn't get into that."

"Kinda. Now go ahead. Tell me about your work with Callaway and what happened."

"Not much to say about our work. We reported to him on a task force that dealt with confiscating and disposing of property seized in federal felony cases. Brody and I were still fairly raw and unseasoned back then, both intending to shake the world — but not the way that was being done, with members of the task force taking property for themselves. When we learned what was going on right under the government's nose, we figured the higher-ups would appreciate being told — but instead the shit really hit the fan. They couldn't make us the scapegoats, since we'd already made noise and it would be obvious what they were doing. Dubbs — later known as Doe — agreed, for a price. They even found a way to fudge his fingerprints in AFIS. But he grew more and more angry and disillusioned — probably encouraged by Callaway and his crew, even while he served time in prison. I'm sure they prodded him to get his revenge on us for giving up what was going on — and shut us up, too. Now, some of this is our surmising — Brody's and mine."

He looked at me, and I nodded that I understood. He couldn't actually know all this, but his guesses would be more than educated.

He continued, "Doe's initial purpose was to scope out what I was up to and find a way to dispose of me quietly, and Brody next. Most likely, Callaway helped him develop a fake identity and background. And he was definitely younger than his purported age — closer to Brody's and mine. Fortunately, there were enough impediments to stop his plans to kill us. Like Krissy stealing the wolf, and Doe finding out about it."

Aha! That was undoubtedly how Callaway had learned where mama wolf had gone — via Jon Doe.

"Doe threatened to squeal on her, so she wanted a way to get back at him — and hung around him when she could. That was how, eavesdropping on Doe's conversations with Callaway, she learned he intended to get rid of me. In her own misguided way, she did kill him for my sake. But she got angry when she kept seeing how I felt about you, after you kept coming to HotWildlife with me — and leaving with me, too. She decided both to protect herself and, like Doe, get her revenge on me by framing me. Brody, too, if it worked out that way. She didn't care. And I'd not be at all surprised if she also had a plan to get rid of you — unless she thought that sending me to prison for life would hurt you enough."

"Nice lady," I said sarcastically. "So she left me those threats?"

"Probably, and I suspect Callaway encouraged her. Doe/Dubbs probably told him all about Krissy when things started to happen around here."

"Interesting," I observed. "So they were in touch, too, and he apparently used her for his own nasty purposes. It's additionally interesting that she never did anything to follow through. She never actually harmed me."

"That might have meant revealing herself

earlier," Dante said.

"Maybe." Now, I would be the one getting revenge — since I felt sure she'd be convicted of Doe's murder.

"And as for the local sheriff's department identification of Doe/Dubbs, with or without fingerprints . . . I can only speculate on that, but I figure Callaway, whether or not in his official capacity, dropped a few hints on their doorstep."

I'd assumed that, too, but was certain Callaway wouldn't confirm it.

"So what about Callaway?" I asked, my concern suddenly spiking as my mind mulled over the situation. "If he wanted Brody and you dead, and now apparently has it in for me, are we safe?"

"Pretty much. I've discussed it all with Brody, and he's been in touch with Callaway's superiors, including some who hadn't liked Dubbs's taking all the blame to begin with. I suspect our buddy will be too busy covering his own butt to even consider coming after us — especially since his threats are part of the whole updated, ugly story that Brody revealed, including Callaway's possible complicity in Dubbs's plans against Brody and me, and even in Dubbs's death. So . . . is that enough detail for now?"

"I think so, but I'll ask if I come up with

any other questions. And I do expect you to keep me in the loop if you learn more about how Callaway's being investigated by his superiors."

"I'll tell you as much as I legitimately can, considering the classified nature of what's going on."

"I guess that's got to be good enough." I was still somewhat concerned, but knew that Dante, and Brody, would have my back. And I'd stay especially alert while Dante was healing.

"So, unless there's anything else you need to tell me — do you want to watch your money shows again?" This subject had been covered enough . . . for now. I had brought along some fascinating legal stuff, and could always play with e-mail on my laptop computer.

"In a minute." He reached out his arms, and, smiling, I settled into them, careful not to touch his injured side. We kissed. And again. And again.

And I wondered how much it would hurt him if we adjourned to the bedroom.

Hell, that could wait. Something to look forward to.

Absolutely.

He pulled slightly away and got an extremely serious expression in those deep, dark eyes of his. "I think you know by now, Kendra, that I've fallen in love with you."

Oh, lord, that particular L word made me crazy. Heat, cold, and terror all tumbled through me.

I'd always been so awful at picking men. And this time, if I let my feelings go wild, would I lose him? Or would he turn out to be a louse like so many of the rest?

And then there was the fact that I'd dumped Jeff Hubbard partly because he'd suspected me in a situation he was investigating. I'd considered Dante a suspect in two murders. Could he — did he — really love me?

Well, he'd said he did.

He'd apparently cared a lot for someone at least once before — a woman who'd died in a car crash. He'd mentioned her, said he'd tell me about her, but never seemed ready to talk about her. I'd already decided it was past history. I didn't really need to know. Hardly even thought about it now.

But I supposed it meant he was capable of love. Did I dare trust him to genuinely love me?

"Aren't you going to say anything?" he asked. His tone was patient, but he looked hurt.

"Well . . . I think that's wonderful, Dante,"

I said brightly.

"That's it? How do you feel? Should I just walk away before it gets worse?"

"No!" I exclaimed, suddenly recalling how scared I was when he was stabbed and I thought I might lose him that way. His walking away would be somewhat better — certainly for him — but it still would be terrible. Yet — "You can't walk very far right now. You've been hurt."

He shook his head, although at least he was smiling. "You do know how to change the subject, don't you? Well, even if I can't walk away today, you can go home."

Home? Without him? Under these conditions, after his amazing assertion? And hadn't I thought, not long ago, that I just might come to . . .

"I love you, too!" I blurted. It popped out involuntarily. And yet, once I'd said it, and he'd taken me into his arms and kissed me, I couldn't help but feel glad.

Would I feel that way in a minute? An hour? A day?

Who knew?

Almost as if echoing my thoughts, Dante pulled back and looked down at me with sensuously flashing eyes . . . and said, "Then what's next, Kendra?"

I wasn't sure how to respond. Not now.

But I absolutely intended to figure it out right along with him. For now. And . . . forever?

Guess we'd find out.

ABOUT THE AUTHOR

Linda O. Johnston is a lawyer and a writer of mysteries, paranormal romance, and romantic suspense. She lives in the hills overlooking the San Fernando Valley with her husband, Fred, and two Cavalier King Charles spaniels, Lexie and Mystie.

You can visit Linda and *her* Lexie at Linda's website: www.LindaOJohnston.com.